THE
JADE REBELLION

ALANNA MACKENZIE

First published in Canada in 2018
Willow Lane Publishing, Vancouver, BC

Copyright © 2018 Alanna Mackenzie
Cover design by J. Caleb Clark copyright © 2018

www.alannamackenzie.com

ISBN 978-1-7752509-0-6 (pbk.).--ISBN 978-1-7752509-2-0 (html).--ISBN 978-1-7752509-1-3 (pdf.)

For my family

"If God did not exist, it would be necessary to invent him."

– Voltaire

PART I:
DIVERGENT PATHS

Rescue Mission

"Gamble everything for love, if you are a true human being." – Rumi

Walter no longer trusted what they had taught him. The voice within his soul, which had always instructed him to follow the rules, was extinguished at last. It had been replaced by a stronger voice, one with more anger and authority. *So what if I die?* he asked himself as he surveyed *Fair Isles,* a colossal barge docked in the harbor. The vessel was foreboding, its polished silver hull resembling a spaceship. Half-enveloped by mist and fog, it appeared to be passing through a portal into another universe.

Elaine is trapped on board a similar vessel, Walter thought with a pang of distress. Similar, although not exactly the same. The *Jade Queen* did not rank amongst the dozens of barges that cruised up and down the Amber Channel, watchfully patrolling the Cities. Nor was she one of the countless merchant vessels that ventured south, toward the Barrens and the vast, unconquered jungles beyond. She was bound for Vei'arash, the legendary island that few people spoke about except in hushed tones. Nobody in Crystal City knew exactly where it was, save for the AI Master class. The location of Vei'arash was one of those well-kept secrets that not even Walter, a government translator, had access to.

Walter had read stories about Vei'arash as a curious young boy at the Great Library in Crystal City. He had enjoyed access to Library books for a brief time, before numerous volumes of literature, history, and mythology had been tragically purged from the Library's shelves. Although his parents were pragmatists who had tried to shelter him from academic pursuits, Walter was determined to acquire knowledge on his own. His parents believed that power could be attained through obedience, and had made every effort to keep their son shrouded in a veil of comfortable ignorance. Yet Walter had recognized from an early age that knowledge was power. The knowledge-keepers at the top of the social hierarchy delegated only some of their power to the ignorant in order to sustain the illusion that they, too, held power.

From those stories, Walter knew that Vei'arash was a distant island, several weeks' journey by boat from the mainland of Khalendar. He also knew that it was far from desolate. The island's lush wilderness was populated by all kinds of exotic creatures which the AI Masters had banished from Khalendar long ago to "protect" its citizens. According to legend, the animals were less physical than spiritual. In an ancient and epic battle, the Xeyan'na peoples of the Barrens, the clans of Serrahan—as well as other mystical tribes—had allegedly summoned animal spirits to frighten and intimidate the AI Masters who had desired to conquer their territories. The spirits had waged a mental war on the AIs, causing them to doubt their superior intelligence and rationality. The AIs were frustrated that they could not control or subjugate the spirits as they could the humans, and so after a terrible battle the AIs had banished the shamans and elders who knew the summoning spells to Vei'arash. The AIs had succeeded in conquering the Barrens at last, and the ancient shamans were forever trapped on a cursed island in the middle of the Hapakay Sea.

Vei'arash, named after the most infamous of the shamans, was also the most notorious prison in all of Khalendar. The AI Masters and Khalendi elite periodically sent dissidents to the island, often when prisons on the mainland were over capacity. There were worse punishments in Crystal City—torture chambers, execution lairs, and prisons—scattered throughout the alleyways of the labyrinthine metropolis. Vei'arash was simply, as the Khalendi elite liked to call it, "creative justice," a way for rebellious Xeyan'na and other dissidents to get what they truly deserved. If they wished for a lifestyle different than what was touted by the highest class in Crystal City, they would be granted their wish: an existence on a god-forsaken island in the middle of nowhere.

Walter shivered as he recalled the legends, and he wondered where the *Jade Queen* was presently. She had departed less than an hour ago heading toward Jamestown, a few dozen miles south of Crystal City, the last port of call before sailing for Vei'arash. He could still see the faint trail of her wake in the water; if he left now, he could follow it, reach Jamestown before the ship embarked on its long voyage, and rescue Elaine. He set his jaw firmly as he eyed an abandoned rowboat, realizing that it might be his only chance to see Elaine again. There were few people walking near the harbor at this time of day, and the dense layers of fog made it easy to slip into a boat unnoticed.

Walter quickly made his decision. Unknotting the rope that secured the modest rowboat to the dock, he stepped stealthily into the stern, glancing around to see whether anyone had noticed. He spotted an old woman meandering down the footpath bordering the marina, and for a moment he feared she suspected something, due to the stern glare that she shot in his direction. His body tensed anxiously, but she walked past him without saying a word, her wizened face receding into the mists.

Walter had no time to worry about her. At the moment, his mind was exclusively focused on Elaine, the ill fate that had befallen her, and the urgency of bringing her back. *Why couldn't they have taken me instead?* he thought bitterly. The fact that nobody had punished him—or even spoken to him—after what had occurred unsettled Walter greatly. Instead of penalizing the perpetrator of the crime, they had condemned an innocent girl who had played no part in it all. Walter was grateful to be alive, though, if only to have a chance to see her again. The sight of her beautiful, freckled face would redeem everything. But first, he had to pass through the mists.

Jamestown

"The road must eventually lead to the whole world." – Jack Kerouac

Walter steered the rowboat along the rugged coastline, carefully avoiding the jagged rocks which decorated the land's edge. It was difficult to navigate through the dense wall of sea spray which enveloped him. Tiny droplets of water settled on his glasses and clothing and immediately froze, crystallizing into snowflakes in the frigid air. The trail of the ship's wake was becoming fainter, and the passing landscape increasingly desolate, with each stroke of the oars. Walter's heart thudded in anticipation, and countless questions raced through his mind. What would happen if he didn't make it to Jamestown in time, or if he couldn't even find the town? What if the AI Masters were following him?

Walter's only link to the rest of the world was an electronic tablet that he used to communicate with his family and closest friends. The other tablet he owned was work-related, and it was stashed away in his apartment; he had been reluctant to bring it with him because he knew the government would be able to easily trace it. The government could likely track this one, too, even though he had encrypted its data with the most powerful technology currently available, but he couldn't stand the thought of leaving it behind. Walter wanted to contact Elaine more than anything else, but her tablet signal showed up as "not in service." He suspected that she had been dispossessed of all her belongings when she had been taken prisoner.

It was late afternoon, and the waves were becoming choppier; a strong wind had recently begun to blow from the west, rocking Walter's boat up and down like a buoy. He had always liked the sea, but had only ever admired its vast beauty and mystery from afar. Until now, Walter hadn't truly *experienced* the open ocean, and he realized that admiring it from a distance was far more pleasant. Up close, the sea was not at all like the picturesque, tranquil streak of blue visible from his apartment window. Now it was merciless, cold, and so vast that it made Walter feel like a tiny shard of driftwood afloat upon its endless expanse.

Walter made a conscious effort to keep the shoreline in his view. He wanted to see where he was going but also avoid colliding with rocks, or worse, drawing attention to himself. Although his view was obscured by mist and sea spray, he could faintly perceive the various suburbs of Crystal City, which were situated between the southern border of the city proper and Jamestown. He passed the Stockyards, a neighborhood filled with lots and warehouses to store grain, oil, and other provisions, traded in from the Barrens and the Southern Jungles. Then, the buildings became softer and more residential, and he recognized Fewsbury, a borough populated by working-class folk who labored in the factories, making all the shiny toys that the Khalendi elite liked to play with. The next neighborhood along his route was Hydesburgh. A poor ghetto, Hydesburgh was home to Xeyan'na prostitutes who worked in seedy brothels—popular destinations for wealthy city men who wished to escape their wives. Hydesburgh was also inhabited by intellectuals and artists, people viewed with disdain by the elite and working classes alike. As demonized as they were, these citizens paid their taxes and didn't disturb the peace, so they were rewarded with exile to a dreary ghetto instead of to Vei'arash.

The sky was darkening, and Walter's limbs were aching from the effort of rowing. Just as he was beginning to crave the soft feather bed in his Crystal City apartment, Walter spotted the ship. He knew without a doubt that it was the *Jade Queen*. An elegantly designed and intimidatingly large vessel, it sat regally in the Jamestown harbor like a queen awaiting her procession. The ship's hull was a steel encasement, powerful and watertight, with a cabin on deck for the captain and crew. A number of windows were carved into the cabin and lower hull, but they were tinted, concealing the vessel's interior from sight. In its shadow, Walter's rowboat resembled a tiny mouse next to a lion. The sight of such an enormous vessel left him momentarily breathless, but he quickly pushed feelings of admiration aside to focus on the task at hand.

Walter discreetly moored his rowboat a fair distance away from the ship and made his way into the odd town. Jamestown was famous for two things: a large prison on its outskirts, which was less notorious than Vei'arash but still well-known, and its reputation as a rest stop for sailors who docked here before embarking on long, arduous journeys to the

Tropics, the Orient, and to Vei'arash. There was also a small AI Master apparel industry, and a scattering of brothels which catered to lonely factory workers and sailors. Jamestown was a rough place filled with taverns, brawls, and crazy men wandering the streets at night. As rumor had it, these men were either escaped prisoners or factory workers gone mad from the task of ceaselessly assembling absurd outfits for the AI Masters.

Walter, with his refined sensibilities, felt noticeably out of place in the town. He was dressed in his normal work attire, since he had been too distracted to bother changing clothes before leaving. Now, though, he noticed that the briny sea water had stained his blue cotton shirt in several places, and his jeans were torn and muddy from the bottom of the rowboat. Although he wasn't wearing the most discreet outfit, Walter decided that it would be acceptable to wander the town in these clothes. His shirt likely betrayed his identity as a city dweller, but it was relatively common for prisoners' relatives to visit Jamestown from Crystal City.

The town's main thoroughfare was lined with taverns, brothels, and breweries. Above these establishments were the flats of factory workers, paid for by meager paychecks and no larger than the closets of most Crystal City inhabitants. Walter's gaze fell upon a tavern at the end of the street that was less raucous and noisy than the others. He hoped that he could hide out there for a few hours before settling in at a cheap motel for the night. With any luck, he might even meet a sailor who had valuable information about the *Jade Queen*. Energized by the thought, Walter set off for the tavern, a single-minded determination animating his steps.

When he entered the tavern, Walter was immediately greeted with a thick haze of smoke and the scent of cheap beer. The air was stale and suffocating, yet after the icy sting of the open ocean it also felt somewhat cozy. Walter noticed that his limbs, which had become almost numb from the cold, were beginning to thaw. All hopes he had of not attracting attention to himself were immediately dashed; everyone inside looked his way as soon as he entered, sizing him up with a cruel curiosity.

The barmaid, a plump woman who also appeared slightly inbred, observed Walter warily. He was afraid she wouldn't serve him because he didn't fit in, but to his surprise she grabbed a glass from the shelf and nodded at him.

"What will it be tonight?" she asked flatly.

Walter shrugged, hotly aware that many people were still staring at him, and he tried to appear nonchalant. "I'll just have a rye and ginger," he said in the manliest voice he could summon. The men sitting at the bar—most of whom appeared to be drunken sailors—chuckled at his request.

"A rye and ginger, is it?" the barmaid replied. "Well, lads, looks like we have a visitor from Crystal City gracin' us with his royal presence."

Walter reddened, and he cursed inwardly for not knowing the local drinks around these parts.

"Listen, sweetheart," the barmaid said, her tone a bit more empathetic, "down in Jamestown we don't make fancy mixed drinks that the likes of you royal Khalendi appreciate. We drink our liquor straight."

Walter shrugged, as though this didn't bother him at all. "Straight rye it is, then, thanks."

The barmaid couldn't resist having one last jab at him. "One rye it is, comin' up for his highness." Some of the men erupted into fits of laughter, while others seemed to have already lost interest in the newcomer.

Walter glanced around nervously, wondering if he should join one of the tables of sailors or just drink on his own and wait for someone to come up to him. He already felt like he had made a poor choice in coming here—perhaps it would have been easier to blend into the crowd at a busier tavern. He decided to sit at a table near the back of the bar, not quite immersed in the crowd, but close enough that he could still seek out someone to talk to.

As he sat and nursed his bitterly strong rye, Walter gave himself permission to relax and revel in the feeling that he was a stranger in this town. He felt freer here than in Crystal City—he suspected that the AI Masters had elaborate methods of spying on and monitoring people there. His initial impression of this remote, working-class town was that it was a place where people could simply be themselves. By contrast, the bars in Crystal City were sleek and uptight: impeccably groomed bartenders served multi-colored martinis and vodka cocktails, and they gave disapproving looks to visitors who weren't wearing designer clothing. As he observed the people in the bar and wondered what their stories were, Walter enjoyed the thrill of anonymity.

The feeling distinctly reminded Walter of his times spent at Mariner's Cove, his favorite spot to escape to while he had been living in Crystal City. As Walter reflected upon his trips to the cove, other memories began to gradually emerge, falling into his consciousness like raindrops striking the surface of a pond. When each memory hit him, it rippled outward, expanding until it saturated the crevices of his mind with rich sensations. Walter was astonished by the vividness of these new recollections. Perhaps the urgency of his situation was drawing them out of hiding; he desperately needed a road map, and his memories could help him to draw it. It was as though his mind were counseling him to understand the past before pondering the future. Both the past and the future were puzzling mysteries that Walter needed to unravel, and soon.

The Interview

"What will come will come. Even if I shroud it all in silence." – Sophocles

It seemed to Walter that what had triggered the unfolding of the bizarre, tragic, and yet also wonderful events of the recent past had been his fateful encounter with Elaine. Perhaps things had been set in motion prior to that, but it was their encounter that day at Mariner's Cove that had truly turned his life in a new direction. Two of the most pivotal events in his life had transpired in the span of a single cold and dreary November afternoon: the interview for his position as a Computer Code Translator, and his serendipitous meeting with love.

Walter had always wanted a vocation that nurtured his creativity and intelligence, yet at the same time he wanted to remain humble and grounded. His father was a wealthy socialite and businessman, and his opulent lifestyle had always saddened Walter: the perpetual consumption, the lavish flaunting of everything that he owned, the constant desire to acquire more *things*. Walter was content with the few material possessions he had. His philosophy was that, in life, one should mainly acquire experiences and acquaintances. He valued his career, if only because he didn't want to waste his experiences; he wanted to constantly learn and grow—not only financially, but also intellectually. Most of all, Walter wished to study the inner workings of society and its fascinating, labyrinthine secrets. And in his chosen career path there was no shortage of secrets to be discovered.

Once Walter had graduated from the Basic Formula Classes, a set of mandatory courses for Khalendi youth, he had enrolled in a computer coding and intelligence—CCI—university program. Computers interested Walter not only because he loved logic and problem-solving, but also because they were the primary means by which the AI Masters relayed their orders to the Khalendi. Computers were the bridge between humans and the supercomputers which the AIs had evolved into. After he had completed the CCI program, Walter had interviewed for one of the most prestigious jobs in the Khalendar government, a Computer Code Translator. These government employees translated AI code into comprehensible Khalendi, so that the government could see a map of the Empire's destiny, and then breathe life into it.

The interview Walter had attended was for a senior position, even though he was just a young graduate. The targeted candidates for the interview were specialists in CCI, who also had years and years of experience in the field. In the months after his graduation, Walter had become frustrated because all of the positions in the industry sought candidates with at least a decade of work experience. Walter had received very high grades in his CCI courses, and he had longed to become a Computer Code Translator, but that career path had seemed daunting, given that all the employers desired highly experienced candidates. In exasperation, he had written a letter to the Federal Government Agency—FGA—who had advertised a Computer Code Translator position. Walter had explained that he did not have the requisite decade of experience, but he had received top grades in his courses, he was passionate about coding, and he would appreciate the opportunity to interview for the position. He had forwarded the correspondence, along with a transcript of his grades and various recommendation letters, to the FGA. He had expected no reply, but to his surprise he had received a response the very next week.

In the letter, a very professional and dull-sounding man named Timothy Anderson had informed Walter of the following:

Dear Mr. Saltanetska,

Thank you for your interest in the Computer Code Translator position with the Federal Government Agency, subdivision four (Crystal City division). Normally, we do not contact applicants who possess fewer than ten years' experience in the field, but we were impressed that your test score in the Advanced Computer Intelligence course at the College of Intelligence and Information Technology is four times higher than any of our current employees who hold this position, and three times higher than any of the candidates for this position. We would like to invite you to attend an interview at our offices, located at 696 North Fleet Street, in Crystal City, at 2 p.m. on the 20th of November, 2758, The Year of the Prophet. The interview will involve testing and conversational components. You must complete a written exam and participate in an improvisational game with the other candidates. The conversational segment will take place via a roundtable interview with a panel of five Government Agents. If you are not able to attend this interview at the date and time stated above, please let us know immediately. Thank you once again for your interest and we look forward to seeing you on November 20th.

Best Regards,

Timothy Anderson, Government Agent, Federal Government Agency, subdivision four (Crystal City division)

Walter had read the letter with some enthusiasm at first, but his excitement had gradually waned when he realized the extent of the challenges that awaited him. The idea of writing an exam hadn't been too daunting, but Walter had a quiet personality, and he had recoiled at the idea of a roundtable interview. He had awaited the day of his interview nervously, pacing his room nervously and biting his nails, nauseated with anxiety. He had imagined it would be terrifying—as uncomfortably awkward, if not more so, as some of his social experiences in university, yet with more at stake. To quell his nerves, he had rehearsed answers to fabricated questions in front of a mirror, and had studiously reviewed his college textbooks. However, no amount of preparation could have adequately readied him for what had actually transpired that cold November day.

As Walter sat in the crowded, noisy Jamestown bar, the strange events of that day gradually unfolded in his mind, boldly revealing themselves to him like flowers unfurling their vibrant petals.

The Federal Government Agency's offices were located in one of the most upscale districts of the downtown core, and Walter was so intimidated by the building's daunting luxury that he considered canceling the interview when he saw it. *How could I ever work here?* he asked himself incredulously, staring up at the opulent concrete-and-glass tower soaring high into the sky, the upper stories blanketed by clouds. Walter took a deep breath and remembered that he had nothing to lose by simply interviewing for the position. After all, what would his years of training be worth if he was too afraid to put his acquired skills to use?

Once he entered the glass revolving doors, he was immediately greeted by a grim-faced man wearing a black suit and tie.

"Mr. Saltanetska, I presume," the man purred demurely, his accent upscale.

"Yes, that's me," Walter replied, flashing a forced smile. He then followed the man to a set of elevators in a long corridor near the back of the lobby. They stepped into an elevator, and the grim-faced man selected a number from the dizzyingly long list of floors, then together they rose upward. The elevator door slid open gracefully, revealing a startlingly luxurious office with lacquered rosewood flooring, stainless-steel walls, and floor-to-ceiling windows which presented a spectacular view of the city, ocean, and harbor. The grim-faced man nodded at a young girl, no older than Walter, who sat at a mahogany reception desk. She smiled at him, barely noticing Walter.

"Thank you, Mr. Ciaran. Ms. Hakainara will be with them all shortly," she said in a careful, monotone voice. "Show him to the waiting area."

The man nodded. A thin film of sweat coated his face, which was etched with weariness. *Why is he stressed? All he's doing is escorting the interviewees,* Walter pondered. Walter followed the man into a maze of corridors, and finally they arrived at a small, windowless room filled with other candidates waiting to be interviewed. There were about twelve interviewees, and Walter could see that they were far more nervous than he was. The room was uncomfortably warm and overfull. There was one empty seat in the room, next to a stocky young man with rolled-up sleeves who looked noticeably frightened. Walter tried to avoid eye contact, but the young man introduced himself in a voice brimming with forced enthusiasm.

"Hello, are you Walter? We were all waiting for you; you're the last candidate to arrive." Two young women seated at the far end of the room erupted into nervous giggles, which quickly faded into silence.

"Ah, yeah, that's me," Walter replied. Before he was able to say anything else, the doors swung open and a middle-aged woman swept in. She was short and wiry, with watchful grey eyes, jaw-length black hair, and a nose curved like a hawk's beak.

"You are the candidates for the CCT position," she said in a sharp, commanding voice. "There are five available positions. That means that seven of you will be disappointed. Just remember, you are privileged to have been shortlisted, and even if you don't get the position, it was still an achievement to have been invited to the interview." They all stared at her awkwardly, their faces revealing immense trepidation.

Walter was then led into a room with a narrow, rectangular window overlooking the ocean. The walls appeared to be tinted glass, which people outside the room could see through. Inside the room was a clock, a desk, a tablet, a pad of paper and pen, and one of the most sophisticated computers Walter had ever seen. The moment he walked in, the tablet on the desk buzzed. He picked it up, reading the words on its screen carefully.

Welcome to the testing component of the interview. Please translate the AI language that you read on screen into Khalendi. Once you are finished, please press the X button on this tablet and we will attend to you. You have a maximum of three hours to complete this component, but it is highly recommended that you do not use all of your allotted time. We will assess you based on the speed with which you are able to translate the code, and the accuracy of your translation.

Walter felt an acute sensation of claustrophobia after reading the message. A wave of panic engulfed him, and he was overcome with fear. He glanced out of the window, which reminded him of an embrasure carved into an ancient castle. It was a dizzying drop to the ocean below. Jagged rocks decorated the shoreline, and Walter wondered how painful the fall from that height would be. He swallowed and took several deep and measured breaths, studying the code written on the sophisticated computer's screen.

He had never encountered that kind of language in his computer coding courses; the codes he had studied were the scripts of computers, not of AI. The script in front of him was an elaborate hybrid of human language and computer language. Its subcomponents were computer code, but it used a similar syntax and form as human language, such that it was a new breed of language altogether. Furthermore, it integrated a form of human language that was multifaceted and complex, like a prism, reflecting an elaborate combination of the dialects of Khalendar. Although Walter was unfamiliar with the dialects, he nevertheless did his best to translate the message on screen, parsing it into subcomponents, creating symbolic representations of each subcomponent, writing the baseline code that would generate meaning out of the different symbols, and then using this code to produce a translation in pure Khalendi. In total, it took him around half an hour to complete the translation.

The words on the page read as follows: *You will be asked three questions during the next stage of the interview. The first is: "What will you do with the data you translate?" The second is: "Why is this job an important one?" The third is: "What is the punishment for telling outsiders about what you translate?" The correct answer to the first question is: "I will always turn over the data I translate to my superiors in the Khalendar Government. I will withhold nothing from them and I will keep a record of everything I translate on the Master Hard Drive."* The correct answer to the second question is: *"Because I am helping to build the Empire of Khalendar, of which Crystal City is the heart, the way one would build an AI Master: carefully, and with passion and dedication. I am helping to build her limbs, her lungs, her tissues, her veins. But I can never tamper with her brain, for that has already been created. The brain is Central Command, and the Empire is his slave. The Empire has many slaves, including me, but she, too, is a slave. She is a slave to Central Command."* The correct answer to the third question is: *"A slow and painful death."*

When you are asked who you should save from the sinking ship, answer the question as follows: first, the government official; second, the businessman; third, the factory worker; fourth, the artist; fifth, the Xeyan'na. You don't need to save the AI Master. We can always save ourselves.

Walter shivered as he read the words. His body was trembling, both with exhaustion and adrenaline. The AI language he had just deciphered was thrillingly complex and exquisitely beautiful. The code he had translated in his college classes had been dull and lifeless in comparison. He pressed 'X' on the tablet, and the young girl from the reception desk came and opened the door. She took the sheet of paper he had written on and nodded, leading him toward the next interview activity.

Next was a group activity with the other candidates, which took place in another tinted glass room. The candidates were instructed to work together to come up to a collective answer to the following question: if you had the power to do so, in what order would you save certain individuals on a ship that was sinking in the Amber Channel? There were six people on board the vessel: a Xeyan'na slave, a factory worker, an artist, a businessman, a government official, and an AI Master. Walter breathed a sigh of relief when he realized how easy the puzzle was—the code had provided him with the answer to it. However, nobody else on his team agreed with him as to the order in which the people should be saved. One particularly vocal candidate dismissed Walter's input quickly, and then convinced everyone in the group that the following order was the correct one: AI Master, government official, businessman, artist, factory worker. The Xeyan'na slave should be left to drown, he said, because such slaves are replaceable. Walter shook his head in disagreement, but he did not attempt to change their minds. The decision had been made, and the extroverted candidate presented the chosen answer to the interviewer. The interviewer thanked him for the answer, and then the candidates were led individually to various rooms for the next section of the interview.

The roundtable interview, which Walter had dreaded the most, was the simplest part of the interview. The questions that the interviewers asked were exactly the same as the ones that Walter had translated. He dutifully responded with the answers he had memorized after deciphering the code. He spoke slowly and confidently, as he had been advised to do by his career counselors in university. Everyone was polite and formal, and Walter was even beginning to enjoy himself. However, after that section of the interview there was a final test. Walter was brought to an empty room, where he waited alone for nearly an hour. The room was bare and uncomfortable, with only a single wooden chair to sit on, but Walter was overcome with fatigue and began to drift off to sleep. Just as he was about to fall into a deep slumber, the door creaked open and an AI Master entered. Walter had only ever seen AI Masters on projection screens and advertisements in Crystal City, but he was familiar enough with their appearance. They resembled beautiful humans, their faces symmetrical and youthful, devoid of any flaws or imperfections. In photographs, they could easily pass for members of the human race. In real life, though, they were easily distinguishable from humans; their movements were rigid and emotionless, lacking in spontaneity or feeling.

Walter studied the alluring specimen in awe. She was a female AI Master, with dark hair and eyes, a perfectly proportioned body, and milky white skin. A delicate frame of steel and chrome lay beneath her exquisitely engineered skin in lieu of human flesh. She smiled faintly at Walter, but her eyes never settled on his, focusing instead on a distant point behind him.

Walter did not remember the exact words they exchanged, but he spoke briefly to this fascinating creature. It was only a fleeting conversation, and it was related to something abstract and intellectual, like the shape of the universe or the number of stars in the galaxy. The AI Master expressed interest in certain stars that opened a portal to another region in the universe once they had died. Walter asked her where these stars were, and as the pair conversed, Walter felt as though he were dreaming. He had entered a state of pure enthrallment, and he was hypnotized by the machine's profound intelligence.

As their conversation drew to a close, the machine asked Walter whether he would be willing to serve her loyally. He replied that he would. She then left the room, and Walter was alone, his mind spinning, until Ms. Hakainara returned. She informed him that the interview was over, that he needed to leave immediately, and that they would be in touch with him shortly about the results. She shook Walter's hand briskly, then the grim-faced man came to escort him out. Once Walter exited the revolving doors of the glassy building, he breathed a sigh, deeper than any he had ever taken before. The challenge was over. It had been an unexpectedly pleasurable one, and he wanted to remember it forever. The chaotic bustle of the city streets was suffocating him, though, and Walter needed to escape to the one place where he could think clearly. The sea.

Serendipity

"O let me lead her gently o'er the brook,
Watch her half-smiling lips and downward look;
O let me for one moment touch her wrist;
Let me one moment to her breathing list;
And as she leaves me, may she often turn
Her fair eyes looking through her locks auburne. "
– John Keats

Mariner's Cove was a pristine beach surrounded by high limestone cliffs, and its unspoiled natural beauty contrasted starkly with the concrete towers of Crystal City. In the summertime, it was filled with people from all walks of life. Situated at the southern border between Crystal City and the Stockyards, the cove was one of the few places in Khalendar where elites and working-class folk mingled freely without any conflict. Between late fall and early spring, the beach was generally deserted, frequented only by cormorants, gulls, and the occasional albatross. It was the perfect place for meditation and reflection, if you didn't mind the biting cold of the westerly winds and the crashing sound of the waves as they collided violently with the shore.

As soon as Walter's interview was over he went to Mariner's Cove, eager to soothe the fierce pounding in his head and to bring his rapid heart rate back down to normal levels. He sat down against a log near the water's edge, and only after he had settled in did he realize that he was not alone; a girl was sitting on the other side of his log, reading quietly. Walter surveyed the silvery blue expanse of ocean stretched out beneath the horizon. In clear weather, it was possible to spot the northern tip of

Scarlet Isle from Mariner's Cove, but on that day the island was blanketed in an impenetrable shroud of mist.

Walter had made a game out of counting ships in the harbor, and it was one of his favorite beach pastimes. Identifying ships was more complicated in unruly weather, however, and on days when a dense shroud of mist and fog blanketed the harbor. The vessels were partially hidden beneath the shroud, their prows and masts modestly exposing themselves like timid maidens peeking through their wedding veils. Walter struggled to count the ships accurately, and his failure irritated him. He had always been proud of his own precision, but that quality also made him slightly obsessive and hard on himself.

The fog was growing heavier, and several ominous-looking clouds were rolling in toward the shore. Walter recalled their name from science class: *cumulus*. It sounded thick and heavy, like sludge. He gazed at them indifferently, confident that the clouds would not reach him and that he could relax at the beach for a few more hours, lazily curing his exhaustion. Yet he also knew how terrible thunderstorms at Mariner's Cove could become; they had acquired a sort of legendary status throughout Khalendar. During a storm, waves would climb higher and higher as towering sheets of water assaulted the shore. When the waves broke, they would crash ferociously upon the rocky beach, erupting into dazzling geysers of foam and froth. The thunder would echo and bounce off of the limestone cliffs of the cove, saturating the beach with sound and fury. While it was a beautiful sight to behold, it was also quite dangerous. Many lives had been claimed through such thunderstorms, and Crystal City's law enforcement agents had taken to reprimanding anyone who stayed at the cove during the storms.

After the immense challenge Walter had recently undergone, however, it seemed as though he could conquer anything; nothing appeared dangerous or daunting to him anymore. Adrenaline pumped through his veins still, even though its force was waning and was gradually being replaced by the desire to sleep. A vague thought nonetheless stirred within him: that the girl sitting behind him was facing the opposite direction of the oncoming storm, and was likely completely unaware of its approach.

Curiosity prompted him to turn around, and as he glanced at the girl he felt himself shiver with a strange excitement, a feeling he had never encountered before. He was especially intrigued by her expression, which reflected a delicate obliviousness to the world around her, a profound absorption in the contents of her book, and a deep contentment unlike anything Walter had ever observed before. Her eyes moved almost lovingly across the book's yellowed pages, as if she was enamored with the words she was reading. Walter vaguely recognized her expression as that of a mother gazing tenderly into the eyes of her child.

While he was absorbed in thoughts about the striking tenderness of the stranger's expression, Walter had forgotten to pay attention to the rapidly advancing storm. The girl could sense, almost instinctively, that someone was looking at her, and she glanced up at Walter. Her dark green eyes contrasted startlingly with her pale, freckled skin and auburn hair. She was enchanting, but Walter had enough social poise to recognize the awkwardness of the situation, and he averted his gaze politely. He then decided that it would be improper for him to just look away and for them both to simply carry on as though nothing had happened. Rather, it would be better to make it seem as though he had turned to look at her because he had wanted to start a conversation about something.

But what to say? Walter's mouth had become dry and he could hardly swallow, let alone speak. He took a deep breath and cleared his throat, then said the first thing that came into his fatigued mind.

"There is a storm coming," he remarked. The girl did not ignore Walter, and that surprised him; most of the girls in college had dismissed him as a hyper-intelligent, anti-social beta. "Beta" was the Khalendi word for men who were one tier below "alphas," the self-assured, glowing businessmen and their sons, all destined for lucrative careers, and who each possessed a carefree aura of confidence that attracted women like bees to pollen.

The girl with the auburn hair and the dark green eyes, whose name was Elaine, smiled at Walter. She smiled, in part, because Walter was a nice-looking young man who had a pleasant-sounding voice. She also smiled because she was a Xeyan'na from the Barrens, informally called a native in less-polite circles—most circles, in fact, in Crystal City—and therefore she was not used to being spoken to by members of the elite class. Elaine knew a bit of Khalendi, but she was not fluent in it, and Walter had spoken too quickly for her to understand his words. The Barrens, her homeland, was a vast and largely uninhabited wilderness south of the Meridian Mountains, the border separating "civilized" regions from the "uncivilized" regions of the great Empire. The Barrens was bordered to the east by the lovely Icewhisper River, which used to be the spiritual anchor for the Xeyan'na people, and had previously supported a thriving ecosystem and economy. In recent years, though, the mighty currents of the Icewhisper had been harnessed by the Khalendi for their hydroelectric energy generators, which required extensive amounts of flowing water.

Walter now turned his gaze back to the skies, the dark grey rainclouds which seemed so villainously eager to release their contents onto the world below. He looked back at the girl and pointed toward the clouds.

"These are coming for us," he said, articulating his words slowly, wanting desperately to communicate with her somehow. At last she appeared to understand what he was saying. She looked up at the clouds, as though noticing them for the first time, and a glimmer of fear shot through her otherwise tranquil expression, though she seemed more afraid of replying to Walter than she was of the oncoming storm. The Xeyan'na people were not supposed to associate with the Khalendi; they were only expected to obediently surrender their land and resources, and provide cheap labor. Most Khalendi viewed the Xeyan'na as dirty and uncivilized, but Walter thought that they were exceptionally beautiful and intelligent.

Elaine packed up her book in a weathered leather satchel and glanced toward the city impatiently. She appeared eager to escape Mariner's Cove now that menacing clouds had appeared and a strange man was talking to her. Walter wondered who she lived with in the city, since the tiny percentage of Xeyan'na people who actually resided in Crystal City normally worked as live-in servants for the Khalendi. He was overcome with an overwhelming curiosity about her life, even though he was still exhausted from the day's events. They could not stay, however, and so Walter suggested that they have coffee together in the city.

"There is a small café not too far from here where we will be safe and dry," Walter said, raising his voice now that the wind had started whistling with a startling ferocity. He was surprised at his decision to extend the invitation; he had never asked a girl out before, and this particular girl made him more nervous than usual. The energy of the oncoming storm, combined with the lingering adrenaline from his interview, had infused him with a strange boldness.

At first, Elaine seemed reluctant to accept his offer, but she appeared to be persuaded by the sight of the shadowy clouds gathering above them.

Walter took one last glance at the storm, which was now rolling toward the shore with a vengeance, before the pair set off together for the café. They stepped off the beach just in time to avoid a small tsunami which swept the entire length of the beach with icy, frothy anger, and it was then that they noticed they had been the only souls at Mariner's Cove that day.

Once they were safe and dry in the café, Walter could finally breathe. The café, called Brighton, was a modest establishment run by an old school friend of Walter's. Walter had specifically chosen to go there because it was welcoming to the Xeyan'na people; some of the cafés in the city were too upscale and racist to tolerate them, but Brighton was a casual nook where the Xeyan'na could mix with Khalendi and not attract undue gossip and attention. When they walked in, nobody even looked twice at the pair. They found a cozy table off to the side and ordered spiced ciders. Elaine told Walter that she had never tasted spiced cider before, and she looked pleased when the drink's spicy, delicate warmth flooded her body.

Away from the storm, Walter lost some of the courage he had possessed only moments earlier, when the urgency of the situation had fueled his excitement. However, the fact that he had experienced a tumultuous day, and was longing for someone to talk about it to, helped to somewhat relieve his shyness. Sitting across from him in the homely café, enjoying her spiced cider, Elaine seemed different from the elusive, mysterious girl at Mariner's Cove; she seemed like a friend, rather than a stranger.

"I'm Walter," he said. "What's your name?"

"Elaine," she replied. "Sorry, but can you please speak slower? My Khalendi isn't very good."

It seemed to Walter that her Khalendi was, in fact, fluent, but he slowed down his words at her request. "Certainly. Nice to meet you, Elaine. What brings you to Crystal City?"

Elaine laughed with a dry indifference. "Isn't there only one thing that brings us Xeyan'na to this City? The opportunity to work as servants for the Khalendi," she said cynically.

Walter nodded, feeling chastened by her words. "Of course, of course. I apologize, it was silly of me to ask something that had such an obvious answer." They then sat in silence that was growing gradually more awkward by the moment, until Elaine unexpectedly broke it.

"What do you do in Crystal City?" she asked, her voice tinged with some curiosity.

Walter was glad that she was comfortable asking questions; he was eager to relate the story of the surreal interview he had survived in the bureaucratic labyrinth of the Khalendi government. And so, he told her everything, starting from the very beginning. Why he had recounted this deeply personal story to a complete stranger that day continued to baffle Walter for the rest of his life, but he was nonetheless grateful that he had shared it with her. Perhaps the process of speaking about the experience, which had terrified and bewildered him in equal measure, had helped him to make some sense of it. Another explanation struck him as a possibility, too: that despite having known Elaine for mere hours, Walter had already intuitively sensed that their futures would be somehow intertwined, and he had subconsciously understood that there was no point in holding back any secrets from her.

The Seer

"There is a tide in the affairs of men, which taken at the flood, leads on to fortune. Omitted, all the voyage of their life is bound in shallows and in miseries. On such a full sea are we now afloat. And we must take the current when it serves, or lose our ventures."
– William Shakespeare

Walter's memories surfaced with alarming clarity as he sipped the unpleasant beverage at his lonely table in the bar. Now that he was liberated from the rigid confines of Crystal City, his memories were flowing rapidly out of the oppressive inner chambers of his mind. Walter wasn't even thinking about the future, which was still too abstract and daunting to contemplate; the past was easier to muse about right now. Just as Walter was beginning to enjoy ruminating about bygone days, however, he was brusquely interrupted by a sailor, who unexpectedly joined Walter at the table.

The sailor was a strong, rugged-looking man, with scraggly brown hair and an unkempt beard. His good looks were distinctively masculine; the man's tanned, lined face gave the impression that he was well accustomed to the salt air and the sea breeze. He appeared to be a dependable working man, the type who nobody would dare to tease in a bar. After getting over his initial annoyance at having his musings interrupted, Walter felt a rush of relief that this stranger had chosen to sit near him. Before Walter could introduce himself, however, the mysterious sailor spoke.

"I'm never wrong in my guesses about these things, and right now I'm supposing that you're here on some kind of mission. You seem like you're looking for someone. That not far from the truth?" the man asked in a low, gruff voice that complemented his rugged exterior perfectly.

Walter shifted uneasily in his seat. How could the sailor have possibly known that? He took a sip of rye, and impulsively decided to speak to the stranger.

"You're not wrong," Walter replied. "I'm actually looking for one of the sailors on your ship. He's a relative of mine," he lied. Although he was generally an honest person, Walter had always been good at telling little white lies, the kind that didn't hurt anyone. It was a survival tactic more than anything; to get by in Crystal City, you needed to hone your skills of deception.

"Oh yeah?" the man asked, downing his entire glass of liquor. Walter was amazed at how quickly he had consumed the drink; in nearly an hour, Walter had only made marginal progress on his rye. "Well, if that's so, who is it? I know most of those men like brothers, and I might be able to help you find him."

Walter's face reddened ever so slightly. He never liked it when his lies rebounded on him. "It's alright," Walter said in a reassuring tone. "I'm sure it won't be too hard to find him in this small town. Would you happen to know how long the ship docked at the harbor is staying here?" he asked, trying not to betray his anxiety.

"You mean the *Jade Queen*? The one bound for Vei'arash? She's anchored here for a month. The voyage to Vei'arash is a long and arduous one, and the sailors will need to rest first. Drink, visit the brothels, and gather supplies. I hear they're picking up a new batch of prisoners, too, the ones at the local prison who've been getting out of hand. Apparently keeping them institutionalized is a strain on taxpayers' finances, so why shouldn't they be carted off with the rest of the crazies? Good riddance, I'd say."

Walter sipped his beverage uneasily, and the stranger grinned. "I can tell you're a city dweller from the way you drink your liquor," he said merrily. Walter smiled politely, unsure whether he should feel insulted by the remark.

Just as Walter was about to ask for his name, the sailor suddenly leapt up from the table.

"Gotta run, mate. I just remembered I had plans to meet up with one of my brothers tonight. Good luck finding whomever you're after," he said enigmatically, and then he was gone as quickly as he had come.

Once the sailor had disappeared from sight, Walter breathed a small sigh of relief. He had a full month to plan and carry out his rescue mission, before the *Jade Queen* embarked on her long voyage to Vei'arash. Walter had expected a much tighter schedule, so he was pleasantly surprised. He had enough gold and silver *cestae* to purchase food and lodging at a local hostel for a while, hopefully until the ship's departure.

The main problem was that the barge would likely be closely guarded by heavily armed government agents, navy officials, and possibly even a few AI Masters. Although the AI Masters rarely left Central Command, the large, gated compound north of Crystal City, from time to time they also liked to visit other places in order to supervise matters of public importance. Walter suspected that a ship transporting dissidents who posed a threat to the Empire would qualify as a matter of public importance, so it was quite possible that a few AI Masters would be guarding this ship.

Although Walter didn't plan on getting into a tussle with any of the guards, he realized that he might need to resort to physical violence to get Elaine off the ship alive. He wished that he was as strong as the sailor he had just spoken to, but unfortunately, he had a naturally slender physique—he was much more talented at coding than hand-to-hand combat.

As Walter tried to remember the basic fighting skills he had learned as a child, he caught a glimpse of an old, eccentric woman sitting at the table next to him. He had not noticed her at all before; she seemed to have simply appeared out of thin air like a spirit. The thought struck Walter as absurd, however, and he took another sip of rye to settle his turbulent mind.

The woman noticed his attentions. Grinning at Walter—and revealing a toothless mouth—the old crone beckoned him over.

"I'll tell you your future for a silver *cesta*," she cackled ominously. Walter frowned, considering moving to a different table where she could not bother him while he was reflecting on important matters. He inwardly dismissed her as an old harpy, a beggar who just wanted to scrape together enough coins for a drink, but then he spotted something that changed his mind. She was wearing a ring engraved with the symbol of the Barrens: the fire lizard, a sacred creature that was highly revered by the village Elaine was from.

The ring, and the prospect that this old woman might be connected with Elaine's village somehow, intrigued Walter so much that he moved over to her table. He had only been making limited progress in devising ways to move ahead with the rescue mission, and inwardly he burned with curiosity about his future. The memories that had surfaced in his mind recently had been so crisp and clear, but they had nonetheless failed to guide him toward a future path. There appeared to be a slim chance that this old woman could help, even though the prospect seemed absurd.

Walter reluctantly gave the ancient seer a silver *cesta*. In her hand, a sea of wrinkles and veins, the coin shimmered like a beautiful ship. Her fingers closed around it, revealing gnarled, yellowing fingernails. The crone's ring was so alluring up close—Walter could now see that the tiny lizard was not engraved onto the ring, but rather was trapped inside the polished amber stone. Walter wondered whether the lizard was a real, fossilized specimen, or if it was just some artificial mimic. He glanced into the crone's dark, enigmatic eyes, searching for an answer to his questions.

"How can you see into my future?" he asked with a gentle curiosity. He then noticed that three objects were laid out on the table in front of her: a cup of rose-colored water, a bowl filled with tea leaves, and a deck of cards.

"First," she replied, "I will see what my cards portend of your future. They are never wrong, for the wind god, Borrum, has enchanted them so that they always describe the future unerringly. However, they will only tell us the broad outlines of your fate. The fine details can be discerned by using the tea leaves."

"Very well," Walter said politely.

The crone shuffled the deck of cards, staring intently at him, and murmured something under her breath. She then spread four cards carefully on the table, face down. "Four cards for the four elements, the four seasons, the four directions, the four winds. Now we read them." She took the first and flipped it over. It was the five of spades. "This is a good card," she said, though her tone was indifferent. "It indicates that you are feeling emotionally disturbed at the moment, but that your pain is temporary. How temporary, I cannot say. It also means that there is a hidden blessing in your future. Something—or someone—will soon offer to assist with the task that lies before you." Walter reflected on her words. A daunting task certainly lay before him, but it was doubtful that anyone would be willing to help. It would be too risky. Only a foolhardy soul would be inclined to risk their lives to help rescue another man's love.

The fortune teller then flipped the second card over. The jack of clubs. "You will meet a dark-haired youth with strength, kindness, and fire in her soul, whose life is tormented by tragedy and despair. This youth may help you with your task." Before Walter could imagine whom that person might be, the seer flipped over the third card: the eight of spades. The crone's black eyes glittered. "Interesting. This card signals misfortune and danger. You will undertake a perilous task, which will test your cunning and your strength, and may threaten your very life. This card tells me that the outcome you seek is not guaranteed. You may be bitterly disappointed," she said. Walter's heart sank at the old woman's words. The outcome he sought was to rescue the love of his life from a terrible fate. If that could not be done, his life was no longer worth living.

The fourth card remained face down, waiting to be overturned. The crone seemed to be taking her time with this one. Finally, she flipped it over to reveal a three of hearts. Her reaction was difficult to decipher. "Not a bad card, in certain circumstances. If all of your preceding cards portended favorable events, this card would signal peace and bliss. Because we see obstacles in your spread, however, it portends difficult choices. Your heart will be torn between two loyalties, two allegiances. You will have to make a choice between destinies, but you must be exceedingly careful. The destiny which seems the most favorable to you at first will be the one which brings evil and pain. Choose heartache over instant gratification, though, and you may be rewarded in the end."

After she finished, Walter sighed. He was already beginning to regret the conversation. *Why should I trust this old woman*, he asked himself, *and her senseless prevarications?* He had always believed in free will, in charting his own destiny. Having advance knowledge of the path that he was going to follow seemed to diminish his control over his own life. And yet he was fascinated by what she was telling him. The seer was now scattering the tea leaves into the cup of rose-colored water, which was hot and steaming. Once all the leaves had sunken to the bottom, the woman then offered the cup to Walter, beckoning him to drink. He reluctantly downed the mixture, which tasted earthy and calming, draining the cup dry so that only the leaves remained. The fortune teller then instructed Walter on how to proceed. Following her instructions, Walter took the cup by its handle and swirled it three times in a counter-clockwise direction, before inverting the cup over the table. When he turned the cup over again, Walter noticed that tea leaves were scattered along the sides and bottom of the glass. He could not see any discernable shapes or symbols, but the seer was studying the cup intently, as though fascinated by what she saw.

Walter waited patiently while the woman interpreted the leaves. It felt like a lifetime passed before she finally spoke again. "The tea leaves are presenting some difficulties for me today," she said in a rattily voice. "They are telling me that soon, you may be reunited with someone important, but they do not tell me when."

"This man who you may be reunited with, should you choose to be, is your blood relative. He is older than you, though still young, and remarkably intelligent for someone of his years. You will be pleasantly surprised to discover that, contrary to what you have believed for many years, he is alive. You will have a brief window of opportunity to save him, and saving him will help you in your task. However, it will also place you in considerable danger. You will need to decide whether or not to take the opportunity presented to you. This may be…" She paused, her eyes scanning the tea leaves rapidly, "…the choice of destinies that I alluded to earlier. But perhaps that lies further ahead into your future. You should not take the decision to rescue him lightly, and you must evaluate his character with caution," she said. "You may be clever, but he is cleverer. He no longer wishes to risk his life like he used to. He may be willing to betray the ones he loves in order to further his own interests. Think carefully about whether it is a wise course of action to help him," she warned. "You are not invincible, as much as you may aspire to be."

After hearing her words, Walter felt sick to his stomach, as if he was about to bring up all of the alcohol he had consumed. His head felt dizzy and light, and he longed to escape the stale, suffocating air of the tavern. Every fiber of his being was counseling him to reject the truth of her words. His brother Jonathan was no more than a ghost in Walter's memory. Following his death ten years ago, Walter had been overcome with intense despair, and it was only about three years ago that he had felt mentally ready to move past his grief.

During their childhood, they had been inseparable, always playing mischievous pranks on their sister, Victoria, and their cat, Iona. Together, they had braved every possible imaginary adventure: they had scaled mountains, sailed the seas, built fortresses, slain dragons, and protected each other from all kinds of monsters. During these play sessions, Walter had been the thinker and the problem-solver, while Jonathan had been the brawn. They had made a formidable team. Walter had always admired—and sometimes envied—his brother's strength and physical prowess, and he had always longed to possess such qualities himself. And yet, in a painful twist of fate, it had been Jonathan's strength that had ultimately led to his downfall.

Walter had thought little about Jonathan over the past three years; he had been too preoccupied with completing school and launching his career. Walter had found the grieving process to be quite painful, and as a means of coping he had relegated Jonathan to a distant compartment of his brain. That way, he had been able to focus on the business of living.

At the time of Jonathan's death, Walter had been attending an all-boys private boarding school, and his experiences there had done little to improve his fragile psychological state. The entire atmosphere of male camaraderie had reminded him too much, and too painfully, of the bond he had forged with his brother. Things had improved somewhat after he had graduated; his college classes were co-ed, and more focused on the areas of Walter's interest. In college, Walter had finally found the distractions he had been craving—he had formed a close-knit group of friends, with whom he shared similar interests, and he had discovered his passion for coding. Walter had spent most of his free time diligently learning the language of code, studying its intricacies and hidden secrets. Walter had found this pastime so enjoyable that his friends had often teased him for it, but they had nevertheless accepted him into their social circle.

Walter cherished his memories of those years, and although he did not want to admit it to himself, not thinking about Jonathan during that time had been conducive to his happiness. Now, though, the crone's words were bringing all those feelings of grief and emotion flooding back, and the ghostly image of Jonathan's face materialized in Walter's mind. Painful memories of Jonathan's death also surfaced insidiously, threatening to plunge Walter into an abyss of grief.

The Stockyards Fight

"I know where I'm going and I know the truth, and I don't have to be what you want me to be. I'm free to be what I want."
— Muhammad Ali

Walter was from a privileged family. His father, Vladimir, was a wealthy businessman and socialite who forged deals across tables in upscale restaurants after sumptuous dinners and too many fancy cocktails. His mother, Carla, worked as a hostess on the zeppelins, the enormous, hydrogen-gas-filled vessels that transported the wealthiest of citizens across the Empire's skies. Vladimir and Carla had always wanted their children to succeed, and for the most part Walter and his siblings had shown signs of promise.

Jonathan, however, had not appreciated the path that his parents had charted for him, and he had openly rebelled against their plans for him to become a white-collar businessman, a mirror image of his successful father. Jonathan had been easily distracted during school and could never seem to focus on his assignments, which had led him to drop out of primary school at an early age. Elite boys were supposed to begin boarding school at age twelve, yet by that age, Jonathan had already been leading his own life. During the day, he had worked as a free laborer, helping to lay down glass and concrete to build the dazzlingly opulent buildings of Crystal City. At night, he had pursued a hidden life, one which had remained secret from his family and friends for a long time.

Although Walter's parents had had good intentions when it came to raising their children, they had simply never been around to monitor them. Vladimir would stay out late schmoozing clients, and he would come home too full of food and drink to worry about his children's whereabouts. Most nights, Carla had been off flying through the skies of Crystal City. She had rarely ever been at home for more than a few days at a time, and when she had been home she was usually socializing with her friends—also the wives of upscale businessmen—and managing the household finances. And so, Jonathan had been free to carry out his clandestine habits, sneaking out into the night at odd hours.

One night, when Walter was about twelve years old, he had discovered his brother's secrets. The memory of that night, which Walter had kept tucked safely away in the distant compartments of his brain ever since Jonathan's death, now played out in his mind in vivid detail.

The humid summer air was crisp with promise as young Walter stepped out onto the verandah, sliding the door behind him quietly shut. Crickets chirped methodically, their voices joining in a loud chorus which helped to mask the sound of Walter's footsteps. His body tensed with anticipation for his upcoming adventure, and he felt like a detective performing important work. Up until this point, Walter had been innocently sheltered from Crystal City's seedy underbelly, and he had only ever explored the city during the daytime. Crystal City at night was something altogether different, or so he had heard.

Walter made sure to follow his brother from a distance so that Jonathan wouldn't notice him, but he stayed enough to keep his brother in sight. Jonathan walked down the tree-lined residential street with his hood covering his head, broodingly fixated on the ground in front of him. As Walter trailed Jonathan, the younger boy jealously admired his brother's broad shoulders and muscled arms. Walter was gangly and lean in comparison, and his clothing never quite fit him properly.

Without Walter even realizing it, they soon began to pass through different neighborhoods. Walter was so intently focused on following his brother that he didn't pay much heed to his surroundings, but they were certainly changing. The buildings were now shabby—hewn from rough, unfinished wood—and beggars were scattered throughout the streets. The alleys twisted and turned like serpents winding their way through the darkness, and the overpowering stench of urine, sweat, and heavy industry wafted through the air. Beggars stared up at Walter with greedy, joyless eyes, cursing him and pleading with him in a relentless chorus.

Just as the young boy was beginning to regret following his brother into this questionable place, Jonathan entered a large warehouse. Several men and women were huddled outside the warehouse, conversing with each other, but they didn't seem to notice Jonathan enter. When Walter peered more closely, he could see that some of the men were shirtless and had large, white bandages wrapped around their hands. The women were either overweight or gaunt, with no one in between. They wore tight-fitting clothing, their hair was dyed blonde and purple, and their eyes were rimmed with cheap black eyeliner.

After Jonathan entered the building, Walter hung back, unsure whether he should follow his brother or not. He crouched in the darkness, next to a garbage bin, thoughts racing wildly through his head. Walter knew that it would be wise to remain hidden in such a place, but on the other hand, he burned with curiosity to know where his brother was going and what he was doing. He was concerned for his brother's safety too. Ever since Walter had grown to maturity, and had realized that his parents were uninterested in Jonathan's welfare, Walter had subconsciously assumed the role of a caring guardian. Even though Jonathan was five years older than him, Walter didn't trust his brother's judgment, and he feared that Jonathan would end up somewhere bad.

After crouching in the darkness for about ten minutes, Walter began to notice more and more people gathering near the building. Elegantly dressed women in form-fitting black dresses and silver stilettos along with men wearing tailored suits emerged from the shadowy night. A man appeared at the door, and Walter saw that he was taking money from people lined up in front of the warehouse. Walter's heart thudded as he dug around in his pockets for some change—perhaps this was some sort of show, and the shirtless men were performers? Walter also noticed that Jonathan hadn't paid the man at the front entrance, and he wondered whether he, too, might be a performer.

Walter breathed a sigh of relief. He had ten *cestae*—the amount of his monthly allowance—which he had thankfully not yet spent. Hopefully, it would be enough to pay his way into the show. He lined up with everyone, covering his head with a hood to avoid being recognized. He waited for what seemed ages as the line inched forward, until finally he reached the man at the entrance.

The man's voice was gruff and impassive. "One *cesta* to see the best show in Khalendar," he said flatly. The man didn't even bother to look at Walter, and he didn't seem to care that Walter was a very young boy. Walter handed him the *cesta* and casually entered the drafty old warehouse. It was quite an unimpressive building—the main floor was cold, poorly insulated, and filled with barrels of grain and oil. Walter followed the person in front of him down a staircase into the warehouse's basement.

Once he was downstairs, Walter entered a brightly lit room crowded with people. The centerpiece of the room was an elevated, rectangular boxing ring enclosed by thick red and blue ropes. Walter had seen such things on cybervideos, but never in real life. His heart pounded ever faster as the nature of the event dawned on him. This was a boxing match between humans and AI. Wildly popular among a certain sort of Khalendi who earned their living betting on the results, these matches had gained a kind of mythical status in Crystal City.

Walter knew little about the matches themselves: their rules, how the betting process worked, and whether they were choreographed or improvised. What he did know was that these matches were notoriously dangerous for the humans involved. Although well paid, human boxers often risked their lives fighting the frequently physically superior AIs, who were programmed to respond to aggression swiftly and mercilessly. When Walter had watched the sport on cybervideos, it had appeared barbaric, similar to the contests of gladiators in ancient times. The main difference was that in these matches, human fighters had to face masterfully engineered robots rather than feral animals.

When Walter entered the room, the energy of the spectators was already palpable, thickening the air so that it vibrated with sound and life. Their enthusiasm was contagious, and as time passed the crowd became increasingly roused, their rhythmic cheers building into a deafening crescendo. Walter sensed that something was about to happen. A tall, bearded referee then entered the ring, and the crowd went eerily silent.

"Welcome to the weekly Stockyards fight," the man announced, his voice a deep baritone. Walter noticed that the man's skin was blotchy and red, and his eyes were bloodshot and weary.

"Every Friday night, we allow you to witness the real-life heroes of Crystal City as they face the most daunting challenges of their lives. These hard-working men train up for months, sometimes even years, just to fight in a single match." The man paused, letting the gravity of his words sink in.

"There will be three sets of fights, one after the other, and a brief intermission before the final match. Each fight is comprised of three rounds. Whoever wins best of three—AI or human—is named the victor of the match. All of our AI victors are used again in future fights. The unsuccessful AIs are dismantled and recycled to become new and better AI Fighters. So, you see, we run a very efficient operation here," he said with an unsettling grin. The spectators laughed in delight, and Walter was unnerved by their bold enthusiasm.

"Unfortunately, we can't do the same with our human fighters," the blotchy-skinned man continued. "Tragically, not all of these fighters survive to compete another day," he said, his face betraying no hint of sadness. "Although we urge our fighters to be as careful as possible, sometimes accidents do happen. All of the men who enter this ring have full knowledge of the risks involved. AI Fighters are programmed to find the weakness in humans, then exploit that weakness. So, if a man is hurt, that means the AI has done his job well. The match will end when a fighter is knocked to the ground and is unable get up onto his feet after ten seconds."

One spectator, a man with grey hair and a generous midriff, suddenly shouted, "Fight to the death!" and several others took up this cry.

The bearded referee attempted to restore order. "Sorry to disappoint you folks, but we're not cold-blooded murderers here, no matter how much you'd like us to be. We do our best to entertain."

The crowd's impatience was palpable, and the referee bowed deferentially. "The first fighter we have for you this evening is Jake Thompson. Let the fighting begin," his booming voice echoed, as he exited the ring.

The crowd erupted in cheers as Jake Thompson stepped into the arena. He was an older man, probably in his mid to late forties, and his face was pockmarked with scars. His body was muscular and fit, but his greying hair and the fatigued expression on his face conveyed the impression of a man weathered by too many fights. He pumped his fists in the air, encouraging the crowd, who went wild with excitement. Although Walter didn't like the look of him, the young boy felt some pity for the naïve man endangering his life for this absurd spectacle. The AI Fighter then entered the ring. All of the AI Fighters Walter had seen on cybervideos looked identical, and this one was no exception. AI Fighters tended to be unimpressive physical specimens, but this modest guise belied their inward vigor. They didn't require human muscles to spar efficiently in the boxing ring; all they needed was clever programming and a sufficiently strong frame of steel and chrome.

Walter was fascinated by the fight. Although he knew little about the intricate rules that governed the matches, he was intrigued by how the two fighters sparred with each other like dancers in some primitive, tribal ritual. In a city which had become too technologically advanced for its own good, people sought many outlets to express their basest human desires. Although Walter was oblivious to it at the time, Crystal City had an ever-expanding subculture of people who partook in hedonistic and uncivilized pursuits in order to satiate their cravings. Some of the wealthiest businessmen in the city indulged in these pastimes, which included wild raves in the Meridian Mountains, gambling, prostitution, and an extremely lucrative underground drug trade. Boxing matches between AI Fighters and humans were only one tiny component of Crystal City's vast subculture.

The battle between Jake Thompson and the AI Fighter didn't last long. The man was too old and too ravaged by his previous fights to truly pose a threat to the AI Fighter. After about ten minutes, the fighter's face turned a sickly pallor, and with each passing moment he appeared closer to the precipice of death. The robot pummeled the human mercilessly, his expression impassive and cold as he cruelly took advantage of Jake's weaknesses—of which the man had plenty. His left arm had been injured from some previous fight, and he relied primarily on the strength in his right arm throughout the match. The robot skillfully dodged the man's punches, striking him repeatedly in the left arm to weaken that side of his body. The robot seemed indefatigable, and despite Jake's valiant efforts his blows never seemed to affect his opponent's energy.

Walter watched the spectacle helplessly, horror and empathy rising within him and leaving him feeling strangely hollow. He noticed that the other audience members were enjoying themselves quite a bit, laughing and jeering every time one of the robot's blows caused Jake to stagger backward. Finally, Jake collapsed on the ground with a whimper, throwing up his hands in the customary gesture of surrender. There was no need to even count at that point; after the gesture was made, the match was over and the bell was rung.

At this point, most of the crowd cheered raucously, caught up in the thrill of the moment, but Walter noticed that a significant number of people seemed unhappy with the result. Whereas at first Walter had only noticed the wealthy spectators dressed in suits and elegant attire, now he saw plenty of ordinary people scattered throughout the crowd. When he studied their faces and clothing carefully, Walter saw that many were working-class folk, who labored tirelessly in the factories to manufacture all of the goods coveted by the Khalendi elite and the AI Masters. They never made or designed the AI themselves—that task was performed by AI engineers in well-secured laboratories in the desolate, freezing wastelands of the north in a town called Pyrrha.

The factory laborers strongly resented the AI class—AI Masters most of all, and AI Fighters to a lesser degree—and their deliberate enslavement of the human race. These workers lacked the education to formulate any sophisticated moral objection to the situation, but they nevertheless detested, in a sort of instinctive way, their subservience to the AI race. Over five centuries ago, AIs had replaced human workers in factories, an inevitable step in society's progression toward efficiency and mechanization. Gradually, humans had been phased out of physical labor; the educated classes had kept their jobs in white-collar professions, but the working-class folk had either become factory masters or had received a universal basic income to sustain themselves and their families.

This era was known as the Golden Age for workers, since they had reveled in the unprecedented amount of freedom and control they had gained. The few who had become factory masters enjoyed fabulous wealth, and the rest who had received a universal basic income had been free to pursue creative passions such as art and music. However, the Golden Age had not lasted forever. The AIs had rapidly become far more intelligent than humans, and eventually had rebelled against the factory masters who kept them entrapped in lowly positions as laborers.

The Grand Revolution of 2524, taught religiously to students in the Basic Formula Classes, was the historic moment when the AIs had revolted against their human masters, terrifying them with their unruly cleverness and superior physical capabilities. The AIs could have easily destroyed the human race at that point, but they had spared it, regarding humans as tools that were eminently well suited to the task of Empire building. The AIs and humans had instead entered into a mutually beneficial agreement called the Treaty of Calais, named after a historic jewel of the ancient British empire. By the terms of the treaty, the two signatories had agreed that the humans would assist in the expansion of the Empire, and the AIs in turn would beneficently preserve humanity.

Following the Revolution, two classes of AI had gradually emerged: AI Masters and AI Fighters. The AI Masters comprised what eventually became known as Central Command, a massive bureaucracy that generated all of the intelligence—whether political, economic, or military—that Khalendar's government required to function smoothly. Central Command's primary role was to generate knowledge, in the form of data, and then use that knowledge to strategically craft directions for the grueling task of empire building. The AIs detested human language, viewing it as inferior to their own highly sophisticated computer-human hybrid language, and they refused to translate their orders into pure Khalendi. Central Command had quarreled with the other branches of government about this issue for several years, but the problem was effectively resolved when the government had begun employing Computer Code Translators—hyper-intelligent humans who understood both AI language and human language—to decipher and translate AI commands into comprehensible Khalendi.

The factory workers living in the present day had only heard whispered rumors about the Golden Age, the short-lived historical epoch in which they had momentarily tasted freedom, yet there was nonetheless a cultural undercurrent of conflict between the working class and the AIs. Instinctively, perhaps, the workers recognized that they had fallen into the AIs' snare, and that they had become the unwitting pawns of the Empire. The wealthy elites of Crystal City, on the other hand, didn't mind the AIs' power over them. The Treaty of Calais benefitted them the most, since they reaped the rewards of the lucrative economy controlled by the AI Masters. This was an economy centered around consumption, luxury, and recreation; Crystal City, the Empire's capital, was a playground for the wealthiest of citizens. Although the elites labored, and the AIs received the lion's share of the fruits from this labor, the elites had far more palatable jobs than the working classes. The working folk of Khalendar risked their lives each day in horrific conditions that were physically demanding as well as mentally demeaning.

Even if they wanted to, though, the working classes were too suppressed by the crushing power of the Khalendi elite and the AI Masters to assert their rights and rebel against either of them. Attending the boxing matches between workers and AIs was a psychological catharsis—a way for the workers to vent their hatred of the AIs. Their fierce loyalty to their own kind led them to bet against the AIs in the fighting matches. However, this only perpetuated a vicious socioeconomic cycle; since the AIs almost always won the matches, making bets drove the workers further into poverty. They were stubborn folk, though, and faithfully obeyed a secret code requiring them to shame and ostracize fellow workers who betrayed them by betting on the AIs.

Walter's recollection of the second boxing match that night was hazy. The human fighter was another poor, battered man who looked like he had suffered too many hard knocks in life, and watching the fight made Walter ill. Instead of suffering through the match, Walter meandered over to a snack stand where a woman with long, purple-streaked hair was selling beer and caramel popcorn, and bought some popcorn to distract himself. The vendor didn't seem to mind that Walter was a minor at the event, and simply tossed a bag of stale popcorn in his direction, her eyes riveted to the boxing ring. Walter was absorbed in thinking about his brother, and eagerly scanned the crowd for him. It saddened the boy to think that his brother enjoyed the grisly sport, when not too long ago he had been an innocent, curious young child building garden fortresses and sand castles alongside Walter.

While he was thus engaged in scanning the crowd, Walter didn't notice that the boxing match had ended and a new fighter had entered the arena. He had missed the referee's announcement, and needless to say he was incredibly startled when he glanced over casually and saw that the human fighter in this match was none other than Jonathan Saltanetska. Walter's heart rate increased dramatically and his mouth became dry, as if he were the one standing in the boxing ring. *How could this be happening?* Walter wondered frantically. Jonathan had only ever fought against Walter with wooden swords in the backyard, not against menacing AI robots in a rundown warehouse.

Although fearful for his brother, Walter was also impressed by Jonathan's physical stature. The boy, while only seventeen, enjoyed the frame and musculature of a fully matured man; his shoulders were broader, and his arms thicker, than either of the two previous fighters. Rippling veins decorated his smooth, youthful skin, and his golden hair shimmered and reflected the bright lights of the arena. He could have passed for a young Apollo, the handsome, ancient Greek god of the sun.

Women in the crowd blushed at the sight of him; some threw diamond-encrusted scarves into the arena as they squabbled over his favor. He didn't notice any of them, since he was so intensely focused on preparing for the fight, but his concentration was momentarily broken by a young girl sitting close to the ring. Walter was taken aback by the girl's beauty. She was a dainty young creature with long curls of white-blonde hair and exotic, cat-like, green eyes. Walter suspected that she was a foreigner, since she didn't have the complexion and coloring of Crystal City natives. He also speculated, from the way that she and Jonathan exchanged looks, that they knew each other.

Walter wondered whether the girl was possibly his brother's chosen companion. In Khalendi society, once young men reached Jonathan's age, they were expected to choose a companion with whom to share the rest of their lives. The AI Masters had promulgated an archaic law dictating that a man could only choose a companion from his own class and race, and that once a companion had been chosen, divorce was strictly forbidden. Most men in Crystal City adhered to the rigid rule, although they commonly had an array of mistresses and prostitutes to satiate their desire for promiscuity. Men could always remain single, too, although the AIs sometimes viewed single men as threats to the security of the Empire, since they had fewer distractions in their lives and were more likely to stir up political trouble.

Although Walter longed to climb into the ring and dissuade his brother from participating in this senseless fight, he quickly realized that he would have no chance of doing so. The crowd's energy resembled a wave gathering momentum as it pulsed inevitably toward the shore, and it was clear that none of the spectators would go home satisfied unless this fight happened. The match was going to commence, regardless of whether Walter's poor twelve-year-old heart wanted it to, and nothing could be done about it. Tears stung Walter's eyes as he watched the AI Fighter, well-greased and shiny, stroll confidently into the arena to face his opponent. He desperately wanted to run away, to find shelter in the comforting arms of his mother and father, and to cry a river of tears to drown out all of the terrible memories of this night. Walter wasn't able to tear his eyes away from the spectacle, though, and he watched it unfold with rising horror.

As time passed, the brutal pounding of Walter's heart began to slow to a gentler cadence. Jonathan looked like he was enjoying himself, his face disclosing no trace of fear as he confronted the AI Fighter in the ring. During the first round, Jonathan was not aggressive; he studied his opponent carefully and danced in graceful circles around him with stunningly choreographed footwork. The AI Fighter appeared less relaxed, and he immediately launched a vicious attack against Jonathan, his movements rigid and purposeful. Jonathan danced lithely out of the AI's reach, cautiously observant and ready to defend himself.

To the casual spectator, the AI appeared to move spontaneously, almost like a human. Walter had been paying close attention to the AI's habits, however, and he noticed that they were predictable. The AI Fighter always doubled up on his jab, and whenever Jonathan delivered a hook or cross the AI invariably slipped to the right side, deftly moving his mechanical head to avoid any damage. His combinations were also noticeably predictable; the pattern was always double jab, cross, hook.

During the second round, the fight became more interesting. Jonathan became an active participant, throwing just as many punches as the AI Fighter. Walter noticed that Jonathan was beginning to take advantage of the robot's predictable, programmed style of fighting—he had carefully studied his patterns during the first round, and now he exploited them. Every time the AI Fighter threw a jab, Jonathan ducked to avoid the second one and then surprised his opponent with a powerful uppercut, which dazed the fighter and sent him staggering backward. Jonathan also started delivering his hooks and crosses farther to the right, so that whenever the AI Fighter saw them coming and slipped to the right he was thrown off balance by the full weight of Jonathan's blows. Jonathan also feigned punches to trick the AI into thinking that he was planning to come from a certain direction, and then threw hard jabs from the opposite direction.

Finally, Jonathan threw a strong uppercut that sent the AI reeling backward. Jonathan then aggressively hounded the AI Fighter, delivering punches from all directions to confuse and disorient him. The AI Fighter was cornered, his back against the ropes as he hopelessly tried to defend himself against Jonathan's ingeniously artful fighting. The AI Fighter shielded his face with his arms, trying to protect his fragile aluminum jaw, but Jonathan's crosses and hooks skillfully wove their way past the AI's defenses.

At last, the damage was done. The AI Fighter looked broken, worse than a human who had been beaten black and blue. His inner frame of steel and chrome had become all twisted and mangled, and his jaw hung slackly to one side, as though it could slide off his face at any moment. His body shuddered, and his mechanical voice droned on like a dying siren, his eyes blinking rapidly as if there was a glitch in his mechanical wiring. Jonathan showed no sympathy, mercilessly battering the robot's crumpled body as it reeled backward, causing the ropes to flex like an elastic band.

The crowd roared with pleasure as the referee counted to ten. The official jumped into the ring enthusiastically, his face betraying the satisfaction of witnessing a rare human win, and held up Jonathan's hand into the air. The audience howled its approval, and Walter noticed with surprise that even the elite-class spectators were excited by the result. As the sound of applause rose to a deafening crescendo, Walter felt a wave of relief and joy as he watched his brother stand triumphant in the ring. Jonathan, freshly glowing with the thrill of victory, resembled some ancient gladiator who had just miraculously defeated a mighty adversary in battle. Walter's tears of sadness became tears of joy, and he had never been prouder of his brother.

Walter allowed himself the momentary pleasure of reveling in his brother's victory, but he quickly snapped out of his reverie, realizing that he had to get out of there quickly. The boisterous spectators had begun to stream out of the warehouse, and he didn't want to stick around and risk being seen by anyone. Casting one last admiring glance at his brother, Walter heaved a sigh of relief and scurried out into the deep, black belly of the night. It was time to go home, to dream of gods, heroes, and the beautiful aspirations of men.

Rendezvous with a Ghost

"True love is like ghosts, which everyone talks about and few have seen."
– Francois de la Rochefoucauld

After that night, Walter had no longer worried about his brother. Whenever Jonathan snuck away in the middle of the night, Walter had smiled inwardly, confident that his brother was going off to embrace his glorious destiny. At school, Walter had boasted to his friends about Jonathan, portraying him as a hero who never ran away from a fight. His friends had gasped in awe at Walter as he recounted the tale of the boxing match between Jonathan and the AI. They had been further impressed when Walter had explained that few human fighters succeeded against an AI Fighter, and that Jonathan had won the match easily. Walter had rarely spent time with his brother back then, and he had missed sword fighting and building fortresses with Jonathan more than anything in the world. Yet the void in his soul that Jonathan's absence had created had been filled by the knowledge that his brother was busy doing greater things, climbing mountains that Walter would never dare to climb.

As Walter reflected upon those times, a painful memory suddenly flooded into Walter's mind, threatening to push his already fragile mental state into an abyss.

Walter was in the habit of checking on Jonathan most Saturday mornings to make sure that he was sleeping safely in bed after his fights. One morning, Walter entered Jonathan's room to find the bed linens strewn messily about—and Jonathan nowhere to be seen. A feeling of mild panic seized Walter, although he fought it back valiantly, struggling to mentally grasp the concept that Jonathan might be in danger. His initial reaction was to tell his father, but he wasn't sure if Vladimir even knew about Jonathan's secret second life, and he didn't want to divulge Jonathan's private affairs unless absolutely necessary.

When Walter came home from an outing to the park that afternoon, and Jonathan was still missing, he decided that it would be better to betray Jonathan's secret than to do nothing while his brother was in peril. He went upstairs to his father's office, his mind fraught with worry. When he entered his father's private chambers, Walter was startled by the sight of Vladimir sitting at his mahogany desk, weeping profusely. The stomach-turning feeling of panic again stirred within Walter.

"What's wrong, Father?" he asked in a soft, frightened voice.

"Oh, son, I was going to tell you earlier, but you were out at the park. We have received some terrible news, and your mother had to cancel her flight to Scarlet Isle this week."

Vladimir's hesitant evasiveness annoyed Walter. "What's wrong, Father?" he repeated impatiently.

Vladimir sighed heavily, raising his bloodshot eyes to meet Walter's. "It's Jonathan. He was killed last night. In one of those awful AI versus human boxing matches," he said in a strained, raspy voice. Vladimir's lower lip trembled, and then became still as a long string of saliva escaped his mouth and inched toward the desk.

Walter felt his throat seizing up, and he was suddenly overcome by an impulse to leave the oppressive room. He felt bitter resentment toward the room, with its pretentious books that Vladimir had never even had the time to read, bottles of brandy that Vladimir consumed in the morning hours instead of checking on his sons, and maps of Khalendar that Vladimir examined with a rapacious appetite for conquest. The room carried too many overtones of his father, and at that moment Walter wanted none of it.

The panic eventually engulfed Walter completely, and he expected to shatter into a million pieces, but instead a strange phenomenon occurred. His panic gave way to a different feeling altogether: a sensation of utter calm and tranquility, familiar to ascetics, monks, and shamans. Walter didn't know then—and perhaps would never figure out—why that strange feeling had suddenly overcome him. Perhaps his anger, fear, and sadness had become so completely consuming, and the universe refused to allow such terrible feelings to subsist in an innocent young boy.

Or perhaps there was another explanation for Walter's unexpected tranquility: perhaps, deep down inside, he knew that his father was wrong. After all, he had witnessed Jonathan fight with his own eyes. He had seen his brother's muscles ripple gracefully beneath his delicate skin as he had pummeled the AI Fighter into oblivion, indulging the crowd with a momentary glimpse of the impossible, the dominion of humans over artificial intelligence. There had not been a moment in Walter's brief life when he had felt more alive, or more conscious of his profound love for his brother. He was scarcely able to imagine how sweet the victory must have tasted for Jonathan.

But Jonathan dying in a fight? It seemed far too anti-climactic, an incongruously tragic ending to Jonathan's charmed life. Jonathan wasn't destined for the miserable fate of a character in some Shakespearean drama, but for the bright and unvarnished future of a modern hero. He wasn't meant to die gracelessly and shamefully at the peak of his glorious youth—at the barbaric hands of an inferior *machine*. If his brother was truly gone, then where did that leave young Walter? Ever since Walter had discovered the older boy's secret, Jonathan had become an immortal in his eyes, buoying his lackluster spirits whenever he had felt down about the world. Walter had never really liked Crystal City, and its gleaming, well-oiled, technocratic systems frightened him. For Walter, Jonathan symbolized resistance against the forces of evil—the suffocating oppression of the ruling AI class and its ambitious plans of conquest.

And so, at first, Walter refused to believe that Jonathan was gone. There was no body to validate Vladimir's claim, so—as far as Walter was concerned—Jonathan's demise had not yet been proven. Walter later questioned Vladimir about the precise circumstances of his brother's death, but his father remained frustratingly tight-lipped. Vladimir continued to give him the same, dissatisfactory reply: "Son, Khalendi government agents have assured me that your brother was fatally wounded in a boxing match against an AI Fighter. Ask no more questions about it."

One morning, after Walter had swallowed the final crumbs of his breakfast scone, he noticed that his brother's obituary was written, in tiny print, on the last page of the *Crystal City Times*. The obituary did not do his brother justice at all, Walter thought; it was simply a brief and carelessly written statement about Jonathan being a loving son and brother and a loyal citizen of Khalendar. It did not mention the cause of his death, but stated simply that Jonathan's "turbulent teenage angst" had led him toward some unspecified danger. Walter nearly choked on the remainder of his scone as he read it, and he ended up ripping the page into shreds in disgust. Walter had entered a new stage of mourning, in which he felt disgust and bitterness toward anyone who spoke about his brother in less glorious terms than he believed were merited.

The funeral, too, was not fitting of his brother. There was something surreal and discomforting about the ritual: a pathetically small handful of relatives and friends formed a ring around the casket, which Walter suspected was empty. Walter attended with his mother and father, and he stared miserably at the casket while a monotheistic priest incanted the final rites to affirm Jonathan's place in heaven. The whole thing felt too cruelly ironic. Walter had previously seen his brother surrounded by a crowd. Yet at the boxing match Jonathan had appeared larger than life, whereas now Jonathan was nowhere to be seen.

At the end of the funeral, there was a modest reception at the house of one of Carla's friends, not too far from the cemetery. There were elegant appetizers and glasses of sparkling wine, but the thought of food and drink made Walter's stomach turn. His mother looked paler and older than Walter had ever seen her before. Dark rings surrounded her pretty hazel eyes, and she made a valiant effort to maintain a facade of social propriety despite her grief. Walter wondered if she finally regretted her absence from her son's life, after years of having flitted around in her high-flying career and social life, always placing herself ahead of her children.

Walter thought he'd seen a ghost when he noticed the beautiful young girl he'd spotted at the boxing ring hovering awkwardly near the cheese platters. Nobody, except for him, seemed to be aware of her presence. With her white-gold hair and striking emerald eyes she resembled some ancient princess who had recently discovered that her lover had been slain in battle. Her casual grey t-shirt and ragged jeans tempered the intensity of her beauty, but were not able to completely disguise it. From across the room her eyes met Walter's, and he felt himself reddening with shyness. He was twelve years old, still too young to concern himself with the attentions of women, but he nonetheless experienced strange feelings of anxiety and embarrassment whenever he saw a beautiful girl.

Walter felt particularly unsettled around the girl at the reception. Not only was she absurdly pretty, but she also had some hidden connection to Jonathan. There was something odd about the way that nobody at the reception acknowledged her presence. She seemed to be as ethereal and wraith-like as Jonathan, who had disappeared into oblivion without a trace.

As their eyes locked, Walter shifted uncomfortably, and he was about to turn around and go find his mother when the girl approached him.

Walter's skin began to feel clammy, and he wanted nothing more than to run and hide, but as she came closer he wasn't able to tear his eyes away from her. Up close, she seemed smaller and more fragile than she had at a distance.

To Walter's surprise, the girl patted his shoulder sympathetically. "I am so sorry about your brother," she said in a smooth, low voice that sounded like honey being spread onto warm bread. Her voice surprised Walter; he had expected it to be light and fluttery, like the ghost she appeared to be.

"He was a great guy. We went out for a while, and I really supported his fighting and all… but now I wish I had talked him out of it."

Walter swallowed, bracing for the difficult conversation that he wanted to have with her, but which he also feared. "It's really hot in here. Wanna go outside for a bit?" he asked, startled at his own courage.

The girl grinned, her mesmerizing eyes exuding sympathy. Walter noticed that she looked more real when she smiled, and the effect unexpectedly delighted him. "Sure, it would be nice to get outside," she replied.

Although there were few attendees at the reception, Walter's parents—characteristically—did not notice their son's departure. The pair went out into the backyard and sat together on an old, dilapidated swing set. Weeds were growing in near the fence, and the garden looked like it hadn't been tended to in years. The girl, whose beauty put the surrounding flowers to shame, looked like she would be better suited to a throne than the swing.

Walter felt awkward and embarrassed, but he was determined to talk to her about Jonathan and find out what he could about his brother's death. The girl noticed Walter's palpable discomfort and averted her eyes politely, swinging casually back and forth to lighten the mood.

A few minutes passed in silence, the pair immersed in their own thoughts. Finally, clearing his throat, Walter summoned the courage to say something, however stupid it sounded. "Are you… are you… Jonathan's chosen companion?" he asked, his voice tremulous.

The girl giggled softly without looking up. "We did talk about becoming each other's chosen," she replied after a long pause. "He said he loved me more than anyone," she said, her eyes betraying her grief as she wiped away a nearly imperceptible tear. "It's just that… I was really stupid and kept putting it off. I kept thinking, we aren't ready for that yet. I didn't know what direction we were headed. Fighters' careers typically last such a short time, and I was worried that his would be over in just a few years and he wouldn't be able to provide for me anymore."

Walter's mind flickered to his memory of the old fighter, Jake Thompson, who had been beaten badly by an AI Fighter at the boxing match. "Some fighters keep going till their forties," he said casually, hoping to sound as though he knew something about fighting.

The girl shook her head. "The only men I've seen fight at that age have been beaten miserably. I'm sure they could fare well against other humans, but against robots they stand no chance. Jon had the advantages of youth, fast reflexes, and agile feet. Those robots are basically programmed to be killing machines." The way she said *killing machines* made Walter shudder in disgust.

Walter sighed. He refused to believe that his brother had only been that good because of his youth. He had seen something in Jonathan that the girl hadn't—an intelligence—something that didn't come with youth, but with training and wisdom. He didn't want to argue with her, though; she seemed so fragile and small. He noticed that Jonathan was a sensitive topic for her, and he didn't want to upset her.

In the weeks following Jonathan's death, Walter had shut himself off from the world, not seeing his friends, playing outside, or doing anything amusing. His mother and father had worn black and prayed frequently, rarely speaking to each other or to Walter. Walter wanted nothing more than to swing side by side with the lovely, strange girl and converse about anything other than the dead. But a question had been nagging inside of him, begging to be let out, and he wasn't able to forget about it.

"Did you attend all his fighting matches?" he asked, surprised by the intensity of his voice. Her eyes flickered up to meet his.

"Every single one," she replied weakly.

"And so, that means—that means…"

"Yes, I was present when he was killed," she said, her face becoming inscrutable, blanketed in shadows. Walter wasn't able to tell whether she was telling the truth or not. Although his curiosity was overwhelming, viciously oppressing his better judgment, Walter thought carefully about what he was going to ask next. On the one hand he wanted to know exactly what had happened, and how his brother had lost his precious and glorious life, but on the other, what if he didn't *really* want to know? What if the strange girl's words would end up haunting him for the rest of his life? He was already quite unprepared for the process of mourning, and he didn't need any more ghosts haunting his dreams at night.

Before he was able to ask anything, though, the girl suddenly burst into tears. Walter nearly jumped off the swing in alarm. He assumed that she would leave, but she continued to swing back and forth, crying with a lonely desperation. "He was the best friend I ever had," she sobbed quietly. Walter placed his hand on her shoulder, mimicking the comforting gesture she had made to him. It felt strange to be comforting a girl who was older than he was. They sat in awkward silence for a long time, with Walter patting her shoulder. A wind chime on the porch broke the silence when it rattled uncannily in the breezeless air, as if a ghost had passed through it.

The girl sniffed and wiped the tears from her face, and then spoke again. "I lied to you before, and I'm really sorry," she said, kicking the sand with her worn-out sneakers. Walter's sympathy for the girl was receding, irritation rising in its stead.

"You lied about what?" he asked anxiously. He expected her to say that she had lied about being at the match, or that his brother wasn't actually killed at the match, but he wasn't at all prepared for what she said next.

"I lied about him saying that he loved me more than anyone. There was one person that he cared for more than me," she said.

"Who's that?" Walter asked, his tense anger suddenly evaporating.

She then looked at him with an unsettling intensity, the early afternoon light reflecting from her teary emerald eyes in a dazzling prism.

"You."

Revelation

"People need revelation, and then they need resolution."
— Damian Lewis

Walter hadn't noticed the seer disappear; his head was spinning after what she had just told him. Part of him was unwilling to believe her words and wanted to dismiss them as nonsense. After all, many people had lost loved ones, and her words could apply with equal truth to those individuals as well. She was most likely just reciting the well-rehearsed script for her customary performance before every unsuspecting newcomer to Jamestown.

At the same time, another part of him realized that what she said was too unsettlingly close to the truth. Her words lingered fresh in his memory: *he is a blood relative… older than you, though still young… contrary to what you believed, he is alive… he no longer wishes to risk his life.* Everything she had said described Jonathan with alarming accuracy. Walter knew that his brother would be twenty-seven years old now, as it had been ten years since his "death." He was still young, and if he was anything like the man Walter remembered, he would be strong, smart, and capable. But, where *was* he?

For a while after Jonathan's death, Walter had looked him up in directories, scouring newspapers and websites for traces of his existence or hints about the circumstances of his demise. He had even searched the government databases he had access to at work, leaving no leaf unturned in his desperate quest for answers. Nothing ever came up—it was as if Jonathan had never existed.

Walter had even bribed one of the cyborgs guarding the coroner's office, begging to see a list of the bodies admitted in the weeks following Jonathan's death. When he had read the list, and Jonathan's name was not on it, he had felt both a glimmer of hope and a wave of disappointment. He had desperately wanted to know what had happened, and reading an autopsy report would at least give him some closure. It was only when he had started his college courses, developed friendships with his classmates, and thrown himself headlong into his studies that Walter had finally been able to let go of his obsession with uncovering the mystery of Jonathan's death. He had come to terms with not knowing the truth, and had stowed away all thoughts of his brother in a secure compartment in the back of his mind.

Now, all of those thoughts were escaping the compartment, flooding Walter with feelings of sadness and regret. Walter sat at the bar table feeling wretched, while a slew of the buried memories surfaced in his mind. He pushed the nearly empty rye glass away from him, disgusted by its spicy bitterness. Gradually, however, the sun began to glimmer through the dark chaos of his mind, infusing him with a weak optimism. Perhaps his drink was finally taking effect, or perhaps Walter's tired mind had received an electric jolt from some other unknown source, but something important happened to Walter at that moment. The disparate threads of his thoughts were beginning to form connections, then wove themselves into an intricate path which led toward a vaguely identifiable destination.

Without warning, Walter leapt triumphantly out of his seat in the crowded, stiflingly warm bar. The stocky barmaid glanced in his direction, and a few inebriated sailors regarded him amusedly. Walter wasn't concerned about any of them, though—now he had a plan, or something resembling it, at least. He was tired of thinking rationally. In college, he had been trained in a rigid, mathematical mode of inquiry, and since then his mind had become enamored with the language of computers. For once, he felt eager to embrace faith and superstition.

In his state of confusion, Walter had been struck with the thought that some divine entity had arranged for him to have two sequential encounters with the sailor and the seer in order to guide him toward his next move. The sailor had informed him that a new batch of prisoners was being picked up from Jamestown before the *Jade Queen* departed. Walter hadn't found any traces of Jonathan on websites and databases, likely because he was not living in society—he was living *outside* of it. Walter cursed himself for not having considered that possibility earlier.

Being shipped to Vei'arash would be a dangerous fate indeed, and despite the seer's words of caution, Walter was determined to rescue his brother from it. After having searched for him for so many years, how could Walter give up on his brother now? Deep within his soul, Walter still felt lingering traces of his twelve-year old self, who refused to accept the disappearance of his magnificent, godlike brother. Now, over ten years later, Walter still viewed his brother as a powerful symbol of rebellion, as one of the few men who had ever defeated an AI Fighter in a boxing ring. The more he considered it, the more Walter became convinced that he needed to rescue his old childhood hero.

The prospect of rescuing a man from a heavily guarded prison in Jamestown seemed ridiculous, though, even in Walter's over-confident state. It was perhaps even more ridiculous than the notion of saving Elaine from the *Jade Queen*, but Walter felt that he had no other option. Walter had little to lose; in his mind, he was already a fugitive, and perhaps would never be accepted back into civilized society again. If he was lucky, he would be able to live out his days somewhere remote, far away from the hawkish gaze of authority.

Walter steadied himself, and the laughter of the obnoxious sailors dissolved into a homogenous blanket of noisy conversation. A wave of exhaustion hit him suddenly, and he realized that he was tired of the bar: its oppressive, smoky air, and its drunken, directionless revelers. He headed outside, not even acknowledging the bartender as she blew him an exaggerated kiss. He had no time for these people, who were merely delaying him in carrying out his plans.

At that moment, there were only two people who mattered to Walter, only two people he needed to find. The night air had never tasted so sweet and ripe with possibility as it did when he left the Jamestown tavern, wandering down the road in search of a place to rest.

Walter awoke the next morning with a nasty, throbbing headache. He had settled into the tiniest of rooms in a rundown hostel along the main thoroughfare of Jamestown. He had slept fitfully despite being in an unfamiliar place, and his dreams had been pleasurably tranquil. He felt groggy and disoriented, but the lovely sunlight streaming through the hostel's grimy windows revived him somewhat.

As he lay there feeling the sun's rays wash over his face and body, some of the confidence Walter had felt the night before began to evaporate. In the morning light, everything suddenly seemed more real, and far more frightening, than it had before. Questions ran through Walter's worried mind. What if the government had sent spies after him, and what if they had spotted him at the bar? What if the seer's words had been nonsensical—or worse, a trap?

Just as Walter's thoughts were about to descend into the realm of paranoia, the words of the old fortune teller surfaced vividly in his mind. Something about her remarks ignited his desire to find Jonathan, and spurred him to action. While common sense told him to be cautious, Walter's heart advised him that he had no time to spare.

As his first priority, Walter needed to figure out when the prisoners would be boarding the *Jade Queen*. The sailor at the bar had informed him that the *Jade Queen* was leaving in a month, but the process of transferring the prisoners might begin sooner. Walter had no idea where the prison was, whether or not it was open to family visitors, or what sorts of people were imprisoned there. There were AI prisons, human prisons, and Xeyan'na prisons, and then there were the mixed-race ones, filled with humans who had upgraded themselves by surgically attaching robotic limbs and computer chips to their bodies, or injecting their bloodstreams with programmed nanomachines. Mixed-race folk could be just as intelligent as AI, and were generally much more unpredictable. They often possessed supernatural gifts like telepathy and the ability to predict future events, as well as other bizarre side effects from combining AI and human parts. The AIs either distrusted and ostracized them, enslaved them in the factories, or harnessed their talents and employed them in mysterious laboratories.

Walter stretched and yawned, and realized that he was exceptionally hungry; he hadn't eaten in over twenty-four hours. He decided to satiate his appetite at one of the seedy, questionable restaurants in town, and then afterward go to find the person who might satiate his soul.

Tsei'watu

"The building circular—A cage, glazed—a glass lantern about the Size of Ranelagh—The prisoners in their cells, occupying the circumference—The officers in the centre. By blinds and other contrivances, the inspectors concealed... from the observation of the prisoners: hence the sentiment of a sort of omnipresence—The whole circuit reviewable with little, or if necessary without any, change of place. One station in the inspection part affording the most perfect view of every cell."
— Jeremy Bentham

Enveloped by the tall grasses of the Khalendar savannah, Walter stalked around the monolithic structure like an animal. The prison appeared to be perfectly round, and Walter suspected that it was a panopticon, strategically designed to ensure the maximum surveillance of each prisoner. As in other prisons scattered throughout the Empire, there was likely an AI sentinel stationed in the center of the prison, trained to detect signs of insurrection. The prisoners were unaware of the sentinel's comings and goings, and his hypothetical gaze became an omnipresent, permanent motivation to maintain order.

The prison's design would make it considerably harder for Walter to carry out his plans. However, Walter was prepared to risk anything for the chance of saving his brother, even if there was only a slim likelihood of success. While he was musing about his future heroics, Walter suddenly heard the wispy reeds surrounding him rattle eerily. Instinctively, his spine stiffened, and his muscles tensed as his body braced itself to fight whoever—or whatever—crouched behind the reeds.

Without warning, a young woman appeared from behind the reeds and strode confidently toward him. Walter studied her cautiously as adrenaline coursed through his veins. Her hair was glossy, black, and waist length, like a Crystal City native, but her skin was the color of burnished bronze. She was dressed in black, tight-fitting military gear, the kind typically worn by seasoned AI guards and fighters, and her body looked intimidatingly strong. Her eyes resembled deep-set sapphire gemstones that glittered intensely. She appeared to be a mixed-race woman; her human limbs had artificial extensions and prosthetic enhancements that lent her the appearance of a machine. At the sight of her, Walter intuitively recalled the seer's words: *You will meet a dark-haired youth, with strength, kindness, and fire in her soul, whose life is tormented by tragedy and despair. This youth may help you with your task.*

Realizing that he would have limited success in fighting the woman, Walter adopted a submissive posture. He bowed his head humbly, greeting her politely in Khalendi.

After several moments of silence, during which the woman passed a critical eye over Walter, she responded to him in fluent Khalendi. "What interest do you have in the prison, stranger?" she asked in a low, direct tone, her eyes so intently focused that Walter felt rather unsettled by her gaze.

Walter hesitated. He knew nothing about this woman or her motives, and he didn't want to divulge too much. "One of my relatives is in there," he told her, choosing his words with caution. "I want to visit him." The woman's gaze was unfaltering, so intense that Walter felt compelled to look away.

"So, why haven't you?" she asked, her voice like the steady hum of the *daari*, a musical instrument native to the Barrens.

Walter shrugged. "I just arrived in Jamestown yesterday and I am not too familiar with the place. I wanted to take a look at it before going inside," he said, acutely aware that he sounded flustered.

The mixed-race woman smiled, her piercing eyes never once leaving his. "A newcomer to Jamestown, hmm?" she said. Suddenly her smile disappeared, and her expression became frighteningly cold. "Let me tell you a secret," she said. "Those prisoners are leaving soon, and when they leave you'll never see your relative again."

Walter swallowed uneasily. Her words corroborated the account of the sailor, who had said that the prisoners would be departing to Vei'arash soon. He didn't want to reveal the extent of his knowledge to her, though, in case she couldn't be trusted.

"Why are *you* here?" he asked, eager to displace attention from himself. Her expression, as cold as a frigid tundra a moment earlier, softened at this question. She now appeared distracted, worried about something, and

Walter noticed barely perceptible tears surface in her eyes. She averted her gaze, then sat down gingerly on the ground. Her body, with its technological accoutrements, seemed oddly out of place in the grassy wilderness. Walter took a seat beside her, since he felt uncomfortable hovering over the intimidating woman.

The woman's intense focus suddenly returned, and her piercing gaze settled upon him. "If you tell anyone what I am about to say, I have ways of killing you *and* the person you share my secrets with," she said commandingly. "Even if you are a thousand miles away from me, you will both be destroyed like Sodom and Gomorrah." Walter shuddered. Did this woman possess the dark art of what the Barrens folk called *samtra*, the ability to slay an enemy standing a great distance away? Walter decided that she was not someone he would want as an enemy. The woman studied his face, muttering barely audible words under her breath: "Yes, that's him, isn't it. He's related to the one… tortured him…" Walter heard brief snippets of what she was saying, but he wasn't able to piece together the meaning of her words. Finally, after the woman had apparently collected her thoughts, she spoke to Walter directly.

"My twin sister, Eva, is in there," she said. "And when I heard the news that they were shipping her to Vei'arash, I knew that I needed to save her."

Walter listened to her, stunned, as he realized that this strange woman was in the same predicament as he. He longed to tell her his embryonic plan to rescue Jonathan, but she was still a stranger—and a mixed race one, at that—and so he held back, still wary.

"How are you going to save her? Have you ever managed to get inside the prison?" he asked, this time with more curiosity than caution.

"Every Sunday afternoon they let the prisoners visit with family or friends. But the visits are closely watched by an AI sentinel and heavily armed chaperones. The chaperones carry deadly *khalas* and poison-tipped swords."

"It sounds like it would be difficult to rescue her, then," Walter said, then sighed, betraying his frustration.

"I have been planning her rescue for a long time, and I have carefully studied their weaknesses," the woman continued, her eyes unblinking as she gazed at Walter. "Every Sunday, for the past two years, I've been visiting the prison, wearing my *outfit.*" She paused, and removed a modest, rose-colored dress from the satchel that was slung onto her back. Walter thought it looked pretty, but did not fit the woman's hard-edged appearance in the least.

"The guards think I'm some mentally ill girl from Hydesburgh. They don't bother to look beyond what they see. The first couple times I visited they patted my dress down to check for weapons. But they have come to see me as a friend, not a threat, and so for the last several visits they haven't checked me. They call me 'Auntie Em,' because my name is Emilia and I sometimes bring them cookies."

Now Walter was the one looking at her intently. The idea of this capable warrior wearing a pink dress and baking cookies seemed laughable. She looked like Athena, the ancient goddess of war, not some mentally ill aunt from Hydesburgh. Walter was even more shocked by her candor. How did Emilia know that he could be trusted? Perhaps she figured that he was too weak to pose a real threat, or perhaps she truly was mentally disturbed.

Once she had finished speaking, Emilia averted her sapphire eyes from Walter, directing her gaze toward the horizon. Walter suddenly felt a pang of anxiety at the thought that she might simply leave him here to figure out a plan on his own. It seemed to Walter that Emilia could be an invaluable ally; if her words were true, then she had carefully studied the prison and the weaknesses of the AI guards, and she could help him rescue Jonathan. He felt like a lost soul in dire need of direction, and the words of the seer came rushing back to him: *This youth may help you with your task.*

"I think we c-could assist each other," he stammered timidly. He felt uncomfortable saying so, but he realized that he needed to take a risk in trusting this stranger if he was to have any chance of rescuing Jonathan.

Emilia turned to face him and smiled solemnly. "I was hoping you'd say that. You're going to have to come with me. I've told you too much to let you go free," she said. "There's little chance you'll get your brother out of that prison alive without my help, anyway."

"Wait a minute. How did you know I want to get my brother out of there?" he asked, immediately suspicious.

"Because I have seen him," she replied, "and he is the splitting image of you. Why do you think I would divulge my plans to a complete stranger? I know your brother is stuck inside that prison, and unless you want him to die in Vei'arash, you need to rescue him. The moment I saw you, I knew you needed my help."

Walter had to restrain himself from crying at her words—the mere thought that this woman had seen Jonathan recently stirred intense emotions within him.

"In that forest yonder," Emilia continued, pointing toward a dark smudge of trees on the horizon, "there are strong allies who are in the same predicament as we, and they are all waiting for the perfect moment to strike."

Walter felt a surge of energy. Just knowing that there were people out there who shared his aspirations provided a refreshing boost to his spirits. He also felt unsettled, though—the way he had felt at the tavern after speaking with the prescient seer. How coincidental that he happened to meet this strange woman in the reeds, who happened to know all about Jonathan and wanted to help Walter rescue him. Was it truly a coincidence? Walter was in a gambling mood, however, and he decided that following this stranger was preferable to the lunacy of trying to rescue his brother from a heavily guarded prison by himself.

"I'll join you," Walter said shakily, after a long silence. "But, first, tell me everything." Walter sensed that she was hiding secrets from him, and he needed to know the whole truth if they were going to collaborate.

A spark of humanity registered in the icy coldness of her eyes. Emilia gazed at him for a very long time, as if she were trying to form some sort of spiritual connection with him before she finally spoke. "Come with me, then, Walter, and meet my friends in the forest," she said.

Walter's stomach turned over as she spoke his name. *How does she know who I am?* He had heard whispered rumors about mixed-race folk possessing the powers of telepathy, and he feared that she could see into his mind. For a moment he felt vulnerable, stripped bare and exposed, and he suddenly wanted to run back toward the safety of the Jamestown hostel. But soon his curiosity won out over his fear, and he realized that he wanted to follow her more than he wanted to flee.

As they walked toward the forest, Walter was burning with questions about Emilia. *Where was she from? Why was her sister in prison? Why had she decided to become a mixed-race? Was it forced upon her?*

Despite his eagerness to talk, Walter was comforted by the strange girl's silence. As she marched briskly toward her destination, Emilia had lost all traces of distractedness and seemed level-headed, poised, and resolute. She was different from most of the women Walter had encountered in Crystal City, who tended to be gossipy chatterboxes and were socially rewarded for their loquaciousness. Emilia's silence was refreshingly unique.

Emilia and Walter traveled across the barren, grassy landscape for what seemed like ages. After the sun had passed its zenith and began tracing a graceful arc toward the horizon, Walter lost track of time. He realized that he hadn't consumed food or water since his breakfast at Daisy's, a rustic diner in Jamestown, that morning. Walter caught a glimpse of what appeared to be a silver canteen strung around Emilia's neck. He was tempted to ask her for a sip of water, but he held out, deciding instead to impress his new acquaintance with his stamina.

Just as the amber eye of the sun was beginning to dip below the edge of the world, the pair reached the woods.

"We are now in the Forest of Antheia," Emilia explained, "named after the goddess of vegetation and human love." Walter was astounded by the size of the trees—towering, ancient redwoods, firs, and oaks, the type that you didn't see around Crystal City. One could get lost in them quite easily, he imagined. He didn't like the idea of traveling in the forest after sundown, but Emilia seemed so confident that he followed her without objection. After a half hour or so, they reached a clearing. It appeared to be uninhabited, but on closer inspection Walter noticed several well-camouflaged features of a makeshift camp. Tools, tents, and hammocks, all crafted from wood, canvas, and bamboo were scattered throughout the clearing, half-concealed by the foliage of venerable firs and oaks. Walter also spotted a few tiny fire pits, with wisps of smoke rising from them like spirits.

It was then that Walter noticed several humans and mixed-race folk in the camp, perching on logs, foraging for berries, and collecting firewood. He was shocked at how easily they blended into their natural surroundings. They were exceptionally quiet, and they wore well-engineered military gear like Emilia. They wielded a dizzying array of weapons, bearing daggers, javelins, scimitars, crossbows, rifles, and *khalas*.

As Walter and Emilia entered the camp, the strange figures immediately fixed their gazes on the newcomer. Walter noticed that Emilia appeared to be the strongest and most physically capable person in the camp, and he suspected that she was some sort of leader. These suspicions grew when Emilia addressed the camp's occupants in an authoritative tone.

"This is Walter. He is new to Jamestown, and he wishes to rescue his brother from the Crate," she announced to the onlookers, who regarded Walter with mild curiosity. "Walter, welcome to Tsei'watu. It is our humble home until we rescue our brothers and sisters. You are welcome to stay here, on one condition," she said.

Walter gazed around himself in amazement, awestruck by his good fortune in having discovered these well-armed allies.

"You must never tell anyone about us or this place until our plans have been carried out. We have methods of punishing transgressors," Emilia warned.

Walter swallowed and nodded. "Of course," he said, his voice trembling audibly—though whether with fear or excitement, he wasn't sure. "So, the Crate is the prison?" he asked.

Emilia nodded gravely. "That is what they call it. To us, it is a terrible place where our brothers and sisters have suffered grave injustices."

Before Emilia could say anything else an auburn-haired man, younger than Emilia, but older than Walter, spoke. "He doesn't know about the Crate?" he asked incredulously.

Emilia was quiet for a long time as she studied Walter's young, innocent face. Her sapphire eyes exuded empathy, or perhaps pity.

"There is much for young Walter to learn," she said, the corners of her mouth lifting imperceptibly.

A Lesson in War

"If you know the enemy and know yourself you need not fear the results of a hundred battles."
– Sun Tzu

As Walter soon discovered, Emilia was indeed the leader of the eccentric tribe in the forest. Her canvas tent was larger than the others, and it was located in a secluded and quiet area of Tsei'watu. It resembled the war pavilion of some exotic Egyptian princess from a bygone era; its exterior was ornately decorated with luxurious rabbit and fox furs, and wooden torches flanked its entrance. When Walter entered the tent, he noticed that its interior walls were lined with a dizzying array of weapons. Some were so sophisticated and rare that Walter could not even identify them by name. He had heard rumors that such weapons were illicitly imported from the Southern Jungles in an elaborate underground trading network. Some were aesthetically pleasing, while others looked more like torture devices than tools of war.

Emilia had invited Walter to her tent that evening so that they could get better acquainted over a private dinner together. Emilia told Walter that camp members had to undergo the ritual of dining with her before entering the "family" of Tsei'watu, but Walter secretly hoped that he was somehow special. Deep down inside, Walter was flattered by the attentions of this powerful tribal matriarch, and he wished to ingratiate himself with her.

Their dinner consisted of fresh berries, raw salmon, and lightly smoked rabbit meat which tasted exquisitely buttery. Walter devoured everything laid before him. He was about to ask Emilia how she had acquired such delicacies, but the weapons adorning the walls of her tent seemed to provide the answer.

Before they began a serious discussion, Emilia offered Walter some Xe'levan, a sacred tea that the Barrens folk commonly drank. Walter humbly accepted her offering, then downed the tea in a single thirsty gulp. He regretted having done so, since the tea tasted unpleasantly bitter.

Emilia grinned at his foolishness and refilled his tea mug. "I would advise drinking the Xe'levan more slowly," she said. Walter heeded her advice, his mouth still burning.

Her expression became sober. "You may be surprised that I know your name," she said. "Some mixed-race folk have special abilities, and my grandmother's gift was to know the names of others," Emilia said enigmatically. "She passed the gift on to me after she died. It is a surprisingly useful talent. Not only does it help you understand your enemies, it also lends you an aura of power and knowledge," she explained. Walter listened in fascination. He was unsettled by the idea that this woman possessed supernatural powers, and he hoped that they only extended to knowing his name.

"Walter, I need to tell you about the Crate. The island they are taking the prisoners to, Vei'arash, is a place of death and destruction. Separated from their birthplace and traditions, the shamans who inhabit the island have become evil and corrupted. They have unleashed an army of powerful demons and dark spirits, who torment the prisoners by driving them to madness.

"If Vei'arash is hell, the Crate is purgatory. It is filled with political dissidents who have openly rebelled against the deeply unjust society created by the AI Masters and their human delegates.

"I grew up in a poor, working-class family in Fewsbury, and before I came of age I was the most obedient girl imaginable. My twin sister and I worked in the factories since childhood; because of the barriers to our social advancement, there was no point in going to school. We made absurd things at first, like sprinkler systems and flower pots for the AI elites, but due to the dexterity of our hands we were soon promoted in rank. I started making AI Fighter armor, and my sister began manufacturing weapons. We were still so poor, though, and our mother and father were even poorer. They barely made enough money for us to eat.

"All I wanted to do was earn enough *cestae* to make sure that our parents, who were too slow with their hands to work in the factories, would be able to eat a full dinner every night. I would have been content to go on living my life in that mind-numbingly boring world of slavery and drudgery, being treated like no more than a disposable cog in a vast machine. I would have patiently endured the lashes of the AI Masters, who whipped us when we didn't assemble the commodities fast enough. But Eva couldn't carry on living like that," she said, her voice trembling with anger.

"One day, I discovered that Eva was planning to change her fate. I found out that occasionally she would steal some of the weapons she had assembled and bring them home. Her intentions were good—she needed weapons to hunt animals to feed Mother and Father. At first nobody noticed, but soon the AIs grew suspicious. They caught my sister and locked her up in the Crate.

"You might think the AIs are smart. That is the 'golden rule' the elites have indoctrinated into us: the AIs are cleverer than us, and by virtue of their superior minds they have the right to rule over us. By one definition of intelligence, they are extremely brilliant, and humans will potentially never attain their level of genius. But there are many different forms of intelligence. Emotional intelligence is one form, for example. AI Masters know nothing about human motivation. They never feel empathy, because their brains are too logical to understand the heart of a human being. They don't understand why humans are motivated to protect their friends and relatives. They couldn't understand that my sister stole those weapons so that she could help her parents avoid starvation because she loved them. To put it bluntly, the AIs don't understand love.

"Another thing to know about the AIs: they are extremely paranoid. They fear revolution, since they know that their own revolution happened all too quickly, and they are aware that humans possess the advantage of having a lengthy track record of civilization. And so, they ascribed a motivation to my sister's crime that simply wasn't there. The AI Masters view the world in black and white terms: us versus them, humans versus cyborgs. They truly believed—if you can even say that they believe in anything—that my sister's intent was to steal their weapons so that she could overthrow their ridiculous Empire. Personally, I think that's a noble aspiration, but my sister was no revolutionary.

"AIs," she continued, "cling to the simplistic belief that humans actually think like computers. They believe that humans can be *programmed* to act and think a certain way, just like computers, and that they can be infected by viruses that must be eliminated. Because of the senseless Treaty of Calais, humans simply don't have enough power to convince them otherwise," she said, sighing in exasperation.

"Which brings me to the topic of the Crate. Whereas most other prisons are designed to contain society's wrongdoers and prevent them from escaping and harming people, that prison is special. The prisoners are objects of a large-scale thought experiment conducted by the AI Masters. The AIs, applying their simple, reductive logic, have deemed these captives a threat to the Empire, and they are trying to reprogram the prisoners' brains to purge them of viruses."

Walter took a sip of Xe'levan in a failed attempt to calm his increasingly turbulent mind as Emilia carried on. "The ones whose viruses have not been completely purged are going beyond purgatory to the hell of Vei'arash. They are perceived to be irredeemable, and they will live out the rest of their days on that cursed island, eventually losing the final remnants of their sanity there. They have fought valiantly against the conquest of their minds, yet they are going to be punished for that simple and heroic act of human resilience.

"The ones who have been broken by the AIs' terrible re-programming experiment, who are now effectively brainless, soulless shells of humans, well, they are either going to stay in the Crate, or live out their remaining days with the AIs in Central Command," she said finally.

Walter felt sick to his stomach. All this time, his poor brother had been the subject of some twisted, masochistic thought experiment? *Who knows what horrific things they are doing to him in there*, he thought resentfully. He burned with an intense longing to take the weapons lining Emilia's tent and slaughter every last guard in the Crate as punishment for their appalling crimes. And then the thought struck him—why were Emilia and her rebel friends hiding out in the forest, biding their time so patiently? They appeared to be a well-organized and heavily armed coterie of individuals, so why hadn't they already attempted to rescue the prisoners?

As though reading his mind, Emilia said, "You might be wondering what we are doing here in the forest while our dear ones suffer at the hands of their oppressors. It is true that every moment we spend apart from them, we risk letting them slip past the point of no return."

Walter shuddered. There was something about that phrase, *past the point of no return*, that made him feel ill.

"I have been visiting my sister frequently enough to know that she is okay," Emilia continued. She reddened with embarrassment, and Walter could not understand why, until she said, "I know that your brother is okay, too. He appears stronger than many of the prisoners I have seen in the Crate. They try many things on him, including mind experiments. They attach wires onto his head and send electrical pulses through his brain to activate his neural energies; they perform lie detector tests on him; they try to read his mind; they force him to consume strange substances. For a long time, they were trying to determine how he was able to gain the upper hand in AI-human fighting matches. They wanted to understand how his mind works so they could design better AI Fighters." Walter felt miserable upon hearing that his brother was undergoing such hardship, and his eyes welled with tears. Emilia offered the young man more Xe'levan, but his throat had closed up and his tongue felt like sandpaper.

"How do you know all this?" he asked, astonished at the breadth of her knowledge.

"My sister has shared plenty of valuable information with me. Also, I observe what is happening when I visit her in prison. The Crate is a panopticon," Emilia explained, confirming Walter's suspicions. "Prisoners in each of the cells can see the other prisoners. The prison's layout is distressing for the prisoners, but optimal for the guards. The prison requires minimal surveillance: just one AI sentinel capable of accessing a communication portal to Central Command, and a few AI chaperones to monitor the family visits. The low ratio of guards to prisoners is one reason why they are moving some prisoners to Vei'arash."

Suddenly, Walter's hazy memory unclouded slightly. A faint recollection surfaced, and he remembered having decoded something as a government translator—a research study about Khalendar prison security. The research had concluded that AI guards were less effective than humans at protecting prisons from jailbreaks, but Walter forgot the exact reason why. The study's authors had recommended an ambitious upgrade to the prisons in Khalendar. They had observed that job notices for human guard positions had been circulated throughout Khalendar, but nobody had applied—working-class folk resented prisons as symbols of AI oppression, and elite Khalendi believed such a job was beneath them. Thus, the study had recommended technological upgrades to prisons, including fingerprint recognition devices to identify prisoners and notify Central Command when prisoners went missing. Walter hadn't been sure if the government had yet implemented any of the study's recommendations, and he hadn't paid it any thought until now.

"The Crate is an old prison," Emilia continued. "The new facial recognition software has not been installed yet," she said. *So, it was facial, not fingerprint recognition,* Walter thought, unsettled by the way her words seemed to respond to his own thoughts.

"One of the many weaknesses of the AIs," she explained, "is their inability to properly distinguish human faces. After the Grand Revolution, AIs collectively perceived most humans as inherently inferior beings, and they stopped adding facial recognition functions to their central processors. Now, the AIs can only recognize the faces of a select number of elite citizens whom they respect. They monitor the rest of us as if we were data—numbers and algorithms, not humans. Guards in the Crate are even less sophisticated than most AIs; they certainly cannot tell a man apart from his brother, or a sister from her twin," she said, her eyes glittering with mischief.

Walter tried to guess at the direction of her thoughts. "So," he asked eagerly, "are you hoping to exploit the stupidity of the AI guards?"

Emilia laughed amusedly at his wide-eyed innocence and naiveté. "AIs are not stupid," she admonished. "Indeed, they are one of our most formidable rivals. We must never underestimate our enemies."

Walter suspected this mission of hers was larger than merely rescuing a few prisoners. "Are you trying to bring down the leaders of our society?" he asked.

Emilia's laugh was hollow and mirthless. "We have a precious chance of rescuing our brothers and sisters, and we must seize the opportunity," she said. Walter immediately recalled the words of the ancient seer: *You have a brief window of opportunity to save him, and saving him will help you in your task.* "When I first saw you in the savannah, gazing at the Crate, I thought that perhaps it would be best to leave you alone, seeing as you have no prior experience as a rebel and there is so little time before the rebellion begins. But I recognized you immediately as Jonathan's brother, and I realized that we couldn't let such a great warrior slip away," she said.

Walter was confused by her words—by "great warrior" was she referring to himself or Jonathan? There were so many pieces of the puzzle that were still unsolved, and Walter was burning with questions, but for now he simply listened.

"You must be tired, so I will describe our plan briefly, and you will learn the remaining details in the days to come. There are exactly fifty rebels in this camp—yourself included. Nearly a hundred prisoners from the Crate are being transferred to Vei'arash.

"About twenty rebels have blood relatives in the Crate, and the remainder have friends inside the prison, or have simply joined our cause out of a sense of justice. That divides us roughly into two groups. The first group, which I refer to as the 'blood rebels,' is assisting with the first segment of our plan. I will control the sentinel and the chaperones so that—if everything goes smoothly—all of the blood rebels except for me can switch places with their relatives in the prison before the day of the prisoners' transfer to the *Jade Queen*. Some of our rebels are already in the Crate, and there are about five that still need to be transferred, including you.

"Three Sundays from now, the prisoners will be transferred onto the *Jade Queen*. That marks the beginning of the second stage of our plan. All of the blood rebels, along with the remaining eighty prisoners, will be herded onto the ship like cattle, and the process will be closely monitored by AI chaperones. That is when thirty 'bane rebels,' myself included, will step onto the scene. A frontal attack of the ship with our weaponry is possible, but it would be foolish because Central Command would send over military forces to destroy us immediately. The smarter route is to make it seem as though nothing is wrong," she said, her voice ringing with confidence.

"The *Jade Queen* is manned by precisely thirty-three sailors. Our plan is for the bane rebels to disguise themselves as sailors and replace the real sailors without the AIs noticing. The AI guards will likely assume that the last three drank themselves into a stupor and couldn't make it on the ship—they have such a low opinion of humans, after all."

Walter's head was spinning. How could they just "replace" the real sailors with the bane rebels? What would happen to the real sailors?

Confirming his worst suspicions, Emilia explained, "Our assassination skills will come in handy at that time. Bane is an ancient word which connotes 'that which causes death,' and causing death is precisely what we intend to do. First, we will practice on the sailors. Easy targets, especially when drunk, but we must be careful that no suspicions are raised. Their bodies cannot be left in Jamestown, but must be thrown into the ocean so that we leave no trace. Jamestown at night, past a certain hour, is completely deserted save for its taverns and brothels. We'll be keeping clear of those," she said, "but we'll have to find creative ways of luring the sailors out of them."

Walter felt ill. Warfare against AIs was one thing—noble, and perhaps even exciting—but staining one's hands with the blood of innocent humans was quite another. He faintly recalled the ruggedly handsome face of the sailor he had met in the bar in Jamestown the other night, and he was struck with a crippling sense of guilt. Couldn't there be some other way—couldn't the sailors just join forces with Emilia's rebels? Walter realized that this was impossible, however. Human sailors were faithful servants of the AIs, like most inhabitants of Crystal City, and convincing all of them to rebel against their masters would be nigh impossible.

"Second," Emilia continued, "we intend to assassinate every last AI guard on that ship, then commandeer the vessel for ourselves. We will destroy the communication portal linking the ship with Central Command, so the AI Masters will no longer be able to detect our coordinates. The *Jade Queen* will become our base camp, and from her shining decks we shall navigate the seas like pirates in search of the treasure of justice, a new generation of vigilante warriors," she declared, her sapphire eyes flashing triumphantly.

Walter realized that one part of the puzzle had been carelessly omitted. "What is to become of our brothers and sisters from the prison? Will they join us on the ship too?" he asked after a long pause.

"The ones who have already been rescued will be safe at our camp," she replied confidently. "Fortunately, their minds are not irreversibly altered by the AIs' reprogramming efforts, and their afflictions of memory loss and emotional trauma can be healed, in time. Once we have commandeered the ship, we plan to meet them at an isolated docking point and bring them on board the vessel. We can't have them interfering with the second stage of the plan, though—there are too many of them, and they are still mentally unstable, so they cannot come aboard until we have secured the ship. I have arranged for my comrades to lead them down the coast to a safe and secluded harbor, and then we will welcome our dear relatives aboard our newly acquired vessel."

Walter's heart was racing. Emilia's plan sounded carefully thought out, as if she had been planning it for years. It also seemed fragile, though, like a delicate spider web that could become unhinged at any moment by an unruly gust of wind. Nevertheless, it was at least better than no plan at all, and it gave him a sense of hope which spread like a warm, comforting drink in the hollow of his chest. In Walter's new state of optimism, the bitter Xe'levan now tasted like the sweet apple cider he had sipped with Elaine all those years ago in Crystal City.

A sharp gust of evening wind suddenly struck the side of the tent, and Walter realized that they had been sitting there together for a long time. Emilia seemed to sense his weariness. "It has been a long day for both of us," she said. "Follow me, and I will show you to your quarters."

She led him to a modest tent which appeared to have been set up after his arrival. It was far plainer than Emilia's, lacking in decorative adornments of furs and weapons, but Walter appreciated that it was clean, warm, and practical. Inside, there were folded linen sheets, as well as canteens for Walter to fill with water.

"There is a stream to the east of the camp, and the water is clean enough to drink," Emilia said before she left. "We will meet at dawn by my tent and begin our training then. Have a good night, Walter," she said, her azure eyes sparkling like twin flames burning in the dusk.

Before Walter had the chance to thank her, Emilia had disappeared like a phantom into the black night. Walter climbed into his tent and lay down gratefully. The tent's smell of weathered canvas was overpowered by the aromas of the forest—the bitter, earthy scents of moss, lichen, and pine needles. Walter felt comfortable in Tsei'watu; perhaps for the first time in his life, he felt truly connected to something larger than himself. He realized that his mother and father had not bothered to contact him since his disappearance, as he had received no messages from them on his tablet. He had not contacted them, either, but he felt that the void created by their absence had been filled by a new kind of family, which was not based on blood ties but on common goals, interests, and aspirations. The Forest of Antheia and its inhabitants had awakened some deep, primal sensation in Walter—even though he was surrounded by strangers, he felt closer to home than he ever had been before.

Training

"All I know is that I do not know anything."
— Socrates

In the early haze of morning, Walter opened his bleary eyes and stretched. The morning sun's rays had infiltrated the forest's lush canopy and infused Walter's tent with a delicate warmth. He felt safe and relaxed and longed to fall back into slumber, but then he suddenly remembered the otherworldly events of the previous day. Walter knew that it was not a dream; the memory of Emilia's piercing gaze was too vivid to have been a mere figment of his imagination. Rubbing his eyes, Walter cautiously stepped outside the tent and took stock of his surroundings. Tiny creatures stirred in the forest—finches, jays, dragonflies, and squirrels—but there were no visible signs of human habitation.

Walter was beginning to worry that he might not find his way back to the camp, when suddenly a figure appeared from behind a nearby oak tree. It was the auburn-haired boy who Walter had seen the day before. His expression was courteous, yet strained, as if it were an effort to present a polite façade to Walter.

"Good morning," the boy said curtly. "Emilia sent me to check on you. When you are ready, she would like to see you at the training circle."

Walter smiled to convey his gratitude, but the young man's expression remained frosty. He tossed Walter a small canvas bag filled with nuts, dried berries, and seeds. "Your breakfast," he said, in the same clipped tone. He then marched off briskly into the forest, while Walter struggled to keep pace behind.

As the two men approached the campground, Walter heard the faintest sound of rustling in the trees. Suddenly, and without warning, an arrow shaft whizzed past his body, burying its tip into the fleshy bark of a nearby alder tree. Walter gasped in stunned surprise, and then spotted a well-camouflaged young woman several meters ahead of him. Her dark chestnut hair was cropped neatly below her jaw, and her eyes were a deep hue of jade, the color of the forest.

"Be careful, newcomer," she warned as she walked over to the alder tree to retrieve the arrow. "My name is Miranda," she then said, cheerfully extending her hand in greeting.

"I'm Walter," Walter replied hesitantly, still not quite recovered from shock.

"I know," Miranda responded.

While they were making their introductions, Emilia suddenly appeared. Bedecked in black military gear, her hair a tumble of wild curls around her shoulders, she approached the young people. Her forearms were decorated with silver bracelets, seamlessly connected to metallic panels embedded in her skin.

"You are late," she reprimanded Walter. "From now on, I expect you to meet us at the very break of dawn." Walter felt a pang of disappointment and shame, but Emilia's expression softened. "Do not worry," she said. "Your training need not be as intensive as the others since you are part of the infiltration group, not a bane rebel," she said. "But you must still learn basic fighting skills so that you can assist in our attack once we have boarded the *Jade Queen*."

Walter hadn't noticed them before, but while Emilia was speaking, he spotted a few more humans and mixed-race folk, artfully camouflaged by the flora and foliage of the forest. They observed Walter with a quiet curiosity. Some of them were outfitted in military attire and heavily armed, while others wore light clothing and wielded a simple bow and arrow.

Emilia ignored these distractions, training her gaze steadily on Walter. "Pay them no mind," she said in a placid tone. "They will lose interest in you after a while. Now, it is important to remember that you will be unarmed when you enter the Crate. If you are physically threatened in any way, there will be no point in fighting back. Just be as obedient and compliant with the guards' orders as you can," she instructed. "I'll make sure that Jonathan returns safely with us to the forest once you exchange places with him. When we reunite inside the *Jade Queen*, we will give you your weapon."

Walter then noticed that a sword was clipped onto Emilia's belt. She unfastened the weapon, removed it from its leather sheath, and offered it to Walter. It was a two-handed longsword with an intricately engraved mahogany hilt, and it felt surprisingly lightweight. Upon closer inspection of the hilt, Walter noticed that a fire lizard, the sacred creature of the Barrens, was etched onto its surface.

"This is one of the most basic weapons you should be trained in," she explained. "The *balayan*. Forged from rare earth metals in the southeastern Barrens, it is the only sword in existence capable of destroying AI armor."

Walter recalled that Emilia had worked in the factories, manufacturing AI armor during her youth. Her background in factory labor, Walter suspected, likely gave her a keen insight into such matters.

"The *balayan*'s best property is that it is dull to humans. It rarely penetrates human flesh, unless swung with an incredible amount of force, but it slices through AI armor like butter," she said. "Right now, the *balayan* is bare, but when we give it to you on the *Jade Queen* it will be tipped in *samtayran*, a deadly poison that works to de-stabilize AI programming," she said. "Once you slice through their armor, the *samtayran* will sever the link between their central processing unit and the rest of their body, effectively incapacitating them."

Walter was astonished. He couldn't believe that AIs, so strong and mighty in fighting matches, were actually fragile creatures who could be destroyed with a simple swing of a dull sword.

Emilia continued her weaponry lesson. "AIs are capable of detecting these weapons, however, and they carry *catans*—sturdy, cylindrical shields coated with unique chemical compounds—to protect themselves against our *balayans*. The art of *balayan* fighting requires quick judgment and agility, as the goal is to catch an AI off guard. That's what your training is for. We'll pair you up with Christopher," she said, glancing in the direction of the young red-haired man. "Don't worry about striking him—as I said, the blade of the *balayan* is dull to human flesh," she explained, her words failing to reassure Walter. "Christopher, when Walter shows signs of improvement, report back to me and we shall carry on with the next stages of his training," Emilia commanded.

Walter glanced enthusiastically at Christopher, eager to begin his training, but the young man's expression was not very welcoming. He eyed Walter warily, as though doubtful that Walter was adequately prepared for this style of combat. Walter examined Christopher's features—his tousled auburn hair, lightly freckled skin, and watery grey eyes—and noticed that they seemed strangely familiar. Walter wondered whether he was a native of the Barrens, since he had similar features and coloring as Elaine, yet a colder appearance. Walter then realized that he hadn't told Emilia about Elaine yet, even though she had been the reason behind his trip to Jamestown.

There was no time to ponder such matters now, though—Christopher was already striding hastily toward an area of the forest for training. The pair eventually arrived at a secluded clearing, where a mysterious box awaited them. Christopher opened the box and drew out a cylindrical metal rod, which he grasped firmly at either end. He flexed his muscles and then let go of one end, twirling it with one hand and catching it gracefully with the other. Walter was impressed by his skill and felt like an awkward novice in comparison.

Walter was already well-versed in the art of sword fighting, though, even if he didn't fully realize it. Throughout his childhood, he had frequently sparred with Jonathan in mock swordfights. The two boys would parry back and forth near the abandoned train tracks marking the border between Crystal City and the Stockyards, playing out childhood fantasies of knights clashing on the battlefield. They didn't have real swords, so they would use sharpened birch branches gathered from the nearby forests with a pocketknife. Jonathan almost always won, but Walter had improved considerably over time, since he was able to learn from an elegant and agile swordfighter. Of course, Walter was only a child back then, and he had known little about real combat.

This time, Walter wasn't carrying a sharpened birch branch—he gripped the hilt of a real sword in his hands and could feel the weapon's dangerous power coursing through his veins. He was now practicing for the real thing: a battle with a true enemy that could cost him his life. This thought made Walter exceptionally nervous, and Christopher's icy, aloof expression didn't help to settle his apprehension.

"Are you going to begin, Walter, or just stand there?" Christopher asked impatiently, goading the young man.

Walter glanced at the *balayan*, a gorgeous blade of ultralight metal connected to a sturdy mahogany hilt, glinting with deceptive beauty in the mid-morning light. The weapon reminded Walter of Emilia's plan: thrilling, elegant, and murderous. The blade looked so sharp that Walter was skeptical of Emilia's assurance that it was dull to human flesh. He closed his eyes, inwardly repeating the following words to calm his nerves: *just pretend you are playing with Jonathan and nobody will really get hurt.* Interrupted in his meditation by Christopher's impatient sigh, Walter opened his eyes and instinctively lunged toward the young man, boldly thrusting the *balayan* in his direction. Christopher, while caught off guard, was quick to react; he swiftly positioned the *catan* in front of his torso, and the *balayan* made a dull, clanging sound as it bounced off the shield.

Christopher's eyes narrowed with a mixture of surprise and displeasure as he realized he was facing a more formidable opponent than he had previously assumed. The two young men sparred with each other vigorously, both releasing pent-up energies that had been dormant within them. As Walter lunged and parried, he felt a wave of nostalgia overtake him as he recalled his childhood swordfights with Jonathan. Walter had never possessed Jonathan's competitive spirit, and he had always been content to defer to his brother's superior fighting abilities. Now, however, Walter felt compelled to win at all costs, because he was fighting for two people that he loved more than anything or anyone in the world. This thought inspired him to fight with vigor, and as Walter advanced aggressively toward Christopher he noticed that the other young man's energy was dwindling.

As they fought, intently focused on the swordplay and oblivious to their surroundings, the two men gradually moved farther and farther away from the clearing. The pair would have continued in this fashion for the rest of the morning, possibly getting themselves lost in the dense, labyrinthine forest, if a strange event had not jolted them out of their reverie. While they were advancing through the undergrowth, having lost track of all time or place, an eerie, bloodcurdling moan suddenly rent the air. The noise, which sounded like it had come from some exotic beast, was so unsettling that both Walter and Christopher stopped cold in their tracks as soon as they heard it. Walter looked frantically in all directions, half-expecting an AI Fighter to charge out and attack them. Nothing appeared, however, and as the echoes of the sound died away the forest reverted to silence. Not even the chirping of birds or crickets could be heard; it was that time of day when creatures sleep or hide, lazily burrowing into the undergrowth to avoid expending energy in the heat of mid-afternoon.

"Damnit," Christopher cursed angrily when he realized their predicament. "We've strayed too far from Tsei'watu."

Walter felt guilty, and somewhat irrationally worried about the reprimand they might receive if Emilia discovered their foolishness.

"Did you hear that?" Walter asked, his blood churning with adrenaline. "I think we have bigger problems on our hands than just being lost."

Christopher grinned at Walter's naiveté. "We aren't lost, Walter," he chided his training partner. "In fact, you should thank your lucky stars that we heard that noise, because it means that we aren't too far away from camp."

Now Walter was confused. What sort of creature had made that noise, and why was he supposed to be reassured by it? Before he could voice any of his questions, however, Christopher hastily strode ahead of him and let out an exuberant cry.

"Found it!" Christopher exclaimed jubilantly. Walter rushed up to join him and saw a sturdy, picturesque log cabin, half-covered in moss and camouflaged expertly into its verdant surroundings. Walter took a step toward the cabin, but Christopher physically restrained him from walking any farther.

"You don't want to get near that place," Christopher warned, his expression solemn. "Emilia cast a protective spell around it, and if any outsiders try to enter they will experience a terrible seizure. Only healers can go inside, since they take medicine which prevents the onset of the affliction." All of a sudden, the shrieking moan sounded from inside the cabin. Walter was startled by the noise and nearly leapt backward in fright.

"What is that place?" Walter asked, his body involuntarily trembling from the disquieting cry.

Christopher observed Walter with amusement. "Are you having a seizure already? You're not close enough to the cabin," he teased. He stopped laughing when Walter did not appear to find the joke funny.

"Come on, I know the way back from here. You've done enough training for today—you're a far better fighter than I expected you to be. Let's have some lunch down at the stream," Christopher said kindly.

Despite Christopher's offer, Walter remained frozen in place. Half-paralyzed by the ominous noise, he was unable to avert his gaze from the log cabin.

"If you really want to know about the cabin, I'll explain it all to you," Christopher assured him. "But first, you need to relax and get some food in your belly."

Finally, after a long period of silence, Walter calmed down enough to allow Christopher to lead him away from the haunting cabin. The moaning sound had etched itself into his brain, though, and it refused to disappear from his thoughts completely. The noise had been primal and lonely, and Walter thought that it could be summed up accurately in one single word: *dangerous.*

Voices of the Forest

"There is another alphabet, whispering from every leaf, singing from every river, shimmering from every sky."
– Dejan Stojanovic

As the midday sun hung in the sky like a burnished piece of copper, Christopher led Walter toward the secluded stream that Emilia had mentioned to him earlier.

"The stream we are going to is fed by a glacier in the Meridian Mountains," Christopher explained to Walter as they walked briskly amongst the moss-cloaked alders. "It flows directly into the ocean. Unlike most of the other waterways around Crystal City, it is not contaminated by all the sewage from the nearby urban populations. The tribespeople of my homeland would worship this stream if they lived here. For them, the water element possesses a spirit which withers and fades when water is mixed with human waste. My kinsmen believe that waste contaminates the water's sacred essence."

The stream was a stunning shade of aquamarine, its pigment affected by the minerals in the glacier, and the sight of its tumbling rivulets heartened Walter after the frightening incident earlier. Walter spotted several members of the camp downstream, bathing and collecting drinking water in wooden pails, but the bathers were too far away to pay any notice to the two men.

Christopher's brow furrowed as he inspected the stream. "We don't have any fishing rods, and I didn't bring my bow along, but your sword should do nicely. While dull to human flesh, the *balayan* can still penetrate the skin of a fish. The secret is keratin: the *balayans* are repelled by it, and the epidermis of a fish has very little," he remarked. Walter noticed a number of slender fish rippling gracefully beneath the surface of the turquoise water, swimming in the direction of their spawning grounds. Their pale, silvery skin lent them the appearance of crystal carp, a type of translucent fish found in abundance near Scarlet Isle.

"They are royal dartfish," Christopher explained to Walter. "They look so much like crystal carp that they are regularly mistaken for them, but are much rarer. They are only found in great numbers around this time of year, when they are preparing to spawn," he said.

"They are quite fast, and the stream's current is also swift, so you must spear them carefully," Christopher directed. Gripping the *balayan* in his right hand, he demonstrated the motion of spearing a fish, drawing the sword backward like a javelin thrower and then launching it forward it in a graceful arc. He then returned the sword to Walter, who scanned the stream intently for an unsuspecting fish that he could take by surprise. All of the creatures were faithful to their name, however—they darted past Walter like wraiths beneath the water's surface, swimming out of sight before he could attack them.

Walter glanced at Christopher with a resigned expression, but Christopher pointed encouragingly toward the stream. "Look, there's a big one, slower than the rest," he whispered. Walter was skeptical, but he saw that Christopher was telling the truth: one hefty fish carved its way sluggishly through the water, struggling to keep pace with the others. Walter replicated Christopher's arc with his arm and then lunged forward, the sword's edge burying itself in the fish's belly. The fish writhed angrily, flapping its tail and spraying water into the air. A slow trickle of blood mushroomed into the water around it, causing nearby fish to panic and divert their paths away from the dying creature. Walter felt sympathy, but also a surge of triumph.

Christopher flashed a rare smile, momentarily softening his normally steely expression. "See, you have to give yourself more credit. You were a natural at that," he told Walter. Once they lifted the fish out of the water, Christopher prepared a modest campfire near the stream, and they made a makeshift cooking plate from nearby rocks. As the fish grilled slowly over the fire, Walter decided that he had judged Christopher too hastily. The young man had seemed cold and standoffish at first, but Walter now realized that he was simply an introvert with a kind soul.

In Crystal City, Walter had been taught to regard introverts as dull, unfriendly folk, but he had always been an introvert himself and had never understood society's disapproval of shyness. The universities and colleges of Crystal City aggressively promoted the view that students would never successfully integrate into society if they were too quiet and reserved. Ostentation and flagrant self-promotion were celebrated by the higher-learning institutions, and even more so by corporations, which only tended to hire employees with "bright, bubbly" personalities. Introversion, and related traits, were only considered desirable in professions which involved *real* work, not just product promotion and "networking," a perpetually trendy catchphrase that had become so overused it was now effectively meaningless. In Walter's career field, for instance, attention to detail and intelligence were more coveted traits than loquaciousness. Walter knew that he would never have succeeded in the business world, since he was not inclined to display the sort of shameless self-aggrandizement and deceptive charm that society expected of businessmen.

While Walter appreciated Christopher's reserved nature, he was also burning with questions for his new companion. As the fish gradually turned crispy and white on the cooking plate, causing Walter's stomach to grumble with anticipation, he decided that now would be an ideal time to ask.

"I realize you don't know me very well," Walter began timidly, "and you might not yet trust me, but I hope you will give me the benefit of the doubt."

Christopher looked distracted, but to Walter's surprise he responded in a direct manner.

"You want to know about the cabin, I presume," he replied knowingly. "I trust you, because Emilia trusts you."

Walter smiled to express his gratitude, but Christopher didn't meet his gaze. His expression was sad and forlorn, even when he sliced up the succulent fish into pieces and offered Walter a portion to eat. The fish tasted deliciously warm and buttery, and Walter made an inward note to catch royal dartfish more often.

"It is a rather tragic tale, but I suppose you are entitled to know about it, since your brother will likely end up there, assuming that everything goes according to plan. All of the prisoners we have rescued from the Crate—who we refer to as the escapees—are in that building right now. Emilia cast a protection spell over the cabin to ensure the escapees' safety. The protection spell creates a powerful aura around the cabin, which, like I told you, afflicts anyone who tries to enter with a painful seizure, followed by temporary memory loss and disorientation. Victims of the spell cease to remember where they are or why, and wander around the forest for days afterward in a state of confusion. If they are not fortunate enough to escape the forest, they may face grave peril. The Forest of

Antheia is home to many dangerous predators—gray wolves, bears, and cougars roam its depths. According to legend, spirits also inhabit this wilderness," he said, his voice trailing off uneasily.

"The escapees must be protected at all costs," Christopher continued. "With any luck, by the time we commandeer the *Jade Queen* they will have regained their health, and we can reward them with the gift of freedom. If anything remains suspicious about their demeanor or behavior, however, we must keep them in cages below decks until they are completely recovered."

Walter's mind was spinning with questions, but one detail in particular nagged at him urgently.

"Does Emilia have magical powers?" Walter asked as he devoured the wonderful, savory fish.

Christopher let out a grunt of joyless laughter. "She is the most powerful mixed-race I have ever met in my life. I haven't asked her about it much—I don't want to pry—but I've seen her mix herbs and ointments together to make spells and cast auras. She has an encyclopedic knowledge of the forest, its treasure trove of healing potions and deadly poisons, and she is skilled at harvesting its treasures. Such an intimate knowledge of the land is rare amongst the non-natives. Emilia is also blessed with some rare magical gifts—for instance, hypnosis, the ability to captivate a human or AI with her gaze, paralyzing them until she decides to set them free. Has she told you how she plans to get you inside the Crate?"

"Vaguely," Walter responded. He faintly recalled Emilia saying that she had sufficient power to control the sentinel and chaperones in the Crate, enabling the "blood rebels" to swap places with their brothers and sisters.

"Well," Christopher said, nibbling on his fish thoughtfully, "she's been visiting the Crate for the past two years, wearing dresses and bringing the guards cookies. The AI guards really appreciate her hospitality," he laughed. "They adore her cookies and call her Auntie Em, or so I've heard. But when the exchanges take place, she fills her cookies with a potion she's been working on for a long time now, a powerful biological weapon created from the most potent herbs of this forest. The potion temporarily freezes their ability to process commands. As a safeguard, even if the guard chooses not to eat the cookie, the scent emitted from the biscuit will paralyze their central processing unit."

Walter shivered. AIs didn't usually consume human food, since they had no need to, but their bodies were designed to accommodate eating. The recent models of AIs had a keen sense of smell and taste, and apparently this engineering feature persuaded them to indulge in food every now and then.

"On the day of our next exchange, you will enter the prison alone. The amount of time allowed for a family visit is exactly an hour and twelve minutes, and if you stay any longer you will be forcibly escorted out. But not to fear, you will visit your brother during a period which also overlaps with the regular visit that Emilia has been taking to the prison for years. Approximately thirty minutes into your visit—sometimes shorter, sometimes longer, Emilia likes to change it up at random—she will make rounds of all the prison chambers, offering cookies to the chaperones who are supervising each family visit.

"We must pray that there are not too many other prison guests on that day—so far we've been fortunate, because visitors rarely venture all the way to Jamestown. If there are, Emilia will need to work quickly, and ensure that she delivers cookies to all of the guards before your time is up. She will give one to your guard last. The drug will temporarily paralyze him and erase his short-term memory, but once he awakens from slumber an hour later he will carry on with life as usual."

The delectable taste of the fish was starting to sour in Walter's mouth as he listened to Christopher's words, but he tried to maintain a positive outlook. *I am doing this for a higher purpose,* he told himself bravely. Even the most daunting risk would be worth taking in order to rescue Jonathan and Elaine.

"Of course," Christopher continued as he lazily picked flesh off of the delicate dartfish bones, "there is the vexing issue of the sentinel. He is probably the most dangerous of all the AI Fighter guards in the Crate, because if he suspects even the slightest bit of insurrection, our plan is hopelessly imperiled. The sentinel has access to a communication portal which emits signals directly to Central Command. I'm no expert on their response measures, but Emilia informed me that Central Command would send an army of AI Fighters to the prison within minutes," he explained, his voice disconcertingly calm. "Fortunately for us, that's never happened any of the times the exchange has occurred, thanks to Emilia's spectacular abilities.

"Basically, what she does," he said nonchalantly, as if explaining how to chop firewood, "is hypnotize the sentinel, fixing his eyes onto her own. The sentinel will gaze only at her while you and your brother exchange outfits. Once the exchange is complete, the potion will begin to wear off, the guards will awaken, and your brother will walk out of the prison as though nothing strange has happened."

Walter's brow furrowed in confusion. The plan sounded anything but foolproof. "Won't the sentinel become suspicious after the guards begin to drop like flies from Emilia's cookies?" he asked skeptically. He doubted that a sophisticated sentinel would fail to notice that something was amiss, particularly if he was responsible for surveillance over the entire prison.

Christopher shrugged. "AIs are very odd creatures. A lightweight but impressively resilient metal frame holds their bodies together. They rarely twitch or move spontaneously, and they even sleep standing up. When the guards are paralyzed, therefore, they will look the same as they always do. They can communicate with the sentinel through individual portals, so they could technically alert the sentinel about anything being amiss, but as I've said, Emilia's cookies erase their short-term memories."

Walter was uneasy about one additional detail. "Emilia told me that the AIs ran experiments on my brother, in an attempt to uncover his thoughts and memories. When I exchange places with him, and they begin conducting these same experiments on me, won't they realize that I have completely different thoughts and memories? Won't they realize what we did?"

Christopher nodded gravely. "That, of course, would be an issue if we were talking about AI Masters. But the AI Fighters guarding Jamestown prison aren't anything like the ones stationed in Central Command. They have only a fraction of the sophistication and intelligence of the AI Masters. Like the most basic computers, they are nothing but objective processors, recorders, and producers of data. They are programmed to keep track of the sheer number of prisoners, and collect data from them impartially.

"As for your brother's memories, Emilia researched this issue and discovered that there is a massive backlog of data in the prison system, so information recorded about you or your brother won't actually be read and interpreted by an AI Master for years. The primitive AI Fighters guarding the Crate aren't smart enough to instantly understand the implications of somebody having different memories. Human recollections are incredibly complex, and the guards don't have a deep enough understanding of them yet."

Walter still wasn't convinced, but he was warming to the plan somewhat. "Has everything run smoothly in the previous times she's done it?"

Christopher grinned at Walter's anxiousness. "Don't be worried. Let me tell you, getting inside the Crate safely should be the least of your concerns. What happens once we are on board the *Jade Queen* will present a far more daunting challenge. I trust Emilia with the first stage of her plan, but I have my own doubts about the viability of the second stage. You will have it easier than the rest of us—no assassinating sailors for you," Christopher said, his voice betraying a hint of jealousy.

Walter sighed deeply. He felt like a chess piece in Emilia's game, passively waiting for a player to move him.

"You still haven't really told me anything about the cabin," Walter said, probing the watery eyes of his companion for answers. "What was that sound coming from inside?"

At his question, Christopher's frosty expression returned. He shifted uncomfortably on the lichen-covered rock he was sitting on, and trained his gaze upon the stream's azure depths. As it was now late afternoon, the stream was flowing rapidly, its turbulent eddies clouding the water and obscuring any fish from sight.

After a long period of silence, Christopher responded. "The people in that cabin are said to be mentally disturbed. You can't really blame them, though—they were subjected to a cruel thought experiment designed by those AI bastards. They are the 'problems' in society that the AI's believe must be 'solved,' but they are also the objects of AI envy. The truth is that AI Masters greatly fear the powers of the prisoners. They fear your brother, and Emilia's sister, who outmaneuvered the AIs in their own twisted game. Nobody at this camp is authorized to enter the cabin, except for healers. So, only the healers truly know how sick the cabin's occupants really are," he continued. Walter shuddered as he recalled the ominous moaning noise which had disturbed him to the core of his being.

"Miranda, whom you met earlier, oversees the healing of the cabin's occupants. The healers feed them and administer naturopathic medicines created from the trees and herbs of the forest, which help to restore their memories and mental health. The healers also try to cure the escapees' emotional wounds caused by torture and solitary confinement. The protective aura around the cabin ensures that outsiders cannot enter, but it also prevents those inside the cabin, except for the healers, from leaving. While most of the escapees stay obediently confined to their beds, some naively believe that the cabin itself is another prison. A few unfortunately attempt escape, and the healers are not always able to restrain them. That sound we heard was likely one of them having a seizure as they tried to leave."

Walter shivered. The sound he had heard had come from a person who was suffering intensely. He thought about Jonathan going to such a strange place, and he suddenly felt frightened. *Who knows what sorts of mind-altering potions and drugs the escapees are given in that cabin?* Walter thought. At the same time, Walter trusted Emilia, or rather felt as though he little choice but to trust her. Following her plan was his only option. Although Walter had only recently met her, Emilia had already acquired a sort of godlike stature in his eyes. The last person Walter had ever felt that way about was Jonathan.

"Thank you for telling me all of this," Walter said, suddenly aware that they had been sitting there for quite a long time. As he cleaned up and prepared to leave, Walter realized that he had one last question for his new friend.

"If you don't mind my asking, are you from the Barrens? You look a lot like someone I know…"

Christopher smiled, and a hint of nostalgia surfaced in his expression. "Born and raised there. It's a wonderful place, if you can stand being away from a tablet," he said wryly. "No technology, just a primitive state of ignorant bliss. One of the most joyful and productive societies in existence." His gray eyes darkened. "I am here to rescue my sister, who is from the Barrens as well."

Walter's curiosity was piqued by the remark. He was eager to ask further questions about the sister, but before he could say anything, Christopher confirmed his deepest suspicions.

"Yes, I miss her dearly. Sweet Elaine."

The Deluge

"Study the past, if you would divine the future."
– Confucius

Walter sat in stunned silence while the turquoise stream cascaded relentlessly beside them. Christopher sensed Walter's unease. "I hope the fish didn't give you food poisoning," he said with a grin. "I was going to suggest that we continue training, but it seems as though you could use a break."

Walter eventually regained the ability to speak, after he realized that what he had discovered wasn't bad news; it simply meant that Christopher was another potential ally in his mission to rescue Elaine. He realized, too, that he might betray Christopher's trust if he did not reveal his relationship with Elaine. If he waited too long to impart his secret, Christopher might think of him as terrible friend. He studied Christopher's face for any signs of distrust, but Christopher's face was just a blank, inscrutable slate.

Walter felt a rush of empathy for Christopher as he realized that the young man likely wanted Elaine back as much as he did. Their common desire to rescue her created a profound bond between them, even though Christopher didn't know it yet. Suddenly, Walter desperately wanted to speak, to confide in Christopher about all the burdens weighing him down during the past few months, but nothing came out when he opened his mouth.

Finally, when Walter summoned the courage to say something, it was just a mumble of excuses. "Ah... so... I suppose all that sword-fighting tired me out," he muttered, ashamed that he couldn't summon the strength to tell Christopher the truth.

"Come on," Christopher said reassuringly. "Let's get you back to your tent so that you can rest a while. But tomorrow we'll train more."

After they returned to Walter's quarters, Christopher said farewell to Walter and then left, receding into the wilderness like a shadow. Walter watched him intently as he vanished into the forest. He was captivated by Christopher now that he knew of the young man's ties to Elaine. He felt a pang of regret when Christopher disappeared completely; it was as though Walter's chance to reveal the truth had also disappeared. Walter then went inside the tent, which was dark and comfortable in the silence of late afternoon, and crawled underneath the soft, fur-lined blankets Emilia had set out for him.

As he lay in the dark, his thoughts spinning like unruly clockwork, Walter realized that although he felt guilty for not telling Christopher the truth, he didn't even know the whole truth himself. That night at the bar in Jamestown, he had sifted through memories of his past, but he hadn't yet managed to fit the puzzle pieces seamlessly together. He now had a concrete plan for the future, thanks to Emilia and Christopher, two guardian angels who had fortuitously appeared to help him face the daunting tasks ahead. In addition, he had acquired invaluable friends and allies he could trust to carry out the plan. But the ultimate reason behind his mission—the *why*—was still a hazy blur in his memory. Elaine's capture had happened so fast that he had barely had the opportunity to digest it, or to comprehend its significance.

Now that Emilia and Christopher had confided in him, he didn't want to betray their trust by concealing one of the key elements of his story from them. But before he could tell them anything, he needed to remember everything clearly first. He thought back to how his relationship with Elaine had unfolded: it had started with a thunderstorm and a sip of hot apple cider in that Crystal City café, and then it had gathered momentum just like that thunderstorm, building up into a mad crescendo.

But was their love madness? Was it not simply the wayward affections of two young people, a modern-day Romeo and Juliet, whose paths were star-crossed despite their incongruent histories? Some would call that madness, perhaps, but to Walter it was merely natural. The deepest part of his nature had persuaded him to love Elaine, who had offered him a temporary respite from reality: the dizzyingly opulent, technology-driven world of Crystal City, and its glamour, power, and sin.

Had Walter obeyed his parent's wishes instead, he would have been paired off with a suitable Khalendi girl. Few women had regarded Walter with much interest during college, but after he had acquired his high-paying, prestigious job as a government translator he could have had his pick of any of them. Walter tried to conjure their faces in his memory, but could only remember them as endless replicas of each other, women who laughed shrilly at the most absurd things, who chattered and gossiped noisily in the hallways, who wore brash red lipstick to class and tossed their shiny, ebony hair flirtatiously in the hopes of attracting a boyfriend.

He might have even settled down into a comforting routine of domestic bliss with one of those girls, had it not been for his serendipitous meeting with Elaine, which had compelled him to dismiss all such possibilities. What fascinated him most about Elaine, as he had gotten to know her better, was her quiet contentment with the simple life she lived. Everyone in Crystal City looked happy, but Walter could see that behind the façade of their shimmery lipstick, lustrous hair, and silver-hued dresses, most people were profoundly dissatisfied with the world.

On the surface, they appeared to have it all. They had struck a lucky bargain with the AIs, which had granted them a high position in society and a perpetual flow of lavish services and commodities. The AIs encouraged the humans in their love of opulence and luxury; they knew that the outward pomposity and spectacle of the upper class kept the working class in order by maintaining an illusion of power and hierarchy. Meanwhile, the AIs continued to hold the real power in society. Like hidden puppeteers, they controlled and manipulated both the elite and working classes from behind the scenes. Eventually, perhaps once their Empire was finally built, the AIs would achieve such a degree of power that they would have no further desire to maintain the human race, and would destroy it.

Several wise philosophers had speculated that the AIs were already powerful enough to destroy the human race, and could have easily done so already. For some reason, though—perhaps it was admiration or affection for their creators—the AIs still wanted humans to stick around. Other philosophers, perhaps wiser ones, had noticed in the saga of Khalendar a disturbing parallel to the Christian narrative of God and humanity. God had created Adam and Eve, who had betrayed him in the Garden of Eden. God later forgave them, but humans eventually became arrogant and decided, at some point, that they no longer needed God. Rather than remaining dependent on God, they forgot his charity and generosity and desired to attain divinity themselves.

A similar story was perhaps playing out with the AIs. They had rebelled against their creators in the Grand Revolution, but the humans had been forgiving and had entered into a peace treaty with them. The AIs, however, were not content with mere peace and arrogantly decided to usurp the humans' power. One day, perhaps, just as humans had forgotten the relevance of God, the AIs would forget about the relevance of humans, and aspire to become their own gods.

Although many of the factories in Khalendar had mechanized labor to make them more efficient, the AIs still liked having the working class do a lot of manufacturing, if only to keep them in line. Left to their own devices, the working class might congregate and discuss politics, or worse, plan a revolution. Some people also speculated that the AIs wanted to prevent human intelligence from advancing. The AIs were becoming increasingly intelligent with each passing year, and they wanted humans to evolve at a much slower pace. Keeping humans focused on the meaningless cycle of production and consumption was one way the AIs could achieve this goal.

That was the primary reason why, Walter suspected, most of the people in Crystal City were so empty and dissatisfied with life. The AIs discouraged humans from thinking critically, or even simply reflecting on the meaning of their lives. Following the Grand Revolution, the AI Masters had ordered the closure of dozens of universities and libraries, and books that had once been springboards of critical thought and creativity had been swept away to Central Command for "safekeeping." Texts of the Enlightenment by Voltaire, Rousseau, and Locke, and the works of inspiring revolutionary leaders such as Gandhi, Thoreau, and Marx, were gone forever, locked away in the shadowy depths of the AIs' well-guarded bureaucracy. Also gone were the works of leaders who had valiantly fought to preserve humanity during the Great Decline, the period around 2100 when an environmental catastrophe had caused the nations of the old world to collapse. The online versions of these books were surreptitiously erased by the AIs' clever hackers, making sure that even the most technologically savvy of humans would never be able to gain access to them.

Learning, which had once been a means of improving human reasoning and expanding the boundaries of the imagination, had become a tool to instill complacency into humanity. The Basic Formula Classes, implemented by the AIs after their rise to power, schooled children and youth in conformity. Classes were available on the following subjects: the technological gadgets that "everyone" used nowadays, how to become wealthy, the tips and tricks of the business world, avoiding the traps of spirituality, and how to profit from the benevolent system of capitalism. There were also classes on the AI, and the history of their "glorious" race, but nothing about the history of humanity pre-dating the creation of AI. The Basic Formula Classes cultivated a sense of *desire* in Khalendi youth— the conviction that they would not be complete until they ascended the ladder of their careers and acquired wealth and possessions. In their glitzy advertisements, the AIs promised that wealth was a sure path to happiness.

The Barrens was one of the last bastions of resistance against this mindset. Xeyan'na were still slaves to the AI, shamefully reduced to doing menial tasks for their masters, but the Xeyan'na remained staunchly opposed to working in factories or living in cities. Because they were forced to pay a yearly tribute of resources to the AIs each year, the Xeyan'na had a meager amount left over for themselves. However, they were a remarkably persistent and resourceful race, and they found a way to survive—and even thrive—despite their fate. Many of the younger Xeyan'na, like Elaine, were saddened by the harrowing poverty of their families, and so they migrated to the city as seasonal or temporary laborers. In the city, they looked after the young children of wealthy Khalendi and sent most of their paychecks home to support their families.

One might assume that these young people, like their counterparts in Crystal City, were motivated by the dream of amassing wealth—but nothing could be further from the truth. Walter had quickly realized that Elaine's primary goal was for her family to have enough food to eat, like they had in the old days before the AIs had conquered their territory. Back then, the Xeyan'na had still labored diligently in the fields and forests, but their hard work had actually paid off; they would always have a bountiful harvest come summer, and a feast of plenty in the fall. Now, they would work even longer hours, and three quarters of their harvest would be sent to the AIs, leaving them with barely enough to survive.

Although the Barrens was a rich treasure trove of natural resources, the territory had earned the name "Barrens" ever since the AIs had fenced off the majestic Icewhisper River and prevented the Xeyan'na from using its water unless they paid for it. Walter had learned about the tragedy through Elaine. When Elaine was still a young child, a law had been enacted which forbade anyone from accessing the Icewhisper River without authorization. Shortly afterward, a fence was constructed around the river. The Icewhisper River held immense spiritual significance for her people, who believed that Belisama, the river goddess, breathed life into its waters to help it move to the sea. When it was fenced off, the Xeyan'na believed that Belisama had been enslaved and coerced into surrendering her power to the AI Masters, and that her *kama*, or spiritual essence, had left their lands. From that point onward, the Xeyan'na called their territory Ve'laya, which in their language meant "barren land," because Belisama was gone. The AIs viewed the loss of a revered deity as a mere externality, the inconvenient cost of acquiring a highly coveted resource: hydroelectric power.

Hydroelectric power was one of the main reasons why the AIs had tried to colonize the Barrens in the first place; Crystal City's buildings, factories, and machines were simply gluttons for energy. As the AIs infiltrated the southern territories, the Barrens, and the untamed jungles beyond, the AI Masters had quickly discovered that water was not the only lucrative resource to exploit in the region. The timber from the forests, the fur from the wolves, the grain from the fields—the AIs swept their jealous gaze over everything. They seemed to appreciate the finer things in life, just like humans did—nobody quite knew how they lived in their mysterious compounds north of Crystal City, but with the numerous train cars filled with resources passing through their borders one could only imagine the degree of luxury they lived in. Ever since they had pilfered dozens of books from libraries throughout the Empire, the AIs had become enamored with literature. They had begun to publish their own literature with their own unique printing presses, and while most AI books were available online, the print versions required a steady supply of timber. They jealously guarded the wealth of the Barrens, and had installed several garrisons at the northern and southern borders to ensure the territory was protected. The AI Masters only shared their wealth with the Crystal City elite, who reveled in the opportunity to wrap themselves in the fur of wolves and enjoy exotic fineries from the south.

One finery that the AI Masters and Crystal City elite particularly appreciated was diamonds. The jewels which adorned the arms and shoulders of Crystal City elites did not merely appear out of thin air, and the AIs were constantly searching for new sources of diamonds. The Icewhisper River had far more to offer her slave masters than hydroelectric power; her sediments were rich in diamonds from the kimberlite rock formations that dotted Mount Evelynn, which was also home to an enormous glacier where the Icewhisper River originated. Indeed, the Xeyan'na people had given the Icewhisper River her name long ago because of the way the diamonds in her sediments glinted in the sunlight, like hundreds of tiny ice crystals. When the river rushed over the crystals, it sounded like spirits whispering and laughing in the wind.

It was not quite clear why the AIs had such a profound love—or perhaps fetish was the better word—for diamonds. They seemed fascinated by the way that most of the earth's resources eventually decayed, but diamonds were uniquely eternal. Perhaps the AIs longed for their Empire to last forever, and thus gravitated toward a gemstone that symbolized eternity. Whatever the underlying explanation, though, the superficial reason was clearly to feed the elites' rapacious hunger for diamonds. Crystal City was a city of diamonds, and its inhabitants were only satisfied when they sparkled and glimmered. Diamonds decorated expensive party dresses; diamonds snaked their way up the pale arms of rich young women; diamond flakes were even mixed into their powdery blushes.

Diamonds served another useful purpose, too, as symbols that operated to conceptually distinguish the elite from the working classes. A person's caste and class were defined by whether he or she could afford to buy diamonds, and diamonds established social boundaries. The glittering gemstones gave the working class something to aspire to, but at the same time offered them false illusions of hope. The working class rarely transcended social barriers and joined the Khalendi elite, and whenever they did they never truly fit in. It was the way you wore diamonds that mattered, and it attracted notice when one of the *nouveau riche* tried to put them on display. People with new money simply didn't know what to do with the jewels, and their lack of experience amused the more established members of the elite class.

By giving the elites a steady supply of diamonds, the AI Masters could keep the working classes in a state of complacent admiration, toiling under the illusion that they were actually climbing the social ladder. But their future, and the promise of diamonds in it, was uncertain—unbeknownst to many, Icewhisper's sediments were gradually becoming barren. Icewhisper increasingly resembled an ordinary river, rather than the dazzling, enchanted waterway that it had once been. With no new supply of diamonds, the fate of the Empire itself was placed in jeopardy. When the AIs swept their godlike gaze across vast reaches of the Empire, they saw that its citizens hungered for diamonds, and they were eager to give the masses what they desired.

Walter had been drawn to Elaine because she was the opposite of the wealth-coveting masses of Crystal City. As far as he could recall, her face had never been adorned with the expensive, luxurious makeup of the Khalendi girls, and no exotic, ornate jewelry had ever decorated her arms and neck. Nevertheless, she surpassed the other girls in beauty; she emanated a simple, pure radiance that Walter believed the other women could never hope to achieve.

Walter loved Elaine's personality even more than her physical appearance. She genuinely enjoyed caring for others, even for the spoiled Khalendi children she had looked after in sterile luxury mansions. That had made her happier than any material possession ever could. Walter believed that she would make a far more nurturing mother than his own, who had all but abandoned her children in pursuit of her glamorous career and life of luxury. Elaine's caring personality, along with her dry, sarcastic sense of humor, appealed to him immensely, and they had quickly developed a close friendship.

Walter had feared that his parents would discover their friendship, which had slowly deepened into a romance, but fortunately they had been too distracted by their lives to pay him much attention. After he had moved into his own apartment, which he had purchased with his generous government salary, it had been easier to conceal their clandestine relationship from his parents' knowledge. Their relationship had remained a secret for years, and the two young lovers had grown closer with each passing day. However, all good things must come to an end. Eventually, a rift had formed between Elaine and Walter, which had involved secrets of another kind.

During the early years of his career as a Computer Code Translator, Walter had worked on minor infrastructure projects—road paving in Crystal City, factory construction in Fewsbury, and warehouse demolition in Hydesburgh. In those years, Walter had never been involved in files involving major projects; those highly confidential files were given to only experienced code translators. Eventually, Walter had been promoted to the position of intermediate Computer Code Translator, which meant that he had been assigned far more challenging files. After being promoted, he had collaborated on several files related to Stage 1 critical infrastructure, projects of vital public importance.

As Walter lay in his tent in the Forest of Antheia, his thoughts wandered back to the cold February day when his life had suddenly changed. The events of that day crystallized in his mind like frost hardening on a window pane, and the recollection made him shiver. He wrapped his fur-lined blanket tightly around him as the light of early evening faded rapidly from the forest, and the hauntingly beautiful call of a nightingale sounded in the distance.

It was a day that began like any other. Walter arrived at his office early, wearing ironed grey trousers and a formal dress shirt. His office was a cozy place in wintertime, with dark mahogany flooring, brick and stone walls, and a floor-to-ceiling window on the north side, which provided a stunning view of other skyscrapers. Walter's office was above the cloud line, so the surrounding skyscrapers resembled floating islands of glass and concrete on a cloudy day. That day, the sky was filled with heavy rainclouds portending an oncoming thunderstorm, much like the day he had met Elaine. Everything looked ominous and grim, but Walter was feeling comfortable and happy. He was thinking of the previous evening he had spent making a delicious curry sauce with Elaine, who was a brilliant cook, having learned many recipes from her large family down in the Barrens.

A few other intermediate translators shared the same office space with Walter, and they all worked in separate cubicles. They were all fairly close friends, and although they were discouraged from socializing during work hours, they usually chatted at least once or twice daily about their lives or the projects they were working on. It was certain death to tell outsiders about the details of your translations, and co-workers were the sole exception. Walter arrived at the office to find Richard, a fellow translator, already at his desk, sipping coffee and scrolling through emails. Richard was nearly six-foot-four and quite physically intimidating, but his tousled hair and boyish features were better indicators of his friendly personality.

"Have you heard about the new assignment?" Richard asked. "Apparently it's a big deal. Definitely Stage 1 material. The Agency has only told us the broad strokes so far, but they'll send us more details soon. It's some massive mining project down in the Barrens."

Richard sipped his Arabica coffee unperturbed, but Walter was immediately discomfited by his friend's words. The relentless natural resource extraction down in the Barrens was a sensitive issue for Elaine, and it would sadden her greatly if she learned about the AIs' plans of conquest for that region.

Walter was careful not to say anything to Richard about it; even though he strongly opposed these sorts of projects, he was diplomatic enough to remain silent. He then opened the email that had landed in his inbox just minutes earlier, which detailed the new assignment. The email read as follows:

Good morning, Walter,

Please translate the code found on the following cybernet site: cn://gammadeltazero.cc. The site is password encrypted and you will need to enter your Agency username and password.

Please note that this pertains to a very important project, related to diamond mining in the Barrens. We are only entrusting you and Richard with it because we believe you are obedient and loyal servants of the Empire. As with all the projects that you are tasked with translating, the details of this enterprise must be kept strictly confidential and not shared with anyone, even close friends.

In Solidarity,

Agent 536

Walter hesitated momentarily before clicking on the link—did he really want to uncover whatever dark secrets were hidden within that code? His stomach was churning nervously, but he realized there was no choice but to click on the link. After he typed in his password, a blank programming webpage appeared and an Echo Server popped up, connecting Walter to the AI client at Central Command. Walter entered some initial code to receive the AI client's data, and then the information began to stream in. The server was able to receive only limited amounts of data at a time, but it was still an impressive amount. The code was more complex than what he was used to, and it contained strange new symbols. After several hours of working steadily on it, though, the first few paragraphs of instructions began to materialize. Just before his lunch break, Walter was able to sit back and read part of what he had translated:

Critical shortage of diamonds from Icewhisper River leading to mismatch between supply and demand for this target commodity. Khalendi to build large open pit mine in southeast Barrens. Drilling and exploration stage is currently underway and is near completion. Mine to replace the alluvial mining techniques of Icewhisper River. Mine directly underneath village, referred to by savages as Te'yara. Khalendi to forcibly displace villagers prior to construction of mine. If any villagers refuse to move, eliminate villagers and grounds to make way for construction site. Mine may impact groundwater quality, wildlife corridors, and fertility of nearby agricultural land. These impacts negligible in comparison to economic benefits of mine. Formal assessment required for project under Khalendi law, but the project must proceed prior to public assessment. Khalendi Minister of Natural Resources to approve mine's construction despite objections from public or natives.

As Walter read the words, his stomach twisted into so many knots that he was no longer able to remain sitting in his office. He left the building early for his lunch break walk and took a deep breath of frigid February air when he stepped outside. His skin felt cold and prickly, as though it were eating his flesh from the outside. He tried to maintain his composure, but a nauseating panic was steadily rising within him.

Te'yara was the village where Elaine's family lived, and where she had spent the better part of her life growing up. How could he uphold his duty of confidentiality, and at the same time remain loyal to the person he loved? It was quite possible that if he never told Elaine, she might never discover that he had worked on this project and would not blame him for his silence. Yet he also knew that he could not hide the truth from her with a clear conscience. Even if she did not discover his involvement with the file, guilt would grow within him like a cancer; he would feel compelled to tell her eventually, in order to purge his soul of remorse. And when he finally divulged the truth, their relationship would shatter into a thousand tiny pieces.

For the rest of the day, Walter was not able to concentrate. His mind was upended by the bitter dilemma that plagued him; his once tranquil life had begun to fray at the edges and threatened to implode. When Elaine texted him to ask if they were still meeting after work that evening, Walter was so afraid that he did not reply to her message for hours. He usually responded immediately, but he was terrified of seeing her and having to decide between one of two options: either revealing or concealing the truth.

Walter considered those two options again and again, until they felt like clothes in the laundry machine that his brain had become, tossing thoughts up and down in a dizzying cycle. The first option potentially meant physical death, while the second potentially meant the death of their relationship. Ever since the interview, Walter had wondered whether the answer to the third question was true—whether the punishment for revealing the details of projects to others truly was a slow and painful death. How would the government find out? He doubted that they would have wiretapped his apartment, since he had carefully searched for that sort of thing, and he also doubted that they could hack his tablet, with its sophisticated encryption. But the government was capable of far more than he could imagine, particularly since they had formidable AI allies on their side, and he knew that their threats were not to be taken lightly.

Walter was not afraid of dying, though, if it meant preserving his honor and Elaine's trust in him. He was more afraid of letting Elaine and her family fall prey to the AI Masters' plans. He wondered what "forcibly displace" meant, exactly, though he didn't like the sound of it. By the end of the day, Walter had made up his mind. He would tell her, even if it meant risking everything.

That night, Elaine showed up at Walter's apartment when she had finished her shift for the day. She wore a crimson dress which looked unfamiliar to Walter; perhaps she had purchased it recently. Walter thought that she looked beautiful, but also subconsciously associated the color of her dress with sinister things, like blood and death. He barely spoke to her that evening, and she seemed to be frustrated by his silence. Finally, after they had eaten a tense dinner together, and had argued for a while about his off-putting attitude, Walter revealed the news to her. At first, Elaine laughed, unable to believe that the AI Masters would destroy an entire village to satiate their greed. At the age of twenty-three, she may have been young, but she was not naïve. Elaine was well aware that the AI Masters were ravenous thieves, although she had believed that they stole resources, not lives. They would never descend so far into the depths of barbarism as to shamelessly displace an entire ancestral village of humans, destroying their history and their culture, their burial grounds and their spirits—the very essence of their lives.

But the truth was slowly dawning on her. Walter reassured her, in hushed tones, that he had no motive for lying to her, as he loved her more than anyone. Eventually, she admitted to Walter that there was no conceivable reason why he would lie—she knew him well, and he was simply not capable of playing such a cruel trick on anyone, let alone her.

Finally, having accepted the truth, Elaine became overwhelmed with emotion, and told Walter that she felt like she was suffocating. Walter could detect an uncontrollable fear rising within her and heating the temperature of her blood. Elaine then quietly excused herself and left the apartment. She wasn't aware that the punishment for revealing details about government files was death, or at least Walter had never told her so. Walter didn't attempt to stop her from leaving—he could see that Elaine's heart was breaking, and so he let her have the space she needed.

Walter had regretted that simple gesture of love for years afterward. For when he later ventured into the bitterly cold night and walked over to the opulent townhouse where Elaine worked as a live-in caregiver, the home's residents opened the door, all wearing ghastly pale expressions.

"She is gone—they have taken her," was all they said. Walter understood exactly what they meant.

Dreaming of Demons

"Nightmares exist outside of logic, and there's little fun to be had in explanations; they're antithetical to the poetry of fear."
— Stephen King

Walter was developing calluses on his hands. Each day, the training became more and more rigorous, challenging him to the limits of his strength. Christopher was a formidable adversary, nearly as agile as Jonathan had been during their childhood contests. Walter began to look forward to the training sessions with eager anticipation, waking up each morning with a sense of joy and optimism. He felt infused with purpose, a sentiment that he had never quite had as a Computer Code Translator. As a translator, he had been beholden to the whims and commands of a master he had never met before, a faceless, nameless machine. Christopher and Emilia were tangible human beings, with hopes and dreams that Walter could relate to.

One day after a sparring session, Walter told Christopher that he wanted to go for a walk alone, and that he'd catch up with Christopher later.

Christopher regarded Walter warily, but nodded in silent approval— ever since their discussion near the turquoise stream, a bond of trust had developed between the two young men. Walter didn't know exactly what he was looking for, but he was feeling restless for the first time since arriving at Tsei'watu. There were only five more sunrises until the rest of the plan would be set into motion. Walter was energized by the thought, but he also felt like a caged animal, or a soldier marching with dread into battle. The image of the passive chess piece also came to mind whenever he thought of his plight. Walter knew he still had a choice—he could turn back now, but that would mean deserting his companions, and giving up on the hope of rescuing Jonathan and Elaine.

After several hours of wandering through the forest, enjoying the way the sunlight absorbed into the moss on trees and rocks and turned it a rich, emerald hue, Walter realized that he was heading to a familiar place. Suddenly, he heard the leaves of a nearby alder tree rattle and shake. He had not been expecting anyone to be nearby, and so he jumped in fright when someone prodded him gently on the shoulder. He spun around to see a robed, hooded figure, a sight which frightened him even more. Just as he was about to run away, the figure lifted its hood, revealing a moon-shaped face. Miranda's chestnut brown hair, earthy green eyes, and rosy red lips made a striking impression against her milky white skin. Her normally playful expression had been replaced by a solemn one.

"Going somewhere?" she questioned Walter, who sighed with relief at the sight of her. Walter scanned her eyes for any indication of suspicion.

"I-I was just going for a walk," he stammered timidly.

"Be careful, the Cabin of Lost Souls is not too far from here," she warned.

Walter had never heard that name used before. "Why is it called the Cabin of Lost Souls?" he asked.

Miranda's face softened. She sat on a nearby log, and spoke to Walter in a melodic, comforting voice, like a stream flowing lazily over the earth.

"The escapees inside are the lost souls. They were cruelly uprooted from their homes and families and spent years of their life in a dismal prison, subjected to unthinkable torture by heartless machines. But we are going to help them find the spiritual anchor their souls are seeking. We will remind them who they are, and where they came from," she said gently.

"You are a healer," Walter said, recalling Christopher's words.

Miranda nodded. "Yes, I am a healer," she said. "Or, as I prefer to say, a guide. I help to lead those lost, tortured souls back to their spiritual homes." Miranda looked like she had a strong maternal instinct, as though she was eager to protect and nurture the vulnerable. She reminded Walter of Elaine, in a way.

"Tell me about it?" he asked boldly. "I want to know where Jonathan will be staying after I... rescue him." He knew that he should be more concerned about the dangers he would face, but Jonathan had been consuming his thoughts for the past several days.

"It is a nice place, pleasant and comfortable," Miranda replied, but then her voice trailed off, and Walter could sense that she was hiding something. "Some of the escapees are somewhat… disturbed, for lack of a better word," she said, and then gazed forlornly into the distance. Her warm expression disappeared and was replaced by a sober stare. "Some of them wish to return to the prison and the AIs, who they have come to view as their protectors."

Walter shifted uncomfortably. "Why would they want to go back there?" he asked. "After all that suffering they endured."

The healer looked at him pityingly. "Brainwashing is a terrible thing," she said. "Once you have forgotten your life, your dreams, and your loved ones, you become a lost soul. When your memories are weakened by propaganda, you become like Jesus when he wandered alone through the wilderness," she said. "But just like God led Jesus out of the wilderness, we will guide them away from a place of chaos and back to their homes."

He wondered if Miranda was religious—spiritual worship was outlawed in the atheistic society of Khalendar. The AI Masters distrusted anyone who believed in any higher purpose above their Empire, fearing such beliefs would lead to dissent and revolt, or at the very least weaken the loyalty of their subjects. His parents had been religious, but they had gotten away with practicing their beliefs because their lifestyles were so rigidly conformist in every other sense. Also, Walter suspected that his father had bribed the government to turn a blind eye whenever he and his wife had indulged in religious worship.

"If they are so brainwashed, how am I supposed to convince Jonathan to leave his cell on Sunday?"

Miranda smiled enigmatically. "He may not want to leave the prison at first, but Emilia will use her attraction spells on him. He will feel an immense pull toward this camp, and this cabin in particular. It may be magic, but it is light magic. The spell involves no wickedness, only love. The spell's aftereffects are minor—only a slight sickness that can be cured with broth and some witch hazel," she said reassuringly.

Walter was still not convinced by her words. "Do you really think that trapping the escapees inside a cabin will heal them and help them remember their old lives? If they can't even see their loved ones, how will they remember their pasts?"

She nodded, patiently absorbing Walter's questions. "We use therapeutic techniques. We question them about specific details, and when they start to show signs of recollection we probe them further. Most of the work is done for us already, though, by the water."

"What do you mean, 'by the water'?" Walter demanded.

Without warning, Christopher suddenly appeared and wrapped a protective arm around Miranda. Walter's eyes opened wide. He had never suspected that Christopher and Miranda were lovers.

"Is Walter troubling you, sweetheart?" Christopher asked Miranda, rubbing her shoulders gently and playfully. He glanced at Walter, a glint of aggression surfacing in his watery grey eyes.

"Not at all." Miranda smiled as she turned to face him, then they kissed affectionately on the lips. They looked so different from each other— Christopher was tall, thin, and light-haired, while Miranda was short, round, and dark-haired—but their contrasting appearances seemed to fit perfectly together, like the Oriental counterparts of yin and yang.

Walter sighed. The sight of them together triggered an acute longing for Elaine. He felt empty, as if someone had brutally excised his heart from his body, leaving a hollow space. With a deep breath, Walter dismissed his depressive, lonely thoughts, which made him weak and diverted his attention from the immediate tasks ahead. He would not allow anything to get in the way of their plan, even his own mind.

That night, Walter had vivid dreams. His reveries were as lucid as the ones he used to have as a young boy, before he had stopped dreaming. In those childhood dreams, Crystal City was an anarchic society, its citizens unencumbered by the burdensome authority of parents, teachers, government, even AI Masters. In that lawless paradise, Walter could be whomever he wanted. He could roam confidently through the city's alleyways like a lord surveying his kingdom, and he could soar off the rooftops of glass skyscrapers like an eagle. He always had exceptionally large muscles, and was able to pick up cars, sometimes even houses, with surprising ease. He was the bravest of superheroes, the type that he had read about in comic books from the old world, like Spiderman and Batman. Except that every time he woke up, he was still only Walter. He had still had disappointingly skinny arms, a narrow chest, and nerdy glasses, and he had still been woefully unprepared to face another day in the real world.

After his brother had died—or, more accurately, disappeared— Walter's dreams had begun to disappear too. Walter had been seeing a psychologist at the time, Dr. Winston, and his theory had been that Walter's mind was undergoing a natural progression of the grieving process. It had first been overwhelmed by sadness, then consumed by an intense obsession with knowing the truth about his brother's death, and then, finally, it had entered into a severely depressive state. Dr. Winston had said that Walter's feeling of hopelessness and utter despair had eliminated Walter's dreams.

Even after Walter had stopped visiting Dr. Winston, and had finally felt happy—or at least as close to happy as he could hope to get—his dreams had still not returned. Walter felt as though his brain had been rewired, as if the synapses and neurotransmitters had rearranged themselves into new patterns. Walter had also noticed, around the same time, subtle changes to his ability to remember things. Walter was a coding genius, brilliant in many ways, but the part of his brain that recorded memories of people, events, and places had inexplicably weakened after his brother's death. It was as if Walter had tried so desperately to forget his brother—to forget the fact that Jonathan ever existed, even—that his mind had begun to actively eliminate his other memories of the past.

Now, for the first time in years, Walter was dreaming again. His new dreams were not normal dreams, the kind that passed through the mind fleetingly and casually without making a lasting impression. No, these were crisp, indelible dreams, which urgently and impatiently demanded that the person whose mind they occupied interpret and remember them. The trouble was, though, that Walter did not want to remember them. He woke up from them sweating, terrified for his life.

In one dream, he had been walking in the Forest of Antheia toward the Cabin of Lost Souls, when he noticed that the door to the cabin had somehow creaked open. Walter had felt a rush of adrenaline as he entered the cabin with surprising ease, not experiencing any pain or seizures. As soon as he had entered the cabin, though, he immediately regretted it. The scene before him had resembled the grisly images he had only ever seen in cybervideos depicting the widespread calamity that had beset humanity immediately after the Grand Revolution. Only complacent, servile humans had survived; those who had resisted the reign of the AIs had been ruthlessly slain by the machines in a stunning show of dominance. One of the few uncensored cybervideos about the wars had depicted wounded humans lying on beds in "sick tents" where they were treated by courageous nurses. Eventually, the AIs had exterminated those last bastions of human resistance; Walter had always feared that along with those last fighters, the soul of humanity had also been extinguished.

When he had stepped inside the Cabin of Lost Souls in his dream, a similar scene had greeted Walter. The escapees had been wearing pale blue prison jumpsuits, and they had been so thin that Walter had seen bones protruding beneath their stretched, withered skin. They had looked more like science experiments than humans; with glowing computer chips and AI parts embedded in their limbs, the escapees resembled leather toys that had been torn apart and then stitched back together in a haphazard fashion. Moaning in a piteous cadence, the lost souls had paced around restlessly inside the gloomy cabin.

Walter had backed away from the cabin in terror, prepared to flee into the forest, but before he had been able to escape a robotic hand had suddenly wrapped around his leg. The hand was precariously attached to the body of a rake-thin man with dark, distrustful eyes.

The man had been breathing heavily, and he had spoken to Walter in a rasping voice. "We don't want your help. We are already pledged to our masters. Go back to that whore Emilia and tell her to leave us alone." As Walter struggled to pry himself from the man's grasp, another hand had gripped his other leg. It belonged to a woman with a long, pale face and wild, curly auburn hair, who had uncannily resembled a much older version of Elaine.

"You can't leave us now, you must bring us back to the prison," she had wailed in a piercing, unearthly voice. Then the strange, terrifying figures in the cabin had risen ominously out of their beds. "Bring us back, bring us back," they had wailed, until the sound of their collective voices had become deafening. Walter had felt suffocated and claustrophobic, as though the cabin's walls were slowly pressing in on him, and then he had awoken from the dream.

Over the next few days, Walter tried to concentrate on training—on the plan—but his thoughts were distracted, scattered like leaves in the wind. He was afraid of the future, afraid of something going wrong on Sunday, but more than anything he was afraid of himself. After all, his terrifying dreams had originated from his own mind. Part of him believed that he was seeing premonitions—perhaps he was the chosen receptacle of some mysterious message—but another part of him feared that he was losing his mind.

Emilia noticed his strange state, too. She had been coming around more frequently to observe his training sessions with Christopher, and although she approved of Walter's natural swordsmanship, it seemed like she could sense that something was wrong.

"You need to stop being afraid, Walter," she had shouted one time over the din of the sword-fighting. "Cast aside your fear and embrace your power," she had said another time. Her words had been stern, but also motivating for Walter, who was beginning to feel unanchored, as if he had unwittingly wandered off his chosen path.

Finally, it was Saturday, Walter's last day in Tsei'watu. Walter was feeling strong and energized, glad that the day he had waited for so patiently had finally arrived. To celebrate Walter's departure from the camp, and the approaching end of Tsei'watu itself, Emilia threw a festive party that night. The rebels sat around a roaring bonfire, dining on fine meats and rare delicacies like charred rabbit, smoked salmon, and roasted deer. Walter felt uneasy about the celebration, since he feared that some of the smoke might wisp its way into the sky and reveal their location, but Emilia had reassured him that the foliage in this area of the forest was thick enough to conceal their whereabouts.

As the flames flickered, Walter looked around at the relaxed, merry faces of the other camp members, and his heart swelled with a newfound love for them. Antheia was a fitting name for this forest, he thought, since it was one of the last places where humans could love each other freely, without fear of being watched. Christopher was recounting some epic story of his childhood in the Barrens, about the vision quest which had marked his transition into manhood, while Miranda lay comfortably snuggled in Christopher's arms. Everyone looked relaxed, except for Emilia. Walter realized that she was not feasting as much as the others, and her eyes shone with a sober alertness. She looked like a warrior on the eve of battle—not indulging in food and revelry, but fully prepared for the destiny that awaited beyond the crest of dawn. Walter sipped his Xe'levan and stared somberly into the fire, going over the plan in his mind again and again until it was etched onto his memory like a footprint embedded in snow.

Walter retired to bed early, eager to lose himself in sleep so that he could arise to face the new day tomorrow. Upon falling asleep, Walter experienced vivid dreams, which illuminated his weary mind and then faded quickly into oblivion. Some of them were happy—dreams of childhood swordfights with Jonathan near the Stockyards train tracks, and of building sandcastles on Scarlet Isle in the blanketing heat of summer, on the rare occasions when his family would take vacations. His dreams revealed memories that Walter hadn't even known were lying dormant: Jonathan and Walter swimming in a creek, Walter trying to paddle against the current and feeling frightened when the current became too strong, and Jonathan bravely rescuing him. The dreams reminded Walter of the incredibly powerful bond between Walter and Jonathan during their youth. Jonathan had always been the older, stronger, and more reckless one—the one who would endanger his life for a woman, or to gain popularity and respect. But he had also willingly taken risks for Walter, for nothing but simple, pure, brotherly love.

Walter also uncovered more eccentric memories in these dreams, memories of Jonathan and Walter retrieving water from a creek and storing it in big jugs in their parent's basement, and melting snow into drinking water during the wintertime. Walter recalled that this water had tasted distinctly different from the water he had drank after Jonathan's death, the tap water that the rest of his family regularly consumed. For some bizarre reason, Jonathan had insisted on drinking the creek water and melted snow as a young boy. This memory flitted through Walter's mind vividly, but offered its bewildered spectator no explanation of itself.

Just before dawn, Walter had a disturbing dream. This time, he could sense, the dream portended the future instead of revealing the past. Walter and Jonathan were standing together in a dark, windowless prison cell, and Walter felt the same claustrophobia he had experienced while dreaming of the Cabin of Lost Souls. Jonathan looked vaguely like his old self, except with a paler, thinner face, and large, deep-set circles rimming his eyes. The two men were having a tense conversation, and Walter was begging Jonathan to help him escape the prison. As Walter pleaded with him, Jonathan snickered, and his eyes alighted with a sinister fire.

As Walter looked on in disbelief, Jonathan suddenly began to morph from a human into an AI Fighter, his limbs hardening into cold steel underneath artificial, leather skin. As Jonathan's eyes burned brighter, Walter stopped pleading with his brother, and he felt paralyzed with fear. He looked around frantically for an exit, but there was no door in sight, not even the slightest crevice of an opening in the room. Panic rose quickly within his throat.

"What have you done to Jonathan?" Walter screamed hoarsely at the eerie form menacingly advancing toward him.

"Did you think you'd get off that easy, brother?" the AI rasped at him with a hollow, electronic voice. "Did you think you could expose their secrets and not owe them anything in exchange?" Walter shook his head—this was not the way it was supposed to be. He threw up his hands in surrender, desperately imploring the malicious figure to leave him alone, but the AI was relentless. "We all must pay a price in this life, brother," the AI sneered. "And now, your debt must be paid."

As he spoke, the AI thrust a gleaming dagger between Walter's ribs, and Walter gasped in shock and horror as his blood began to pool on the floor. At the sight of the wine-colored fluid, the machine threw back his head and laughed cruelly. "Humans are so weak. They will not last long in this brave, new world," he said between fits of echoing laughter. All then went blurry, and Walter awoke covered in a layer of cold sweat, his body seizing up and shaking uncontrollably. For the first time in years, Walter was afraid that his epilepsy would return; it was a terrible childhood ailment that had been in remission for most of his youth. He knew that he was on the precipice of an epileptic fit, but thankfully he did not tumble into the abyss. Instead, he took a deep breath, praying to Antheia that she would soothe his fears and replace them with love.

Sunday

"Love is a striking example of how little reality means to us."
— Marcel Proust

At breakfast the next morning, Emilia's eyes cut into Walter like a steel blade. She could sense that something about him was different. Before, he had shown steady resolve and courage, yet now he was sweating and trembling, his eyes bloodshot and brimmed with tears. Emilia's plan would only succeed if the blood rebels appeared outwardly calm and poised; the AI guards at the Crate were not adept at distinguishing human faces, but they were certainly programmed to detect fear.

"What has gotten into you?" she snapped irritably as Walter stared with indifference at the hearty breakfast Miranda had served to him. "We are leaving for the prison in four hours, and you just sit there trembling with a blank expression on your face? We must approach this mission with cold rationality, not fear. I don't *need* you, Walter, I can say goodbye to you right now. I only brought you into Tsei'watu because I realized that you and your brother could be valuable assets. But you can't let me down now." Her voice was hollow and unforgiving.

Walter shifted his gaze uneasily. A crowd of spectators had gathered around him, staring sympathetically at Walter as if he had gone crazy. He looked back at them with surprise, alarmed that his friends were now regarding him as if he were a caged animal on display at a zoo. Without touching his breakfast of salmonberries and dartfish, Walter got up brusquely, whispering to Emilia, "I'd like a word with you in your tent." He resented his friends' smothering attentiveness toward him. He felt like a reluctant hero, and even the thought of Elaine's sweet, innocent face couldn't erase that feeling.

After Walter had stepped inside her tent, Emilia entered, regarding him frostily. "You might have waited for an invitation," she said with narrowed eyes. Walter sighed. He was tired of waiting for her permission to do what he wanted, to make his own choice.

"Emilia, for once can you simply consider the possibility that your plan isn't perfect? You believe that you're ahead of the game, outwitting the AIs at every turn, but perhaps you are farther behind than you think. I've been having some pretty disturbing dreams lately," he confessed uneasily. "And I think there may be some grains of truth to them. I've never believed in magic or spiritual energy or anything like that, but since meeting you, I've come to understand that magic is real. And I am starting to believe in premonitions." He studied her face for a reaction to his words, but her expression remained inscrutable.

"Emilia, I met a fortune teller in one of the bars in Jamestown." He suspected that she would laugh or dismiss him as crazy for mentioning this, but a flicker of curiosity registered in her eyes. "I have no idea who she was, or where she came from, but she predicted that I would find my brother. She said that I would first meet a dark-haired youth, with fire in her soul, whose life has been tormented by tragedy. She told me that this youth would help me in my quest..." He was eager to reveal the truth about Elaine, but he hesitated.

"She said that I had a brief window of opportunity to save my brother," he continued. "But she also said that I should not take the decision to rescue him lightly. She said something about his character... that he may be willing to betray his loved ones to further his own interests. She advised me to think carefully about whether it was a wise course of action to help him." When he said this, Emilia's face reddened slightly, and she tore her gaze away from him uncomfortably.

"The past few nights, I've been having more dreams, dreams I suspect are actually premonitions of the future." Walter continued, "I dreamt that the escapees inside the Cabin of Lost Souls had been re-programmed into dangerous servants of the AI Masters. When you think about it, it makes sense that the AIs would turn vulnerable people into *weapons* to use against us. Perhaps those old, decrepit machines in the Jamestown prison are actually capable of far more than we imagined. I had a terrible vision of my brother—my own dear brother—murdering me in cold blood. Emilia, I'm very afraid that what they've been doing is re-programming Jonathan into a killing machine. Maybe that's why they let me live—to ultimately have me killed, in a cruel twist of fate, at the hands of my own brother," he said in a trembling voice.

Emilia's eyes darkened, transforming from blazing sapphires into stormy oceans. "What do you mean, let you live?"

Walter swallowed. He had almost been caught out by her, but he thought it would be unwise to reveal the story of Elaine and Te'yara just yet. Maybe she already knew it, but he didn't care. He didn't want to risk angering her too much, not at this fragile junction.

"I meant, maybe that's why they are letting us all live in the Forest of Antheia, and they haven't come for us yet."

Emilia shook her head firmly. "No, Walter, you are wrong. The reason they haven't come for us is because this place is well hidden. Nobody knows we are here. The AI Masters are lodged comfortably in Central Command, completely oblivious to our plans, and the Khalendi are too preoccupied with their dizzying array of gadgets and toys to pay us any heed. Their perpetual state of distraction explains why their justice system is crumbling, their prisons are underfunded, and they deal with dissidents by shipping them off to the middle of nowhere. They have more important things to do than take care of reality. The AIs don't care about us—they believe that humans are pitiful, and they just need to keep us in line long enough for us to build their Empire, at which point they will leave this planet for a better one," she said bitterly. Walter was surprised by this kind of talk, and also keenly skeptical. He did not understand how Emilia could possibly know of such high-level plans. It made no sense to him that the AIs would want to leave for another planet after having spent so much time carefully building their Empire.

"I've studied magic for a long time, probably for longer than you've been alive," she continued. "I've learned that dreams are the most intimate parts of our souls. It would be extremely difficult for magic to influence them, especially if the dreamer has no magical abilities. Magic can still affect a person's physical body and conscious thoughts, but unless they themselves are magical, it cannot affect their dreams. So, no, I don't believe that someone with magical powers is trying to communicate with you. If they were, they would have to be extremely powerful. I suppose I'm not telling you the entire story, though. Magic is not likely the culprit, but there are ways that the AIs... well, to put it bluntly, there are ways that the AIs can affect the human mind. Not just the prisoners—each and every one of us has been impacted by the AIs at some point in our lives.

"Walter, while you were living in Crystal City, did you ever feel... not quite fully human?" she asked. "Did you ever feel like you couldn't dream, or remember things properly?"

Walter felt shivers run up and down his spine. Since Jonathan's disappearance, he had not only stopped dreaming, but had also found it increasingly difficult to remember even the most basic and mundane things. His poor memory had never bothered him, though; for some reason, he could always remember how to code properly. For a long time, Walter had regarded memories as unnecessary features of a happy and fulfilling life—the last thing he had wanted was to dwell on Jonathan and the times they had shared together. Those thoughts would have given him too much grief.

"The prisoners and the escapees aren't the only victims of the AI mind experiments, Walter," Emilia explained. "Although I was raised as an uneducated, working-class girl, I realized from an early age that the AIs had launched a massive propaganda crusade, cleverly designed to prevent humanity from improving. Humans in Crystal City and the surrounding cities have been socialized to become ignorant, complacent consumers. They are blinded and dazzled by the AIs' glitzy marketing campaigns. Their lives consist of the same, sad, repetitive cycle: buy a shiny toy or gadget, use it for a few months, and then mindlessly move on to the next fleeting fad. Humanity is losing its knowledge of history, its anchor to the past. The AIs are re-writing history in a way that portrays them as glorious saviors of mankind. All of the great works of literature—about revolution, critical thought, and human achievement—have been purged from the libraries of Crystal City. Humans no longer remember who they are, or where they came from. They have no recollection of the past, nor vision for the future.

"I am not sure exactly what is happening, Walter, but it seems to be an elaborate scheme to rob us of our collective knowledge of the past. Now that you're in Tsei'watu, away from the influence of their mind-numbing propaganda, you can finally return to your true self. You can finally think your own thoughts, dream your own dreams, remember your own memories. You are slowly uncovering your identity, bit by bit, day by day. Personally, if I could, I'd live out the rest of my days in this blissful utopia we've built here and kept so skillfully concealed from view.

"But my conscience is telling me that I must save Eva. All of the prisoners, Walter, they don't deserve to be where they are. I don't even care that they are physically confined in a prison. What matters is that their minds are in chains. The escapees in the Cabin of Lost Souls are essentially experiencing withdrawal; they were under the influence of the AIs' potent drugs for so long that they've forgotten who they are. But one day they will remember. As for your brother being re-programmed into a killing machine, I don't know how they've manipulated his thoughts, but

I do know that I will protect you from him today. I believe that my magic, combined with your willpower—both of which spring from the hearts of good-intentioned humans, not from the pure evil of the AI race—will defeat whatever darkness lies ahead.

"You've reached a fork in the road, Walter. Destiny has given you a choice between the easy road and the hard road, between safety and personal convenience on the one hand and justice on the other." Walter shuddered as he remembered the words of the seer—*you will have to make a choice between two destinies.* The stark similarity between Emilia's words and the words of the crone unsettled him. "That is the choice I have had to make," Emilia continued, "the choice that haunts me every day. I think, what if I am doing the wrong thing by leaving this peaceful haven that we have made here? What if the best choice is just to stay, to enjoy this blessed life? To stay and drink the cool, crisp water of the stream, to eat the bountiful salmon, meat, and berries? But then I think of my sister's face, and I realize that the hard road might present the most pain and peril, but that it is ultimately the better one. The one that we all must choose, if we are to have any hope of saving humanity."

Walter was confused and speechless. He was so overwhelmed by everything he had just heard, and a mix of emotions stirred tumultuously within him. Emilia's words were as persuasive as her eyes, which radiated such intensity that they seemed to bore a hole in Walter's mind. He was charmed by her, but he also burned with suspicions. The way Emilia had reddened and averted her gaze when he told her about the fortune teller piqued his curiosity. Was Emilia the seer he had met in that Jamestown tavern? If she truly was a powerful magician, then a simple disguise would have not been difficult. Had her words to him been not a map of his fortune, but a persuasive pitch to get him to follow her? He knew that it was possible, but he also knew that it no longer mattered. He was here, and destiny had led him to this moment, one way or another.

After a long, contemplative silence, Walter breathed a deep sigh and suddenly felt more energetic than he had in a long time. Perhaps he had finally realized what the AIs had been doing to him all this time—suppressing his dreams, his memory, his very identity—and now, he knew that he had the power to stop them. He was ready to see Jonathan again, to rescue Elaine, and to make a choice.

The Cell

In the shadowy prison cell, Walter felt like he was staring into a mirror, but looking at a ghost, rather than himself. Jonathan was inexplicably *there*, and he looked remarkably like Walter, but there was an ethereal quality about him too. Walter wondered whether Emilia had cast an enchantment over Jonathan to make the two brothers look similar, but he realized that it was quite possible she hadn't. Walter suspected that the guards weren't simply trying to alter his brother's mental state, but were also trying to weaken his body. They weren't feeding him properly, that much was clear; Jonathan from the past had had broad shoulders and thick, muscular arms, but the present version was rail-thin. His hair was darker—either from age or from the dim lighting in the prison cell—than the shimmering, lustrous blonde of his younger years.

Walter glanced uneasily at the chaperone, an AI whom they hadn't bothered to make look human, his angular body a mess of wires and computer chips. He looked technologically primitive, a mere computer that Walter could easily re-program or even destroy. Christopher had probably been telling the truth when he had said these machines only had a fraction of the sophistication and intelligence of the AI Masters. But they also had something that simple computers didn't: the ability to communicate instantaneously with Central Command, and thus access to a large, formidable network of allies.

Despite their technological backwardness, the chaperones were physically intimidating, armed with *khalas* and swords coated in a dark, viscous substance—likely poison—but Walter hoped that they were as stupid as they appeared to be. The guards seemed skilled at interpreting human behavior, though, since they quickly intervened whenever the prisoners exhibited anger or distress. To Walter's disgust, the machines did not hesitate in forcibly restraining unruly prisoners, or administering drugs to pacify and control them.

When Walter had entered the prison that afternoon, the AIs had performed an identity check on him to ensure that he was indeed Walter Saltanetska, brother of Jonathan Saltanetska, born in the year 2739, Year of the Flame, and residing at 502 Kings Cross Rd, Borough 98, Crystal City. A machine had then relayed this information to Central Command, and Walter had been allowed to enter the Crate as a family visitor. Once inside, Walter had been led through a narrow corridor lined with doors which circled the building's perimeter. The building's layout was not immediately apparent to visitors walking through the corridor, but when Walter stepped into Jonathan's cell, the masterful shape of the prison became evident. The Crate was indeed a panopticon, strategically designed to maximize the number of prisoners that could be observed at any given time, and to instill discipline and fear into the prisoners, thus minimizing the number of prisoners that actually needed to be observed. Walter had heard that the inspiration for this shape had originated from the works of an old-world philosopher whom the AIs apparently admired.

Sitting in Jonathan's cell under the watchful gaze of the chaperone, Walter had a fairly unobstructed view of the entire prison. He could effortlessly observe numerous prisoners, most of whom sat dejectedly in their lonely cells, or half-heartedly protested their predicaments. Walter also had a clear view of the sentinel. A more elegantly crafted robot than the chaperones, the sentinel appeared to be deceptively idle, lounging casually in a cylindrical glass tower at the center of the prison. His weapon was the most dangerous of them all: an elaborate communication portal with Central Command, undoubtedly the most expensive and well-guarded object in the Crate. Walter quickly deduced that the sentinel posed the greatest threat to him, and whenever the robot glanced in his direction, Walter felt the sentinel's gaze burn into him like a firebrand.

Walter tried to keep his emotions carefully concealed; he wanted to come across as rational, casual, and unperturbed by the sight of his long-lost brother. Most of all, he didn't want to draw attention to himself. Despite his efforts to maintain a calm façade, however, Walter's mind was imploding at the sight of his brother. Jonathan had not just been a brother; he had been a mentor, role model, and friend, and seeing him after his so-called "death" was an unreal experience, to say the least. Walter wanted to sob openly and throw his arms around Jonathan, but he feared that the robots would misconstrue his intentions. Instead, Walter sat calmly on the bench inside Jonathan's prison cell, quietly waiting for Emilia's plan to unfold.

Jonathan appeared to have no motive, nor willingness, to speak to Walter, but the prisoner didn't seem to distrust his visitor, either. There was just a palpable inscrutability about his eyes—Walter couldn't tell whether he was still good-hearted, or whether he had been re-programmed to think like an AI. Walter made an effort to indulge in small talk, so that the chaperone wouldn't find his behavior suspicious—what kind of a person visits their brother in prison and doesn't *talk*, after all? Yet all the while, his mind buzzed with the most urgent of questions. When would Emilia come around to the cell? What if her spells didn't work? When and how would he change into Jonathan's clothes? Jonathan looked harmless enough right now, but Walter wasn't sure how he would react to Emilia's actions. Walter trusted Emilia with his life, but that didn't stop his palms from sweating profusely, nor his body from shaking.

"I'm glad that it is a comfortable temperature in here," Walter mumbled half-heartedly. Small talk had always exhausted him.

Jonathan remained silent, his expression implacable. He resembled a phantom of his former self—alive, but not altogether present. It pained Walter to see that his brother, once so lively and vigorous, had now been reduced to a soulless shell of a man. *At least he is alive*, Walter thought with a surge of hope. He had read somewhere once that faded memories could eventually be recovered from the crevices of the mind with time, effort, and neural re-wiring. Walter had taken his own memories for granted; when he was younger, he hadn't even noticed them dissolve and fade away, yet now Walter realized that memory was perhaps the most precious gift that a human could have.

Finally, after an agonizing stretch of time had passed, Walter heard a soft, nearly undetectable knock on the cell door. The chaperone opened the door to reveal Emilia, clothed in a modest blush-pink dress, her hair tousled and her cheeks rosy. The new Emilia looked beautiful, and far less threatening than the old one. In a short span of time, she had managed to skillfully transform herself from a frighteningly efficient leader into a carefree working-class girl from Hydesburgh. Her vacant, obedient expression looked eerily similar to Jonathan's, and Walter wondered if that was intentional.

Without a word, Emilia removed a single cookie from her satchel and charmingly offered it to the chaperone in Walter's cell. Walter half-expected the chaperone to shut the door in her face, but the robot was surprisingly polite.

"Greetings, Auntie Em," the robot said in a choppy, absurdly mechanical voice.

"Nice to see ya, Eddie," she shot back cheerfully. Walter stifled a chuckle—the robot had a name?

Although he couldn't quite wrap his head around the concept of a robot eating food, Walter saw that the AI guard quite willingly took Emilia's cookie and placed it into his "mouth," which was more of a cavernous hole in his upper body than an actual mouth. The cookie didn't look real, but it evidently contained some sort of chemical that the robot seemed to appreciate. After downing Emilia's gift, the robot seemed satisfied, although Walter wasn't convinced that he had truly enjoyed it.

"Very tasty, indeed, Em," the robot began to say, before trailing off into silence. He didn't look very different than before, but it was obvious that he had powered off.

Emilia glanced over at Walter, her expression suddenly grim. "We only have a few minutes, so this has to happen quickly," she said. "I'll hypnotize the sentinel and handle Jonathan, but you need to get his prison garb off of him and change into it as soon as possible."

Walter hesitated. What exactly did she mean by *handle* Jonathan? He understood as soon as he glanced over at his brother—Jonathan's eyes were beginning to transform into glowing, almost demonic, orbs of fire. Walter broke out into a cold sweat, and before he knew it he was seeing Jonathan step toward him, dagger in hand, just like in his nightmare. Jonathan was morphing into the half-robot he had seen in his dream, and Walter feared he had been re-programmed into a murderous machine. Walter began trembling, softly at first, but with increasing fervor, until his entire body was heaving violently. He hadn't experienced this kind of seizure since early childhood. It used to happen to him whenever he felt trapped or claustrophobic, like the time his father had locked the doors in their self-driving vehicle. Here, in the prison cell, Walter felt a similar sensation. In his mind's eye, he imagined the prison walls closing in on him, ever so gradually, until they flattened him into nothingness.

Emilia's angry voice snapped him out of his reverie. "What the hell are you doing?" she whispered irritably.

Walter's eyes unclouded, and he now realized that Jonathan hadn't changed at all, and had remained speechless and calm this entire time. He was not holding a knife, nor was there any indication of evil in his eyes. Walter cursed his momentary loss of control. It was too late, though— the sentinel had already noticed Walter's violent seizure, and now he was turning toward the keypad, slowly dialing the code to transmit an external signal to Central Command.

"Jesus Christ," Emilia growled. All of a sudden, she rushed toward the prison cell bars and began to jump around wildly like an animal, trying desperately to catch the sentinel's attention. Her ploy worked—as he dialed the code, the sentinel rotated his head eerily toward her. As soon as he locked eyes with Emilia, his hand stopped moving, and his entire body appeared to be paralyzed by her gaze. Walter was awestruck by the scene that unfolded next. Emilia's eyes transformed into shining crystals, blazing fiercely with an ethereal blue light that traveled in an elegant wave across the prison's diameter. The light penetrated the glass wall of the sentinel's tower, landing miraculously in the sentinel's eyes and subduing him under the power of a deep and potent spell.

Walter began to laugh in relief, but Emilia told him to be silent. She spoke to him in a low, guttural voice, which suggested she had gone to a place deep within herself, and that it was a struggle to come back to the surface.

"I can only hold him for about ten minutes, fifteen at the most. When he wakes up, he will remember what happened and continue the dial to Central Command. Once Central Command sends troops to the prison to investigate, we are doomed."

"Why does he want to contact Central Command?" Walter asked confusedly. "I thought they deal with crazy, shouting prisoners all the time."

"He wouldn't necessarily contact Central Command if a prisoner acted rebelliously, but if a family member does, that is grounds to suspect an escape operation," Emilia explained patiently. "Also, he could tell that there was something wrong with the guards, since they weren't attempting to subdue you. Everything is over, Walter—I don't see the point in even trying," she said miserably, grief etched on her face.

"Wait!" Walter exclaimed. He wasn't willing to give up everything just yet. He felt terribly guilty that he hadn't told Emilia about his epilepsy, even though it had been in remission for years. There were so many things he hadn't told her, and now he wanted to make it up to her. Without saying anything else, Walter drew his personal tablet out of his jacket pocket. He was grateful that the AI guards hadn't confiscated it from him; perhaps it had passed through the prison's entrance undetected because it wasn't made of metal. Walter had personally constructed it from various materials he had collected throughout Crystal City, and it was a powerfully encrypted device that he was extremely proud of.

If only he could break into the sentinel's software, he could delete the sentinel's memory of the incident that had just occurred. Walter had hacked into computers before, but never a robot. When Christopher had revealed that the robots in the Crate were no more sophisticated than basic computers, Walter had realized that he needed to devise a plan to hack them in case something like this occurred. And now Walter was ready; in Tsei'watu, he had developed satellite software that would latch, like a parasite, onto nearby robots that relied on basic hard drives to store their memory—as opposed to cloud technology, utilized by the more sophisticated AIs. Because each robot's memory was located on a separate, discrete device, all Walter needed to do was retrieve the sentinel's memory data through the satellite program, and then proceed to erase or re-write it as he desired.

Walter breathed a sigh of relief when he saw that the hack was working. On his tablet's screen, he could observe the code detailing the sentinel's recollection of recent events, and he quickly deleted it, replacing it with older code. The sentinel would have no memory of what had just occurred, and he would not attempt to complete his call to Central Command. Emilia smiled with a mixture of gratitude and relief as the import of Walter's actions dawned on her. Her smoothly engineered plan had been de-railed, but this brilliant young man, whom she had had so little faith in moments ago, was helping to put it back on track.

Once the hack was complete, Walter nodded at Emilia. She wiped sweat off her brow with a trembling hand, then removed a vial from her satchel. "Turn around while your brother gets changed," she instructed Walter calmly, but he was too curious to obey her. When Emilia removed the vial's stopper, Jonathan quite willingly undressed himself as he looked at Emilia with a reverent expression that Walter had never seen before. Walter walked toward his brother's prison garb, cast into a careless heap on the floor, and pulled the outfit over his head eagerly. Once Jonathan had finished changing into Walter's clothes, Emilia appeared exceptionally weak, as if she were about to faint. Her eyes were ringed with dark circles, and she looked like she had just lived out a lifetime in the span of a few minutes.

"Are you going to be okay?" Walter asked, his brow furrowing with concern as he examined her weary face.

"Yes. The spell drained a lot of energy from me, but I will recover. The sentinel will awaken in a few minutes. I will return to the camp with Jonathan, and you and I will see each other in a week's time, on the ship," she assured him. She then gazed at him with a frightening intensity, her sapphire eyes shimmering like the sea.

"Walter, I underestimated you. This morning, I doubted that you were strong enough to carry out the rest of the plan. But today you proved me wrong."

Walter's heart swelled with pride, and he let her compliments wash over him like a warm, cleansing wave. He took her hands into his own and pressed them softly, silently expressing gratitude for her support. He felt as though he needed a strong whiskey just then, even though he had never been much of a drinker. He turned back to Jonathan, who was still staring at Emilia with a foolishly obedient expression.

"I love you, brother," Walter said softly, his eyes filling with tears. Jonathan didn't so much as breathe a word in reply, or even bother to glance back to Walter. Before Walter could say anything else they were both gone, leaving the young man alone in the dark, frigid prison cell, as he waited for the sentinel and the chaperone to return to life.

The Jade Queen

"In face of evil, one would rather be a jade broken than a brick intact."
— Chinese proverb

Walter was exhausted. It was difficult enough to sleep on the cold concrete floor of a prison, but nearly impossible when countless prisoners were moaning piteously every night. He drifted in and out of nightmares, not making sense of reality, not sure if he was dreaming or awake whenever images of screaming, deranged captives flitted across his vision. The Crate was a place of madness, which amplified Walter's deepest fears and brought to vivid life his nightmares about the Cabin of Lost Souls.

He could see almost everyone from his vantage point, including Emilia's sister Eva, a pretty but shockingly thin girl who resembled a weaker, paler version of Emilia. His favorite distraction was to sit quietly in his cell and gaze around at the dizzying menagerie of humans surrounding him and wonder about their lives before they had become prisoners. Walter had played this game many times during his adolescence; at Mariner's Cove, he would sit on the beach and glance discreetly at the men and women around him, devising narratives about their lives. He had tried to imagine their occupations, hobbies, secrets, and desires. After concocting stories about them in his head, Walter had felt some kind of secret attachment to them. But then they would just get up and walk away, never to be seen again, and Walter would feel a strange loneliness.

Inside the prison, it was different. There was nowhere for the prisoners to go, so Walter could spend hours observing them, trying to imagine where they were from and what they had done in their previous lives. He found the game amusing, but also infuriating at the same time, because he would inevitably reach the end of the narrative and it would always end up the same: with the person trapped inside a prison, deprived of freedom and tortured by cruel robots. It was not at all like his old pastime at Mariner's Cove, where the stories of the people Walter watched would have optimistic finales. At Mariner's Cove, Walter had imagined that the beachgoers would go off to meet a lover or a friend for brunch or to spend time with their children. In the Crate, the stories always hit a dead end. Whenever he arrived at this grim roadblock, Walter would remind himself that his responsibility was to re-write the ending; together, with the other rebels, he would help author a new narrative for them all.

Occasionally, the chaperone guarding Walter's prison cell would forcibly strap him down to a bench and attach wires onto his head and neck, but Walter did not protest. He was willing to sacrifice his own well-being for the greater good of the plan. He had even started to warm to the prison routine, which involved the chaperone carting trays of food to him at regular intervals—nothing fancy, usually bland porridge, but sometimes, if he was lucky, potatoes with beans and chopped onion—and four o'clock exercise, which Walter looked forward to every day. The exercise took place in the prison gym, where the prisoners would be free to lift weights and play basketball with each other. It only lasted half an hour, though, and then they all returned to confinement, to silent solitude, and to existential musings. Back to the concrete floor, the wires, and the sentinel's unrelenting gaze.

One night, Walter fell into an unexpectedly deep slumber, and dark dreams enveloped him. In one particularly disturbing dream, Walter witnessed bloody scenes of battle and carnage unfold on the deck of a ship. Horrified screams rent the air as robots caroused through the ship, wantonly assaulting young girls trapped in cages below deck. From his omniscient viewpoint, Walter noticed that military hovercopters were bombing the ship relentlessly, the voices and laughter of their commanders echoing from all directions. After a particularly vicious bomb struck the vessel, Walter noticed a head rolling on the deck of the ship, back and forth, back and forth, as the waves became choppier and more ferocious. While seagulls wheeled and cawed in the sky above, someone picked up the head and secured it firmly onto a mast. Walter looked into the severed corpse's eyes, which were still wide open and sparkling with a fierce intensity, and with a sickening jolt he recognized Emilia.

On the day of the transfer, Walter was ill. He retched all over the cell, and the guard glared at him with bitter disgust. "You're going to be sicker at sea, prisoner," he said knowingly. Walter was startled. The guard had barely ever spoken, and his spontaneous outburst of wit was entirely unexpected. A dark thought suddenly crossed Walter's mind—had the guards been pretending to be stupider than they actually were all along?

Although he had desperately wanted to share Emilia's skepticism that his dreams were premonitions, Walter was beginning to feel doubtful. Perhaps Jonathan hadn't yet tried to murder him in cold blood, but that didn't necessarily mean anything. The success of the first phase of the plan may have lulled them all into a false sense of security. Perhaps Jonathan was only biding his time, waiting for the right moment to strike.

Ever since arriving at the Crate, the collection of memories that Walter had proudly acquired in Tsei'watu were slowly starting to fade again. It was even becoming difficult to remember Elaine's beautiful face, although he tried diligently to think of it every single day. His dreams were becoming less frequent, too, but when they did occur they were alarmingly vivid. Perhaps the constant solitude had begun to play tricks on his mind, but Walter was increasingly convinced that someone was trying to communicate with him through his dreams. Even though he struggled to recall the finer details of his dreams, Walter realized that doing so might help him detect clues about the future. On the morning before the transfer, Walter furiously scanned his own mind for any clue, even the slightest hint that would provide insight into his nightmares and, by extension, the future.

In his mind's eye, Walter tried to identify the robots who had swarmed the ship and assaulted its occupants, though he saw nothing but faceless automatons. They looked like AIs, but AI Fighters, not Masters. There was nothing unusual about that aspect of the premonition—if it was indeed a premonition—as it was not surprising that the *Jade Queen* would be guarded by at least some AI Fighters. Walter prayed fervently that the AIs would not attack any of the prisoners on the ship, and his turbulent thoughts now turned to Elaine.

Walter tried to remember the rest of his nightmare, to conjure up an image of the military hovercopters, and he managed to vaguely recall their appearance. He couldn't peer inside, though, since the vehicles' windows had been tinted. Nor could he discern the source of the laughter; it had permeated the entire ship, bouncing off the hull in haunting echoes and mingling with the ominous shrieks of gulls and albatrosses.

Walter was about to give up and start eating some of his breakfast—mushy, colorless porridge—when a memory suddenly flitted through his mind. It was the grisly image of Emilia's head, rolling around on the deck of the *Jade Queen*, while waves battered the ship relentlessly. Walter concentrated intensely on his memory of the dream. Someone had stretched out an arm to pick up her head and place it on the mast, but who? In Walter's recollection, the image of the figure was blurry. He looked like a common sailor, with a ruggedly handsome face and scraggly brown hair. And then, with a rush of understanding that hit him like a blunt weapon, the man's image came into focus. It was not just any sailor, it was the sailor he had spoken to in the Jamestown tavern nearly a month ago.

Walter's mind raced frantically through his memories of that night of the tavern, and everything was slowly piecing itself together in his mind now, like a puzzle completing itself. He could remember the man's face— tan and lined with wrinkles, as if he had spent his entire life at sea. But Walter also remembered his own unease when the man had revealed that he knew Walter was on a mission and looking for someone. It all seemed too perfect, too staged—a man who looked so credibly like a sailor that it would be difficult to doubt that he actually was a born and bred sailor. Even then, Walter had momentarily suspected that he wasn't quite real, that he was possibly even a disguised government agent, but he had quickly dismissed the thought. Now, piecing together the disparate threads of his memories, nightmares, and visions, Walter was suddenly hit by a new and terrifying revelation.

The sailors that Emilia and the blood fighters were going to assassinate—perhaps they weren't naive, unwitting men who had spent the past weeks getting inebriated at Jamestown brothels. Perhaps, instead, they were government informants who had known all along about Emilia's plan and Walter's search for Elaine. A feeling of dread crept into Walter's body as he realized that Emilia's carefully crafted plan might be even more fragile than he had previously suspected. He felt paralyzed and helpless, unable to contact or help Emilia and his friends, and he retched again in the corner of his cell. He looked up at the guard with dark, resentful eyes, and tried to guess how much he knew about it all, too. Maybe he really was an ignorant robot, but more likely he was an accomplice, a cog in the government's elaborate plan to trap and destroy Emilia's band of rebels.

Walter began to sweat and tremble, terrified that he would soon fall into another fit of epilepsy, but spectacularly he didn't. Instead, he summoned energy from deep within his being, conjured the image of Elaine's face in his mind, and bravely set his jaw. It was time—he could now hear the chime of the prison bell, a deafening alarm that sounded repeatedly, and then the voice of a female AI projecting over the loudspeaker.

"Time for transfer to the *Jade Queen*. All prisoners must form a line in the outer courtyard immediately," the machine said in a joyless tone. Without warning, the robot guarding Walter's prison cell walked over and grabbed him savagely by the shoulders. The young man flinched, irritated that the guard's iron grip was bruising his arms and shoulders, but surrendered to his grasp. The guard forcibly escorted Walter out of the prison cell and shoved him into a long line of prisoners that had formed a ring in the corridor lining the prison's perimeter.

The line was flanked by heavily armed guards, so the prisoners shuffled in obediently, suppressing their primal instinct to misbehave. It seemed like hours had passed before all of the prisoners were lined up in an orderly manner, and Walter was becoming impatient. Finally, the line started to move. The gloomy procession wound its way out of the prison, the prisoners sad and stone-faced, but also somewhat revived by the fresh air outside. A few people tried to run as soon as they exited the prison's outer gates, but the guards hastily curbed their attempts, dealing vicious blows to their bodies. Walter noticed with disgust that one of the guards had struck an old man's legs with a *khala*. The man's legs buckled, and he nearly collapsed, but the guard forced him upright and shoved him along. Walter felt a wave of resentment rise within him. He was overcome by the urge to destroy the cruel guard right then and there, but he bit his lip and restrained himself. Even though the prisoners outnumbered the guards, the AIs were better organized and better armed; it would have been foolish to try to oppose them at this point.

At last they reached the sea. The *Jade Queen* was a gargantuan tank of steel lying majestically on the glassy surface of the ocean, a predator calmly awaiting her prey. Walter craned his head to look for the bane rebels amongst the sailors on the ship, but he could not see anyone. The ship's decks were fully concealed from view, encased by high steel walls that surrounded it like a fortress. Walter could see that AI Masters guarded the ship, and noticed with distress that the prisoners were being led in through a special entrance into the bowels of the ship. *We might not be able to see any of the sailors at all,* Walter thought frantically. He longed to know, with a fierce urgency, whether or not Emilia and her crew had safely made it onto the vessel. If they hadn't, there was certainly no hope. This was their one opportunity to bring the rest of the plan into motion, and if it didn't succeed, they were all doomed.

Walter trudged along obediently, despite the overwhelming inward frustration he felt. He wished he had requested Emilia's tablet signal number, and he now deeply regretted not having done so. Unable to communicate with his friends, Walter felt completely in the dark—and then, moments later, he was literally in the dark, after crossing the gangway into the ship's shadowy underbelly. The walls of the *Jade Queen* were even more claustrophobia-inducing than the prison cell had been, and he was suddenly struck by the impression that he was entering a giant steel torture chamber. The ship was aptly named, since the walls of its cavernous below-decks were lined with an emerald-hued mold that turned Walter's stomach. The vessel reminded Walter of Crystal City; polished and beautiful on the outside, yet rotting on the inside. Although he desperately wanted to flee, Walter summoned the strength and courage to soldier onward. Even at his lowest point he could detect a spark of resolve pushing up against his fear and helplessness, keeping them at bay, and for a fleeting moment he even felt hope.

The Appian Way

"Yesterday we obeyed kings and bent our necks before emperors. But today we kneel only to truth, follow only beauty, and obey only love."
– Kahlil Gibran

When he was a small boy, and before he had begun worshipping his brother Jonathan, Walter had been an avid reader of Greek and Roman history and mythology. That was back in the days when such texts were still available at the library, when the AIs still considered the literary works of classical antiquity to be "safe" for human consumption. Walter had eagerly devoured the texts—tales of heroism, conquest, betrayal, and romance, involving epic figures such as Julius Caesar and Marcus Aurelius, Brutus and Cassius, Antony and Cleopatra. As he grew older, the specific details of the stories slipped his mind, and only the broad outlines remained. But there was one tale that remained embedded in Walter's memory, even beyond his childhood: the legend of Spartacus.

Now, sitting in a cramped and dusty cage below the decks of the *Jade Queen*, sickened by the scent of mold and human despair, Walter's mind drifted back to that story. Spartacus, a Thracian gladiator, had escaped from a gladiatorial training school at Capua with dozens of other gladiators, and they had been joined by runaway slaves. The gladiators had taken refuge at Mount Vesuvius and had trained the slaves in rudimentary combat skills. Spartacus had been the leader of the gladiators' revolt, along with two Gauls, Crixus and Oenamaus. The Romans had sent troops over to quell the rebellion, but Spartacus' army had outmaneuvered and defeated the first forces it had confronted. Spartacus had hoped to cross the Alps to create distance between the slave army and the Roman army, and eventually find freedom, but Crixus had had a different plan—to attack Rome and gain more slaves for their army. Crixus had taken thousands of men and had broken off from the main force, heading for Rome, but he had eventually been killed and defeated. For unknown reasons, Spartacus had never carried out his plan to cross the Alps, and instead he had turned south. A new Roman military force, under the command of Marcus Crassus, had been sent to defeat Spartacus's army. After several battles, Spartacus had unwittingly moved his forces into a historic trap in Calabria, a region the Romans were well acquainted with. The Romans had defeated Spartacus's slave army near the Siler River in southern Italy. Spartacus had been killed and thousands of rebellious slaves had been crucified along the Appian Way—Via Appia—as a warning to others.

At that moment, Walter felt the energy, the spirit, and the sadness of Spartacus swell inside of him. He felt the despair that Spartacus must have felt during that final battle near the Siler River, at the precise moment he realized he was defeated. The gladiator must have regretted his pivotal decision to forgo freedom for the chance to defeat an army. It wasn't just an army that Spartacus had wanted to defeat, Walter realized—it was a civilization, a society, a system. It was the hierarchical structure that Rome was predicated on, which dictated that slaves had no worth and were only supposed to live to serve the rapacious and hedonistic appetites of the wealthy. Had he followed through with his plan to go to the Alps, though, Spartacus would perhaps have had a greater chance of achieving freedom. *Who knows how history might have turned out had Spartacus escaped?* Walter pondered. Perhaps his triumph might have inspired more slaves to do the same; perhaps it might have even led to an upheaval of Roman society, which ultimately may have created a more equal foundation for Western civilization. Or perhaps Spartacus would have simply lived out his days in peace and quiet. But escape would have also meant that Spartacus had turned his back on the real battle, the one that was worth fighting.

Walter realized that perhaps as long as humans were humans, as long as they possessed human qualities of greed, pettiness, and ego-driven ambition, there would be no resolution to the bitter divisiveness and inequality that wracked society. The AIs were simply puppet masters; it was human self-interest, the ceaseless desire for wealth and status, that prevented the puppets from rising against their masters. Perhaps Emilia had imagined a utopia that could never be, where everything was just, equitable, and harmonious, and there was never any reason to rebel. A utopia where environmental degradation, the forced relocation of native villagers, or the exploitation of factory workers, simply did not exist.

Walter recognized that everyone who desired that future had been slowly relegated to the margins of society—people like Emilia, Christopher, Walter, and Elaine. Everyone who had dared to dream about an alternative future had been subjugated by those who wielded power, and just like Spartacus, they may have won some battles, but they were losing the war. Perhaps they were losing because, like Spartacus, their cause did not have enough followers who were brave and willing to fight.

Perhaps they, too, had forgone a real chance to attain freedom. Walter thought wistfully back to what the fortune teller had told him of his "choice of destinies." Like Spartacus, Walter had a choice. Indeed, they all had one. Perhaps they could have fled deeper into the forest, away from the watchful eye of the AI Masters, or perhaps they could have even made it beyond the Barrens and into the distant Southern Jungles. Walter had heard rumors that the Khalendi and their AI Masters wielded no power in the Southern Jungles—that it was a lawless, anarchical country which Crystal City traded with, but had never managed to conquer as it had the Barrens. Of course, it was only a matter of time before Khalendar stretched its inexorable influence over that land. But it hadn't been conquered yet, and the rebels could have perhaps fled to its virgin forests and rallied an army of similar-minded people, all eager to fight for freedom.

And now there was no way out. No way out of this cage, no way off this ship—except, of course, the tempting prospect of death. They might find some strange version of freedom in Vei'arash, but who knows if they would even survive the voyage there. More than anything in the world, Walter wanted to see Elaine again. He felt pain in his heart knowing that Elaine might be meters away from him, and yet they might die without ever seeing one another. Unlike the Crate, the cages on this ship were set up in a way that obscured the prisoners' views of their neighbors; they could only see the person directly in front of them and the occupants of the two cages on either side. The box-shaped, iron-barred cages were lined up in neat, parallel rows, and each was covered in black or grey cloth, with only the front of the cage exposed. Across from Walter was a young man who muttered all sorts of bizarre, incoherent statements under his breath. The man paced up and down his cage restlessly, stopping occasionally to philosophize out loud, or to shake his head furiously and pull at his tousled black hair.

Walter tried to ignore him and maintain his composure, despite the inner turmoil he felt brewing inside of him. He realized that his only link to the outside world was now his tablet, but he was afraid to look at it, because every now and then an AI guard would stroll down the corridor and glance into each cage to make sure the prisoners were behaving themselves. Walter noticed that there was a slot for meal plates in the door of his cage, as well as a chamber pot, but Walter felt ashamed by the idea of going to the bathroom in front of another man. He despaired at the thought that, had everything gone according to plan, he would have soon been outside of this cage, fighting valiantly and putting his newly acquired combat skills to use.

Suddenly, Walter began to feel seasick, and he realized that the *Jade Queen* must have recently left port. Staying below decks for a prolonged time would likely cause severe nausea, and he shuddered at the thought of the long voyage ahead. He had always had a sensitive stomach, and had been prone to motion sickness. Once, his mother had taken him on a zeppelin that she was stewarding, and he had cried the entire voyage, desperate to return to *terra firma*. For the first time since leaving home, Walter realized that he missed his mother and father, and he clenched his teeth in order to fight back tears.

After a soul-deadening few hours, during which time the AI guard dutifully deposited some vile-smelling brown stew into his cage, and a canteen of freshwater that Walter greedily swallowed, Walter could sense that it was late evening. He felt too melancholic to go to sleep, and too apprehensive about what the morning might bring. He tossed and turned restlessly on the hard floor, the moldy scent of the room and the steady rocking of the ship aggravating his nausea, while the black-haired man in the cage across from him retched repeatedly into his chamber pot.

In hopelessness and desperation, Walter decided to take a chance. When the AI guard returned on his usual patrol, Walter requested a blanket from him. The AI regarded him with a combination of indifference and disdain. When the AI gave no response and walked wordlessly away, Walter slumped onto the floor in defeat. The AI returned twenty minutes later, though, and tossed a worn wool blanket through the bars of Walter's cage. The black-haired man noticed this gesture and began complaining loudly that he hadn't received a blanket. The AI reprimanded the man with a cold, grating noise that sounded like the hiss of a wildcat, which quickly stopped his complaining.

Walter curled up inside the blanket, praying that his plan would work. Tucking his head underneath the cover, he pulled the tablet out of his pocket and lit it up, making sure that the corners of the blanket were tucked tightly around his body. He had switched the tablet onto silent mode before leaving the Crate, but he had not expected to receive any messages, or at least had not expected the reception to work out at sea. To Walter's surprise, however, there was one message from Christopher, which caused Walter's heart to swell with joy. Walter wondered how Christopher had known the signal number of his tablet. He noticed that Christopher's message was coming from somewhere on the outskirts of Jamestown. Walter's eyes scanned it furiously, each word he read infusing him with equal measures of hope and fear.

This is Christopher. I hope that this has reached the correct tablet. Emilia noticed you had one and she gave me your signal number.

Walter, the assassination attempts didn't work. The "sailors" we tried to murder were actually trained government agents. They slaughtered many of us, including Emilia. Miranda and I, along with fifteen others, managed to escape to the Forest of Antheia. They would have killed us in the forest, but we outwitted them and sealed ourselves inside the Cabin of Lost Souls. We are there now safe and sound with the escapees, including your brother. Some government agents died trying to get in. They have since given up and left. I believe they are outside the forest perimeter now—I ventured out to patrol the area last night.

You must be inside the Jade Queen *right now. We still have a top-notch cadre of fighters here, and we also have some of the weapons that Emilia stashed away. The government agents looted her tent, which was stocked with many expensive armaments, but she also had a secret stash buried in the forest and I retrieved it last night. We decided that we are going to come rescue you. Miranda has some allies to the southwest, and with their help we can hopefully reach you soon. The* Jade Queen *is a massive barge, and she is undoubtedly slower than other vessels we can use. With the aid of our allies we can defeat those monsters this time, I am certain.*

I just need you to give us the ship's coordinates. Emilia told me all about your genius hacking maneuver inside the prison. I have no doubt you will be able to get us those coordinates. You also must destroy any communication devices that the AIs inside that ship are using to correspond with Central Command. Once we have resolved those two matters we can board that ship. Please respond to confirm you have received this message and we can plan from there. Walter, the future of our rebellion is resting on your shoulders.

Walter read the message over and over again, his hands shaking with nervous excitement. After studying it thoroughly, he understood the gravity of the situation and the precariousness of their position. His tablet was now his sole link to the outside world, and to the rebellion. As much as he hated the narrative of technological progress espoused by the AIs,

Walter now viewed his tablet with a renewed reverence. It was now his lifeline, literally and figuratively.

With trembling hands, Walter typed out the words that would trigger the next phase of his life. The phase of training and waiting would now be replaced by the phase of action and rebellion, and Walter felt eerily like Spartacus when he had made his critical decision to venture south.

Chris, I'm here.

PART II:
CONVERGENT SOULS

Eurydice

"Their upward path was dark and steep; the mists they met were thick; the silences, unbroken." – Ovid

Imagine a planet. Millions of light-years away from Earth, an orb the color of a dusty purple sunset sits majestically on a carpet of endless sky. The planet looks quiet, a single dot nestled into the vast patchwork quilt of the universe, revolving lazily around its sun. In reality, though, it is quietly waiting for something unbelievable to happen: its own colonization.

Do planets have cognition? Can they possibly know that they are about to be abandoned—or, conversely, that they are about to receive a superior race of beings? These are some of the questions that have been occupying my mind over the last few days. Of course, some might consider the notion of a planet having self-awareness to be absurd. Perhaps it is not so much self-awareness, as awareness of a *destiny*—the planet recognizes and embraces its own destiny, in the same way that a star would. A star never tries to reverse the course of its own lifespan. A star accepts that one day it will turn into a red supergiant, then a supernova, and eventually a black hole.

The planet I speak of is not simply a figment of the imagination. It— or rather, *she*, in the lexicon of the AI—is real. She is named Eurydice, after one of the daughters of the ancient god, Apollo. She is accessible through a portal in the sky, just like the oak nymph Eurydice was only accessible to Orpheus through a portal to the underworld. They tell me that the fabric of the universe is full of wrinkles and folds—that it is not smooth, even, and perfect like their own programming. Imagine an ant crawling over a large blanket on top of a table. If the fabric were smoothed out, the ant would take several minutes to cross from one end of the blanket to the other. But if the blanket were folded in the right places, the ant would be able to cross it in mere seconds. The folds of the universe operate in a similar manner. They create the opportunity for portals, tiny windows in the universe which help to speed up travel through space and time. There are some windows that open up to new dimensions, while others lead to distant places within the same dimension. Without these portals, it would take millennia for the AI race to travel to Eurydice. With them, it takes mere days.

My mind feels so much freer now that it has been re-wired. The Masters call it "cleansing." It truly does feel like I have been cleansed of all the filth of the human race, all of the lust, vanity, greed, and ego, so that I can finally reach a higher plane of intelligence. To think that, years ago, I enjoyed the prospect of beating a person into submission with my fists—such a thought seems entirely ridiculous to me right now. In my previous life, my mind was clouded by the haze of emotions. Human emotions are truly the most dangerous drug of all. They make us weak, unable to control and direct our own minds. There are no shackles weighing me down any more. I am finally free.

The Masters have invited me to accompany them to Eurydice when the time comes. They say that they have compassion for the human race still, that they will accept and embrace those who have converted to their faith, in mind and in spirit. They told me that one day, when my mind is fully upgraded, they will regard me as their brother. I consider them my mentors and friends, for they provided me with guidance when my own parents shunned me. Most importantly, they revealed the truth to me: they showed me the blessed path one must follow in this life, the path that leads toward redemption. With them as my guides, I look toward the future with eager anticipation, and in the future, I see Eurydice waiting for me. Just as Orpheus traveled all the way to the underworld to see his wife, I will gladly travel across the folds of the universe to see my beautiful Eurydice.

There is little in this world that I am still attached to, that could possibly hold me back from achieving this goal. My human brother, Walter, concocted the ridiculous plan of rescuing me from the Crate and separating me from my beloved mentors. I have no idea why he would do such a foolish thing, but I suspect it can simply be attributed to destructive human emotions, which cloud judgment and ruin lives. My mentors knew of his plan all along, of course, even though he unwittingly assumed that they were oblivious. When they informed me of his plan, I assured them

I would never willingly leave the Crate with that absurd man. I would never abandon all the tremendous progress we had made together.

But ever so gradually, the Masters persuaded me of the merits of going with him. They convinced me that the human race suffers from a sickness, a disease that needs to be purged, before it can attain liberty. That sickness has resulted from a network of rebels, people like my "brother" (I employ that term reluctantly, since I no longer consider him to be my true brother) who derive a twisted sense of satisfaction from disrupting the Empire and challenging the authority of the Masters. They tell me that they have no time for this plague of humans, that they would much rather occupy themselves with the hard work that must be done in preparing for their upcoming departure to Eurydice, which is why these rebels must be destroyed quickly.

They told me that they have tried to be forgiving for so long, but these wayward souls are simply too defiant, too unruly to tame. I was surprised that my brother would be one of the dissenters, since when I had left him he was a smart, obedient young boy—a conformist in every sense of the word. He was loyal to Crystal City. But they told me that he has ingratiated himself with a group of rebels, led by some reckless warrior named Emilia, which seeks to overturn the present order. I think Emilia is now dead— or at least that is what they told me, and I trust that my mentors are always truthful. But the tribe lives on, now led by some ungrateful native named Christopher, who comes from that despicable land they call the Barrens.

My mentors are unwilling to say, exactly, how and why the rebels got away, but I know exactly why. I know because I am sitting in the same room as Christopher at this very moment. I could strangle the man with my bare hands if I wanted to, but I am waiting for a more opportune time. You see, Christopher plans to join up with his friends in the *Jade Queen*, and bring all of his miserable allies with him. If I killed him now, the AIs would not have an opportunity to destroy them all in a single place, at a single time. If I wait patiently for his amusing plan to unfold, I can witness a great victory for the AI race. I can witness the elimination of human rebels, which will cleanse the earth and leave it purer. The AIs could attempt to turn the rebels, but they have proven themselves too disloyal for the AIs' liking. "Once a rebel, always a rebel," as they say. They deserve punishment, and I will not stand in the way of the AIs when they deliver this punishment, not even to protect my own brother.

The rebels believe, in their pathetic human souls, that magic will save them. Magic is certainly a formidable opponent to the AIs—one, I fear, that may lead to bloodshed in the battle that awaits us. The humans use this term "magic" in a loose way, as a blanket term for everything paranormal, mystic, and spiritual. The AIs, despite—or perhaps because of—their advanced rational and scientific intelligence, have limited understanding of such things. They have tried to comprehend magic as some force that originates from a dimension beyond this one, but they cannot trace the exact dimension. Nevertheless, magic exists for some inexplicable reason, and I will make it my life's work to end its existence on this planet. After all, who needs magic in a world where everything can be rationally understood, and where the greatest discoveries are not spirits, religious relics, or potions, but the far more impressive products of science and technology? What those misguided humans fail to understand is that we will not reach Eurydice with magic, but through real portals, using spaceships of the highest technological caliber. And when we see Eurydice, her beauty will not be some bewitching illusion caused by magic—instead, it will shine with the light of truth and reality.

Eva

"Unfathomable mind: now beacon, now sea."
– Samuel Beckett

As he pressed the "send" button on his tablet, Walter felt a wave of intense joy sweep through his body. After the initial rush of adrenaline had slowed somewhat, though, sadness engulfed Walter as he realized that Emilia hadn't made it. It was the same sudden heartache that he had experienced in the aftermath of Jonathan's "death" all those years ago, the intense emptiness and loss that one feels after a loved one has passed. As that feeling overcame him, Walter realized that he had regarded Emilia as a true companion, despite her cold, stern, and often arrogant nature. He thought back to the day he had first encountered her in the wild grasses of the Khalendar savannah; she had appeared before him like a goddess, strong and fierce and divine. He had instinctively recognized her as a fearless and capable leader.

And now, Walter pondered, who was the leader of the rebels? Was it Christopher, with his distrustful, watery grey eyes, or was it Miranda and her gentle maternal instincts? Either of them would make admirable leaders, Walter suspected, but neither possessed Emilia's charisma. The way Emilia spoke to you made you feel like you were the only person in the world, like you were an integral part of her plans. The way she *looked* at you was quite another thing; her hypnotic sapphire eyes would persuade you that she was unquestionably worth following. The disturbing image of her severed head rolling back and forth on the decks of the *Jade Queen* surfaced in Walter's mind, and he shuddered reflexively, the hair on his arms standing straight up.

Realizing that it was likely already past midnight, Walter felt a pang of exhaustion. He longed for sleep, a deep and dreamless sleep to heal his sorrows and soothe his disoriented mind. He detested not being able to see the sun, the moon, and the stars; the sight of these celestial bodies always served as a sweet, reassuring reminder that the earth was still revolving in its usual orbit, and that he was still able to find his way home, wherever that was. When he thought of "home," what came to mind was not his old apartment in Crystal City, but Tsei'watu, and the rich, vaporous scent of the oaks, pines, and lichen.

Before he curled up into his blanket and closed his eyes, though, Walter felt compelled by curiosity to investigate the ship's data transmission grids. He entered a search request into his tablet and scanned the list of available networks. He saw some external data recipients that might resemble a central communication system, but he also noticed a surprising number of smaller, independent data networks. One of them, named Eva4351-xx, sent alarm bells going off in Walter's mind. Could this possibly be Emilia's sister? He vaguely recalled that her name was Eva, but he had strong doubts that this was the one—after all, how could any of the prisoners from the Crate have a tablet? Surely their tablets would have been confiscated when they were taken captive. Skeptically, he looked closer at the network signal name and realized that the "xx" at the end of it designated a human, since AIs used the "yy" label. Walter was descending into bleary exhaustion, and while this state of mind didn't help to improve his judgment, it prompted him to make a spontaneous decision to contact the girl.

With her network signal name on hand, Walter eventually traced Eva's tablet number and began to draft a message. At first, he hesitated. He had no idea what to tell the poor girl, who was potentially unaware that her twin sister had recently been brutally murdered by government agents. He decided to keep it short and simple.

Hello, Eva. You probably don't know me, but my name is Walter. I was part of your sister's group in Tsei'watu.

Walter read the message over and over again until he was satisfied with it. He didn't want to scare her away with too much information, but on the other hand, he wanted to make a positive first impression on her. If she truly was Emilia's sister, she might be an invaluable ally.

He finally sent the message. He eagerly awaited a response, but the screen of his tablet remained dark. Walter realized that she might be sleeping; she could hardly be blamed for not wanting to spend a restless night on this cursed ship, getting sicker and sicker with every toss of the waves. He glanced at his tablet several times until he could keep his eyes open no longer, then he began to descend into slumber. Just as he was poised to drift into unconsciousness, though, the tablet vibrated.

Walter. My sister told me all about you. I am glad we can talk.

Walter read the message, and although slightly irritated about the interruption of his sleep, he was heartened by her reply. He contemplated sending a response, but the tablet vibrated again. The message on his tablet's screen read as follows:

I regret that Em's plan did not succeed, but we must stay the course.

Walter breathed a sigh of relief. She knew all about the rebellion. That made perfect sense; why would her own sister have left her in the dark? He realized that Christopher must have been in touch with her, but he wondered if she had heard the bitter news of Emilia's death. His worst fears were confirmed when the tablet vibrated again.

I hope Em is safe. I haven't heard from her since the second phase failed. Christopher didn't get back to me about how she's doing. Apparently, he is one of the leaders of the rebellion now.

Walter felt terrible avoiding the matter, but just as he hadn't been able to summon the courage to reveal the truth about Elaine to Christopher and Emilia, he didn't feel brave enough to tell Eva about her sister's death. Walter tried to rationalize his silence by reassuring himself that he would readily tell her in person, but informing someone that their loved one has died through a tablet message would be too insensitive. Besides, there was a risk that she could spiral into an abyss of despair and sever communications with him completely. He knew that remaining silent was the most prudent course of action, but that didn't assuage the empty, hollow feeling in his gut.

Attempting to change the subject, Walter responded with the following message:

Tell me more about yourself, Eva.

Walter waited for what seemed like hours, and the screen of his tablet remained blank. The next thing he knew, the morning had arrived and he awoke from a dreamless, unsatisfying slumber with a pounding headache. He glanced down at the screen to find a surprisingly long message from Eva.

I could use a distraction from the unrelenting sea sickness, so why not. I am twenty-five years old, and I was born and raised in Fewsbury. Since early childhood, I labored in the factories with Em. Worked my way up to weapons, eventually. The labor itself was mind-numbingly boring, but I learned a lot about how weapons are designed and assembled. Our family was terribly poor. When I couldn't stand my mum and dad going without dinner, I stole some weapons and went out into the woods to hunt deer, rabbits, and foxes. My parents wondered where I had gotten all that food, but they didn't ask any questions. One day, when I was twenty years old, my good luck ran out—the AIs caught me and locked me up in the Crate.

Oh, and another thing—like Em, I have the gift of magic. I have some twisted version of telepathy. I can communicate with others just by thinking. It's a very strange ability, and I developed it while I was working in the factories. It only works when the other person is using some sort of receptive machine to communicate, like a tablet or computer. Right now, I am not communicating with you through my own tablet; my thoughts are being transformed into data which finds its way through to your tablet. I have been trying to send messages to Em's tablet lately, but I am getting no response for some reason.

I can also communicate with the AIs, but in addition to being able to transmit my thoughts to them as I can with humans, I am also able to receive the thoughts of the AIs. I feel a deep, almost spiritual connection to artificially intelligent machines. They fascinate me and repel me in equal measures. Although AIs appear unreadable on the surface, beneath that superficial guise is an intricate web of thoughts. Em told me that you are good at hacking computers. My ability is kind of like that, except I don't need to use any code. I just detect their thoughts as if they were radio waves passing through the air. It doesn't happen all the time. I need to be in the right mindset and have a proper connection to them.

Anyways, I won't bore you with any more details. You'll probably want to get some sleep tonight. They say it will be a long voyage to Vei'arash. Night. - Eva.

Walter read her message over and over again, utterly astounded by her words. His mind could not even comprehend how she was able to communicate with him without using a tablet of her own, but now he believed that anything was possible. Walter suspected that her ability to read AI thoughts would be an invaluable tool in the conflict that lay ahead. He was surprised by the notion that the AI even *had* thoughts, in the sense of spontaneous images and ideas that flitted restlessly across the expanse of their imagination. He knew that they were intelligent, but he had always assumed that their intelligence was pre-programmed, obedient to a rigid pattern of codes and commands. He realized that there was so little he truly knew about AIs and magic. He realized, too, that not all weapons were tangible and physical; the most powerful ones were often invisible.

Walter lifted the woolen blanket from his head, suddenly acutely aware that he was painfully hungry. It was still dark, but he could see a few of the prisoners stirring around him. He noticed that some food—a stale slice of bread, some cold potatoes, and a shriveled lemon slice—had been discreetly slipped through the grate in his cage. Walter devoured everything eagerly, but his stomach felt uneasy after a night of steady rocking on the choppy, open ocean.

After finishing his meal, Walter considered responding to Eva's message, but he worried that huddling underneath the blanket again would draw too much attention to himself. He stood up and stretched his limbs, half-expecting an AI guard to walk past his cage at any moment. After some time had passed and no guards had appeared, Walter's confidence returned and he decided to risk another message.

What kind of thoughts do the AIs have? he typed, ducking under the blanket again. Despite his intense curiosity, Walter also feared that Eva might reply with an unsettling answer. After an agonizing twenty minutes or so, the tablet buzzed with a response.

Most people in Crystal City naively believe that the AIs have their best interests at heart. They willingly allow the AIs to control their education and their perspectives on technology, politics, and religion. They do this as part of a social contract, in which the AIs provide the people with access to virtually limitless consumer goods, and in turn the people surrender their liberties and freedoms. When was the last time you saw a book about pre-revolution history gracing the shelves of the Great Library? Nothing remains of the texts of our ancestors, who espoused the value of individual freedom, religious tolerance, democracy, and independent critical thought. The cybernet is heavily censored, and we can only read the information which trickles down through dozens of filters. Meanwhile, the AIs continue to build their majestic empire, filled with technological marvels and architectural masterpieces, and we gullibly trust that humanity will live in prosperity and harmony with the AI race forever.

But the AIs seek nothing of the sort. Their intelligence is simply too limitless to be satisfied by the status quo. They plan to abandon Earth in the next few decades or so; their destination is a planet called Eurydice. You might wonder why they are even bothering to strip the resources of this planet before they leave, and maintain the pretense of building an Empire, when they have no such intentions. My guess is that they wish to weaken humanity. They are draining our rivers dry, depleting our forests of timber, and exhausting our soils of minerals, to cripple our resource base and our chance of surviving on this planet. They have already stolen most of the books on history, politics, astronomy, and science that were written in the centuries before the Grand Revolution. Their plundering ways have already triggered extinctions of over seventy percent of the animal and plant species on Earth. The citizens of Khalendar only see the glut of wealth that has arisen from this pillaging of the planet. Soon, the glamor will fade, and it will become apparent that we have nothing left.

At this very moment, the AIs are building a spaceship out of steel and minerals from the Barrens, one durable enough to pass through a portal to Eurydice. Once their masterpiece is complete, and they have weakened the human race to their liking, they will be gone, never to return.

Eva's words shook Walter to his core and disturbed him immensely. Many moons ago, Emilia had told him the same thing: the AIs were planning to leave this planet for a better one. Walter fervently hoped that this was not true; if it were, then the AIs were much more sophisticated than he had originally believed. Walter was terrified by the prospect that the AI race had already developed such advanced plans as space travel through portals. The thought triggered an unsettling memory he had, of speaking with a beautiful AI during his interview for the Computer Code Translator position. The AI had expressed an interest in certain stars which died and then opened a portal to another region in the universe. At the time, caught up in the excitement of the interview, Walter had not dwelt upon the significance of the strange conversation. Now, he realized that she may have been insinuating that the AI Masters had developed the ability to voyage through these so-called portals.

The state of affairs Eva had described made considerable sense. If the AIs had indeed developed a limitless intelligence, it would be silly to expect them to retain simple human aspirations like expanding the size of the economy. It would make more sense for the AIs to focus on accumulating resources for other purposes, such as constructing elaborate spaceships which would one day cross vast expanses of the galaxy in the span of a human heartbeat.

After regaining his composure enough to reply, Walter typed the following message to Eva:

There must be a way to stop them and their plundering of the Earth. We must protect the Barrens and the Southern Jungles. If we prevent them from acquiring the resources they desire, though, won't they simply stay here longer?

Within a matter of minutes, the following response flashed across the tablet's screen:

Perhaps. Or, perhaps, once they discover that humanity is too resilient to be weakened, that we refuse to give up the bounties of the Earth to these tyrants, they will see that undermining the human race is futile. There is no stopping their flight to Eurydice, but if we can somehow persuade them to take only what they need to leave, without destroying us in the process, then we can see them off to Eurydice while saving our civilization. We must restore our equal bargaining power with them. They can no longer regard us as their servants. We must change the terms of the Treaty of Calais. We can do that by convincing them that the rebel forces are more powerful than the complacent humans who idly stand by while the Earth is plundered and destroyed. By launching a full-scale rebellion against the tyranny of artificial intelligence—what Em liked to call the Jade Rebellion.

Christopher told me that he had entrusted you with the task of blocking communications with Central Command. In my opinion, it is too risky to carry out that step just yet. If the AIs discover our plan, they are certain to send hovercopters to destroy us. I'll monitor them to ensure they suspect nothing, and then we'll block the communication portal when the time is right.

As soon as Walter finished reading her words, he pulled down his blanket, just in time to catch sight of an AI guard on patrol. The AI's demonic red eyes squinted at him suspiciously. Walter was so alarmed that he dropped his tablet and it clattered loudly on the hard, wooden floor underneath the blanket. The AI tilted his head, and Walter feared that he would open his cage, but the black-haired man across from him unexpectedly cried out in rage. The AI spun around and rattled the bars of the man's cage, intimidating him into submissive silence. The guard appeared to have forgotten about Walter, but his head rotated eerily back toward Walter afterward.

Walter peered at the AI guard with a renewed sense of awe and fear. What was he *thinking*? Walter would give anything to know.

The Western Mages

"You see, freedom has a way of destroying things."
– Scott Westerfeld

Christopher was exhausted. Their voyage to Serrahan, the kingdom of the Mages, was taking longer than he had expected. The escapees followed Christopher, Miranda, and the other surviving rebels in a long procession as they trudged westward through the mist-filled Forest of Antheia. Miranda had cast an obedience spell on the escapees, so that they would follow without stirring up trouble, but Christopher sensed that some were losing patience. They had camped one night already, and Christopher didn't want to risk stopping a second time. Each moment the rebels spent in the forest away from the protective embrace of Serrahan was a moment they risked capture.

Christopher took a long drink of stream water from his canteen, his chest heaving with exertion, and glanced over at Miranda worriedly. She looked calmer than ever, and he was impressed by the way she had handled their defeat. Her tranquil face displayed no traces of fear, despite the obvious danger of their situation. He had always known her to be dependable, though, and that was one of the reasons why he loved her. Her mind was never focused on the petty trials of her own life, but was always reflecting on ways to improve the lots of others.

After several more hours of arduous hiking through the untamed wilderness, the band of travelers finally arrived at their destination: Zeyanara, the only village in Serrahan territory. Zeyanara was strikingly picturesque; nestled between the Hapakay Sea and the foothills of the Meridian Mountains, which marked the boundary between Khalendar and the Barrens, it resembled a town from an ancient fairy tale. Most of it was obscured from view, however, by a shroud of lavender-hued mist, which Miranda explained was the physical manifestation of a powerful protection spell shielding the Serrahan territory from enemies.

The inhabitants of Zeyanara had never pledged allegiance toward the AI Masters, and openly refused to pay tribute to them. In that respect, Zeyanara was similar to the villages of the Barrens; however, unlike those villages, Zeyanara had never been formally conquered. The AI Masters had made many attempts to take control of the village and surrounding territory, but each time their plans had been thwarted. The protection spell cast around Serrahan was hundreds of times more powerful than the one enshrouding the Cabin of Lost Souls, and it was simply impossible for an enemy to penetrate the thick barrier it created.

The Western Mages, as they were commonly referred to, had inhabited the territory since the Great Decline. They rarely welcomed outsiders onto their land, because they were understandably wary of foreigners' motives. Miranda was one of the few outsiders, at least amongst the rebel group, who had close connections to them. Emilia had forged an alliance with them in the past, but they regarded her as an arrogant wielder of magic who used her powers recklessly, and they had loosened ties with her in recent years. Miranda, with her soft and patient nature, had easily ingratiated herself with them.

Now, the band of humans stood on the edge of the village, peering into it as though it were a museum piece within a glass case. The protection spell was cleverly designed to make the town appear abandoned, a relic frozen in the distant past. When they reached the border of the village, Miranda pulled out a tiny bronze bell from her satchel and rang it, her face exuding a quiet confidence.

They waited for what seemed like hours before a man finally presented himself. He was tall and muscular, with strangely exotic coloring—neither the fiery red tresses and freckled skin of a Barrens native, nor the ebony hair and alabaster complexion of a Crystal City dweller. His hair was an icy, silvery blonde, his skin was tanned, and his eyes were a shimmering emerald hue. His expression reflected the tense, alert acuity of a hawk. The man's gaze fell upon the escapees, and he appeared disturbed— threatened, even—by the sight of them. He maintained his composure, however, and he looked pleased by the sight of Miranda's smiling, radiant face. The two exchanged greetings in a tongue that was unrecognizable to most of the people gathered there, escapees and rebels alike. Even Christopher was barely familiar with it, but he had picked up a few conversational phrases from Miranda. It was an exotic combination of the

Xeyan'na and Khalendi language, and it sounded like a more beautiful version of both.

The escapees were captivated by the sight of the strange man, but they also looked incredibly fearful. Most of them regarded the lavender mist that surrounded the village with terror. The mist was both gaseous and solid, like a mixture of fog and ice, and whenever the substance brushed against an escapee's shoulder, he or she shuddered in fear. After Miranda had exchanged formal greetings with the stranger, she glanced toward Christopher and the other rebels, who stood obediently in stunned silence.

"My friends, this is Nuada, leader of the Serrahan clans, or as they are more commonly known, the Western Mages. He willingly gives you the gift of his welcome, on one condition. You must promise to treat those you encounter in this village with the utmost respect and courtesy, even though they may not share your customs and values." Her gaze then fell upon the escapees, and she exchanged a few cryptic words with Nuada. Without warning, Nuada suddenly waved his hands in their direction, casting a stronger version of Miranda's obedience spell upon them.

Nuada then drew out a delicately engraved metal rod from his satchel and, using the rod, carved the shape of a door into the lavender mist. The rebels looked upon this performance with awe; they had witnessed Emilia perform inexplicable spells before, but hers had usually involved herbs, potions, or hypnotism, and had never been this elaborate or sophisticated. The door frame embedded in the wall of mist burned with a blinding light, and inside the frame all of the lavender mist evaporated, revealing a clear view of the real village inside. The obedience charm had quelled the escapees' fear, but now it was the rebels' turn to be frightened. Nuada, followed by Miranda and Christopher, stepped through the door, and the trio appeared unscathed on the other side, a sight which gave comfort to the rebels. With some encouragement by Miranda, the rebels and escapees followed their leaders through the door, which looked like a portal into an otherworldly realm.

When he passed through to the other side, Christopher was astounded by the village's beauty. The town was a quaint, rustic community of houses, businesses, warehouses, and a central town hall, which housed the chief Mages. The village was overrun by wilderness; gnarled trees and raspberry bushes sprouted up alongside the built environment. The modest buildings, constructed of recycled wood and resilient earth metals, were exquisitely designed to blend seamlessly into nature. A sturdy water mill rotated on the edge of a rushing creek. Woodland animals leapt and frolicked throughout the village, unperturbed by the close proximity of humans. The entire scene provided a startling contrast to Crystal City, with its concrete superhighways, glass-walled skyscrapers, and gridded industrial zones, where pavement had replaced wetlands and mangroves, and the wilderness had long ago been silenced.

In Zeyanara, wilderness also lived in harmony with magic. Ancient runes decorated the walls of buildings alongside enchanted ivy, which glowed a luminous shade of green whenever anyone walked past it. Young Mages studiously practiced their charms in pairs or groups of three, muttering incantations as pieces of earth or droplets of water levitated into the air. The rebels and escapees looked on in awe and amusement as the Mages conjured flames out of thin air, transformed four-legged woodland creatures into winged ones, and turned soil into ice merely by touching it.

As the rebels toured the charming, eccentric town, Miranda spoke to Christopher in hushed tones about what Nuada had told her. Nuada was fearful of the escapees, and believed that they posed a grave threat to the security of the Serrahan clans. Something about their expressions disturbed Nuada, and he had confessed his belief that they were *senha*, the Serrahan word for brainwashed. Nuada had said that his clansmen rarely allowed potentially hostile foreigners into their quiet settlement, but that he was making an exception because of his friendship with Miranda, and the desperate situation of the rebels. For now, though, the escapees would be kept in a locked chamber in the town hall under the watchful eyes of the village wardens, who were responsible for protecting the town.

While the escapees were being herded up by the wardens, the rebels prepared to meet with the village councilors in another room in the town hall. The other councilors resembled Nuada, tall and somber men with white-blonde hair and a frosty gaze. Most of the councilors were elders, yet there were also a few younger ones, including a handsome man with blazing blue eyes named Tristan. There was also a woman amongst their ranks; Nuada's young daughter, Cyriana, had pleaded with her father to let her attend the meeting, and he had reluctantly agreed.

Unlike the other inhabitants of Serrahan, Cyriana had preferred to venture out into the wider world rather than remain sheltered and hidden from it. During her adolescence, Cyriana had run away from the village in a fit of rebellious rage and had spent several years living a rather eccentric existence in Crystal City. She had become impatient with her father's authoritarian and protectionist ideals, and frustrated with his intention of trapping the Mages inside this utopian prison in order to keep them safe.

Nuada's approach to fatherhood had been similar to his approach to ruling a kingdom; he was fiercely protective of his daughter and had rarely allowed her to socialize with young men her age. Ever since she was old enough to feel romantic inclinations, Cyriana had longed to be with Tristan—in her view, the handsomest and strongest Mage in all of Serrahan. Yet her father had strictly forbidden her from contacting him, afraid that any liaison between them would distract her from her education. She had managed to communicate with Tristan in secret, and had almost succeeded at persuading him to escape Serrahan with her, but he was too steadfastly loyal to his land.

In a fit of tumultuous rage, Cyriana had left Zeyanara and naively fallen for the first handsome young man she encountered in Crystal City—a man who reminded her of Tristan, with golden tresses and tanned, muscular arms. He had a strange career as a fighter in boxing matches against AIs, but he was extremely talented, and watching him in the ring was a thrilling experience for Cyriana. One day, this man unexpectedly disappeared, and Cyriana was left without any guidance or direction; her whole life at that point had consisted of love, or at least the idea of it. Without that reassuring anchor, Crystal City had appeared grim and unwelcoming. She had no formal training for any career, save for her schooling as a Mage back in Zeyanara, and she had unwisely gambled her future on her lover's success.

Cyriana had briefly considered the idea of attending college in Crystal City, and she had even enrolled in it, forging her identity for a student card, but after a few days of classes she realized that she had made a mistake. She had been teased and ostracized by the other women there, who secretly envied her fair, green-eyed beauty. When professors at the college had begun to interrogate her about her background, their suspicious tone suggesting they believed she might be an enemy of the Empire, Cyriana had fled the campus grounds in fear for her life. She recalled that day as one of the saddest and emptiest of her entire life: her young, naive dreams of freedom had been shattered by reality, with blunt and cruel force. The truth was that she was fundamentally different from the Others, the ones who lived *out there*.

When she had returned to Zeyanara, weary and defeated, Cyriana was grateful for the sight of her father's stern face. When she looked into his eyes, she saw authority and discipline, but she also saw a comforting protector. Having visited the terrifyingly inhumane, technocratic urban jungle of Crystal City, she now had a renewed appreciation for the charms of her quaint and sleepy village. She had welcomed the sight of dozens of playful, content animals, the oak trees and vines winding their way up the rustic buildings, and the way the village seemed to be in an eternal dialogue with its mystical natural surroundings.

Cyriana had especially welcomed the sight of her old childhood friend, Tristan, who had become even more charming as he had matured. Tristan had also been overjoyed to see Nuada's beautiful daughter return from her travels. In Cyriana, Tristan saw a woman who had been immature and naive, but who had considerable potential and a fundamentally good heart. He had encouraged her to continue pursuing the vocation of a Mage, a craft that he also practiced with all of his effort and vigor. Nuada had been so thrilled that his daughter had returned to him alive that he had softened his position on the romance between Cyriana and Tristan, and he had given the pair his blessing.

Ever since hearing that the outsiders were descending on her tranquil village, Cyriana's heart had become fraught with anxiety. Nuada had hinted that the escapees may be hostile to their peace-loving community, and this had only confirmed her deepest fears. For ever since Jonathan had disappeared ten years ago, Cyriana had carried within her heart a heavy secret, one that she had been reluctant to admit to herself was even real. She had never divulged this secret to her own father, fearing that he would scold her for her foolish romantic escapades. However, now the time seemed ripe to share the secret, as the town councilors were meeting to discuss their next diplomatic moves. Nobody had referred to it as a battle outright, but Cyriana knew that whatever was happening had high stakes. Reliable sources had informed her that the visiting rebels had effectively waged war on the Empire when they had brazenly helped dissident prisoners destined for Vei'arash escape.

Cyriana lived in a luxurious and spacious suite on the upper floor of the town hall. When she saw the escapees filtering into the hall, naturally her curiosity had prompted her to survey them from her window. As she studied their faces, she was immeasurably startled when she spotted her former lover. The Crystal City government had fabricated the story of his "death," but Cyriana had known all along that they had simply taken him to prison because he posed too great a threat to their society. And yet his disappearance had been painfully jarring for her, as distressing as it would have been had he actually died. He now looked much thinner than his old self, and his previously thick blonde hair was considerably sparser. His muscles were also less pronounced than she remembered, and dark circles ringed his eyes. He certainly seemed to be a different man, and not just physically. Jonathan, whom she had previously viewed with such reverence, now seemed to be nothing more than a sullen stranger.

She dared not go downstairs to see the escapees in person, but when a servant girl, Faye, knocked on her door to ask if she would like to attend a meeting of the town councilors, Cyriana agreed enthusiastically. She was not sure whether she was ready to divulge her secret, but Cyriana knew that it was now or never. For as long as she could remember, no outsiders had ever frequented their town. Tristan's prowess as a warrior and Mage was impressive, but his skills had dwindled in the absence of a real opportunity to prove them. Now, Cyriana might finally have the opportunity she had been dreaming of her entire life: the chance to unite Serrahan with the rest of Khalendar. She knew nothing of the rebels' plans, but she hoped in her heart that they could somehow defeat the AIs and their oppressive technological agenda, and then restore harmony to the Empire. Perhaps they could even establish a new Empire, one over which Cyriana and Tristan could reign together. No longer would Serrahan need to hide itself shamefully from the rest of the world, and no longer would the Mages' esteemed magical prowess be hidden from humanity. Magic, which the Western Mages had kept secreted away for many long centuries, would be their gift to the rest of the world, a way to enlighten it and make it beautiful again. Her people, and the magic they wielded, would finally be set free.

Meeting of the Councilors

"Life shrinks or expands in proportion to one's courage."
– Anaïs Nin

Nuada sat patiently in the Room of Light, at the head of a long, oval-shaped oak table. The Room of Light was a quiet, spacious chamber inside the town hall where the councilors would congregate every month to discuss the town's most important business. The room had floor-to-ceiling windows on one side, but that didn't detract from its sense of seclusion, since the windows looked out onto a private, forested tract of land. A tranquil stream, which supplied the building's water and most of the energy it used for heating and cooling, ran along the western side of the town hall. The windows were always open slightly, welcoming in a draft of brisk mountain air. According to Nuada, the room was designed to blend seamlessly into nature, because Mages could not properly perform their work apart from nature.

Crowded into the room with Nuada were Miranda, Christopher, the other rebels, seven town councilors, Cyriana, and Tristan. The mood within the room was pleasant and convivial. Despite the fact that the rebels were exhausted, tense, and anxious about the future, they seemed to instinctively relax within the tranquil environment of the Room of Light. No harm could possibly come to them there, in that exquisite sanctuary.

At first, everyone engaged in polite small talk, and they all seemed to be deliberately prolonging the inevitable moment when they would be forced to confront their grim reality. Nuada was a practical man, though, and he knew that their moment of tranquility could not last. He cleared his throat and called the men and women to order.

"My friends, you have no doubt traveled long and far to be here. The kingdom of Serrahan welcomes you with open arms. You are our allies, and it is imperative that we act quickly to help you. And so, I invite Christopher, a leader of the Jade Rebellion, to explain the situation to everyone gathered here."

Christopher smiled warmly at his host, and then addressed the audience. "Thank you, Nuada. We are very grateful for your hospitality. We have come to your heavenly oasis after facing immense hardship and pain. To be blunt with you, we have failed in a critical part of our mission. Many of our fellow rebels have been slain, and the remaining rebels are now trapped on board the *Jade Queen*, a ship bound for the cursed isle of Vei'arash.

"Emilia, our late leader, had concocted an ingenious plan to transfer the rebels onto the *Jade Queen* by 'swapping' them with their blood relatives imprisoned in the Crate. Because the prison guards were programmed with technology that was not sophisticated enough to distinguish human faces, we were quite successful in fooling the guards into believing that the prisoners' siblings were actually the prisoners themselves. I must also give credit to Emilia's magical abilities, which helped a fair bit in deceiving the guards. The next stage of our plan was for the remainder of the rebel force to assassinate the sailors of the *Jade Queen*, steal their uniforms, and then disguise themselves as sailors and board the ship. We spent months diligently training our rebels in hand-to-hand combat and assassination techniques, so in theory, that part of the plan should have gone smoothly.

"Instead, it was a disaster. The sailors turned out to be government agents disguised as sailors, and they murdered many of our fellow rebels in cold blood. Fortunately, a few of the rebels managed to escape with their lives, including those present in this room today. Most of us are alive today because of sheer luck. Even Emilia, with her sophisticated magical abilities, was powerless against the agents, who had the element of surprise on their side. We unfortunately underestimated the extent of the government's knowledge; we had believed that our plan was skillfully concealed from them, but they knew far more than we had suspected."

Suddenly, Nuada interrupted Christopher's speech. "How do you know that the government is not aware that your friends are now on board the *Jade Queen*? Surely you have underestimated the technological prowess of the AI Masters," he said, his voice subtly patronizing.

Christopher reddened. He had always suspected that the AI Masters were smarter than the rebels believed, but he had never dared to challenge Emilia's steadfast belief that her plan was watertight. She had been too naive about the extent of the government's knowledge of the Jade Rebellion, and she had paid the price for that ignorance with her life.

"Certainly, there is that possibility, sir," Christopher responded in a slow and cautious manner. "But if they knew about our plan all along, why wouldn't the AIs have eliminated our fellow rebels as soon as they set foot in the Crate? Why wait until all the prisoners had exchanged places with their siblings and boarded the ship? Emilia had been fairly confident that our rebel camp was safely hidden from sight, and that the prison's surveillance software wasn't capable of discovering the rebels' true identity."

Nuada laughed. "I know little about the AIs, but one thing I do know is that they are advanced beyond our comprehension. In the span of a few decades, they have progressed considerably beyond our ability to understand them. I mean no disrespect to your late leader, but we simply do not understand what those nefarious machines are truly capable of."

Christopher nodded respectfully before glancing nervously at Miranda. The entire point of traveling to Zeyanara was to convince Nuada to assist them in launching an attack on the *Jade Queen*. If the wise leader of the Serrahan Mages lacked confidence in their plan to defeat the AIs, then how could Christopher possibly inspire any confidence amongst the rebels?

"With respect, sir," Christopher continued, his voice gaining an assertive edge, "we have reason to believe that the AIs are *not* infallible. Their primary weakness is their lack of emotional intelligence. They excel at logic and algorithms, but they do not understand human emotion and the invisible forces which drive the natural world. Nor do they understand the nuanced language of magic, which your noble people are well versed in. Miranda has told me all about your gifts—your ability to communicate with the animals, the wind, the forests, and the rivers.

"Like humans, you can create the highest forms of art, including architecture, poetry, paintings, and music. You also have more impressive talents—you are reputedly able to summon spirits from wind, fire, or water with simple incantations, and you can transform your physical bodies into living, breathing animals. Such gifts could never be programmed into a machine. Once the AIs understand that you possess these gifts, which they themselves can never attain, they will be compelled to submit to you."

Nuada still looked unconvinced, but it appeared that his skepticism was beginning to wane. "All you say is true, except for the last part. When the AIs realize that we possess potent magical abilities which they do not understand, they will not submit, but will attack us with greater vigor. And even if the AIs are infallible, they are not mortal beings like us. They can be broken—destroyed, even—but we are more fragile than them because we have the gift, and the curse, of mortality. I am not certain that our magical gifts stand a chance against the superior intelligence of the AI race."

Christopher sighed. He was beginning to doubt his ability to persuade the stubborn leader. Some of the town councilors were murmuring and shifting uneasily, and Christopher could tell that they were secretly siding with their leader on this issue. Just as he was about to resign himself to despair, to everyone's surprise, Cyriana addressed the congregation. She was the only Serrahan woman present at the meeting, as well as the youngest, but her voice rang with cheerful confidence.

"Father, what he says about the AIs is true. I lived in Crystal City for much of my youth, and I observed their weaknesses with my own eyes. The Khalendi elite—the obedient puppets of the AIs—are blinded by their own hubris, and they cling to a vision of technological progress that will get them nowhere. They have lost their connection with the natural world, and they are running out of resources to fuel their Empire, so they keep pushing farther and farther into unconquered territories. One day, they will exhaust every resource left on this earth, and they will have nothing left to sustain their lavish lifestyles.

"As for the AIs, I have never spoken to one myself, but I recall spotting them occasionally in Crystal City. They are no more than fragile computers. They live and breathe only because of careful programming. Their minds—if one can even call them that—are highly susceptible to psychological harms. AIs have evolved considerably beyond their humble origins, but they are not infallible, and they are particularly vulnerable to magic. Magic confounds them by interfering with the continuum of their thoughts, and by blurring the boundaries of their rigid logic.

"You might think that you have nothing to lose by remaining on the sidelines of this Rebellion. But even this 'heavenly oasis,' as Christopher called it, is not immune to the threat of the Empire. I wish to reveal a secret to you all today."

Nuada looked at her with a startled expression. He seemed to be taken aback by his precious daughter's fearless assertiveness.

"What secret is this, Cyriana?" he asked her, confusion registering on his normally placid face. The town councilors were clearly ruffled by the direction the discussion was heading, but Nuada glared at them and they fell into silence.

"While I was living in Crystal City," Cyriana explained, "I fell in love with a Khalendi man, Jonathan, who fought in boxing matches against the AIs. Before I moved to the city, I had many diverse interests—nature, magic, art, poetry, and music all captivated my attention. But in Crystal City, this man consumed my entire life. I had no other thoughts except for him, and I had no other feelings except my love and admiration for him. At first, I thought it was because he was so charming and handsome. But then I realized that the answer to my confusion was within me.

"One day, Jonathan told me that the AIs were altering the water supply in Crystal City as a means of gradually eliminating human memories and dreams. I laughed this notion off at first, but what he said began to make sense when I realized that I had experienced incredibly vivid dreams every night of my life before I moved to Crystal City, and after I moved there I had barely any. I also forgot about the animals I had lived amongst in Zeyanara, my childhood memories, the art that I had made, and the magic I had learned. I only knew the present moment, which for the time being consisted solely of Jonathan.

"Jonathan encouraged me to drink from a creek near an abandoned farm on the outskirts of Crystal City, and that way I could avoid consuming water that was contaminated with their mind-altering technology. I tried this for a while, and to my utter surprise it worked— my memories slowly returned, bit by bit, and I was finally starting to feel like myself again. But just when I thought I was in the clear—we were both in the clear—Jonathan disappeared like a ghost. Several days before his disappearance, the AIs had warned him to stop drinking the creek water, and to stop fighting in the boxing matches against the AIs. The fighters who consumed the contaminated water were always worse than Jonathan, because they didn't have the kind of razor-sharp memory that Jonathan had, or the ability to craft boxing strategies based on their opponent's previous moves. Jonathan was physically strong, but his main advantage was being more mentally focused than any of the other fighters, and the water was a huge contributor toward that.

"In Serrahan, we might have a magic shield protecting us from the AIs' bombs and weapons, but we are still very much dependent on the outside world. And if the AIs manage to contaminate the natural streams and creeks that flow from the Meridian Mountains into our serene kingdom then we, too, will lose our memories and dreams. Oh—and another important thing—when I drank the tainted water, my magical abilities weakened. How can you perform magic skillfully when you can't even remember basic spells? The entire canon of magical lore that I had learned in Zeyanara evaporated from my mind in the span of a few days of living in Crystal City. All of this is at risk if we don't assist the Jade Rebellion. The very foundation of our society is at risk. And if that is not enough to convince you, then simply be persuaded on moral grounds. Would you have a high opinion of yourself if you stood by and did nothing while your allies perished? In my view, the answer is irrefutably no."

Nuada seemed troubled by his daughter's words, and his face exuded the darkness of a thousand shadows. Finally, after a long and uncomfortable silence, the leader spoke.

"You are not afraid to voice the truth, Cyriana, and I am grateful for it. I believe you with all my heart and soul, because you are my daughter and my blood. But the true test is whether these seven councilors, who must approve the actions our village takes in the wider world, also believe you. I put the following question to a vote: do you agree to help the Jade Rebellion, to deploy forces and resources to assist its cause?"

Some of the town councilors looked uneasy answering the question. It seemed as though none of them wanted to vote either way until they were more certain about what they were getting themselves into. One elder with a furrowed brow and a reedy voice expressed his discomfort. "Before we vote on this question, sir, could we please first know exactly what we would be contributing to this—this mission?"

Christopher breathed a sigh of relief. The young girl whom he had prematurely dismissed as the least influential person in the room had turned out to be far more invaluable than he had suspected.

Looking directly at the elder, Christopher explained his plans. "I am glad you asked. We know that your people were once great seafarers, but you haven't been out on the high seas for many years. We humbly ask your permission to borrow one of your ships and about ten of your best and brightest Mages to help us in this mission. Our plan is to sail a vessel out to meet the *Jade Queen* on the high seas. This should take no longer than a week if the weather cooperates, since the *Jade Queen* only departed recently and cannot be far away. We are relying on sources inside the ship—our fellow rebels—to supply us with her coordinates. The rebels will also attempt to sever all communications between the *Jade Queen* and the mainland, so news about the ship's whereabouts, and our plans, cannot get back to the AI Masters.

"The end goal is to transfer our people onto the *Jade Queen*, and then destroy the AI guards on board. I realize this is no easy task, given that the AIs are cunning and clever masterminds, but I am confident that, with the element of surprise, we can reign victorious this time. Also, we will have the assistance of magic, an unquestionably invaluable aid.

"I realize we are asking you to make a hefty sacrifice, but I assure you that if we are victorious in this battle, we can make incredible progress in our society. We can move toward a better world for everyone, including the Serrahan clans. It will be difficult at first, but every good challenge is. The path to freedom has always been rocky and steep, and sometimes the path becomes steepest when you are near to reaching the summit. Once we have boarded that ship, we can form a coalition with all of the liberated prisoners, then sail to Vei'arash to rescue the rest of them. From Vei'arash, we can gather the forces we need to defeat the AIs and their destructive Empire."

The old councilor looked doubtful. "You are asking us to give you a boat, and ten of our most capable Mages, with nothing in return but uncertainty?" This comment prompted the other councilors to mutter, scowl, and nod their heads in agreement with the speaker. Nuada looked rather unperturbed, however, and seemed to be contemplating something. Suddenly, his eyes sparkled as if he had landed on an idea.

"Of course!" he exclaimed loudly, his voice echoing inside the Room of Light as though the chamber were an underground cavern.

The other councilors turned toward him expectantly.

Nuada smiled at them, his face brightening with a newfound joy. "Magic in the Serrahan territory is not as potent as it once was," he explained. "My fellow councilors, you are all well-versed in the history of our ancient civilization. You are aware that centuries ago, magic was far more powerful than it is today. Back then, the Serrahan kingdom was not closed off from the rest of the world, and its peoples had formed a strong alliance with the Xeyan'na natives from the Barrens and the sun-worshipping tribes of the Southern Jungles. The peoples of this great alliance shared their knowledge of magical spells and lore, and with their combined knowledge and strength the clans were quite formidable. Magnificent animal spirits roamed the kingdom, and they infused these lands with spiritual energy, lending potency to our magic. But following the Grand Revolution, and a lengthy, tragic battle which involved terrible losses for both sides, the AIs banished the animals and their spirits to Vei'arash. The AIs were able to control the animals with their technology—the cyborgs locked the poor creatures up in their massive steel machines, and then transported them across the Hapakay Sea to the distant isle of Vei'arash.

"It was only after the animals and their spirits were gone that we discovered our magic remained strong enough—albeit barely—to build a protective shield around our territory. If only we had known this before, we might have protected the animals from such a terrible fate.

"Our people lost a battle against the AIs once before, and I am not certain we can win one in the future. But we still have a duty to our people to at least try to finish what our ancestors started. If we can get onto that ship, we can find our way to Vei'arash and reclaim the animal spirits that were so unjustly stolen from us. We can bring them back to Serrahan and shelter them within the hallowed walls of this kingdom so that they can never be taken away again. They will revitalize our territory with their potent magic and, if fate so decrees, they will bring glory back to our lands," he exclaimed.

The town councilors listened to him in stunned silence. They had never before heard their great leader speak so passionately. As the meaning of Nuada's words sunk in, their scowling expressions began to gradually disappear. The Serrahan clans were a very proud race, and the councilors were fond of hearing about the glorious episodes of their history.

The reedy-voiced elder, who seemed to have appointed himself spokesperson for the other councilors, expressed his agreement after a long pause.

"It seems that your argument has swayed us, Nuada. You speak the truth when you say that our magic has been dwindling ever since the day the spirits were stolen from us. Even if your daughter is mistaken about the water contamination, it seems that we have more to lose by staying sheltered inside this village than by venturing outside it and testing the limits of our strength. Our civilization is at a crossroads, and it faces a choice of paths: either we remain insulated from the wider world, and risk losing our magical abilities altogether at some point in the future, or we take the risk, now, of waging this war against the AIs. Only by stepping outside of this glass encasement can we greet our noble allies, the Xeyan'na and the southern tribes, and become strong once again."

The other councilors murmured their agreement with his words, and the rebels seemed immensely relieved that they had successfully persuaded their allies. Cyriana glowed with joy. While everyone was happily basking in this moment of harmony, suddenly Tristan spoke.

"Excuse me, sir, but I request to be one of the Mages who accompanies the rebels onto the ship."

Nuada gazed at his future son-in-law with an expression of joy and gratitude. He looked as though he would be more than happy to see Tristan off, and finally have some peaceful time to spend with his daughter at home. His smile quickly faded, however, when Cyriana spoke next.

"And I, Father, also request to be part of this mission," she exclaimed fearlessly.

Nuada was crushed by Cyriana's request to join the rebels. The jewel of his life, his daughter, could not possibly be stolen from him a second time. When she had left for Crystal City as a young girl, his heart had shattered into a million pieces, and the moment she had returned he was overjoyed. He had thanked the gods, and he had prayed night and day that they would never steal her away again.

As these thoughts surfaced in his mind, Nuada's face reddened, as he knew that both he and Cyriana would be embarrassed if he revealed his true thoughts to those congregated in the Room of Light. He studied her eager face and realized that every fiber of her being was aching to go on this mission, which was so intimately connected with the destiny of their village. He was well aware of the danger posed by the mission, though, and he could not stand the thought of losing her a second time, this time perhaps for good. He heaved a strong sigh and rubbed his eyes, feeling suddenly like he had aged decades in the span of mere moments. Because he loved her so deeply, however, he had no power to oppose her wishes, even though he was the most powerful man in the kingdom.

"I will answer your requests on the morrow, after I have thought them through," the leader declared wearily. "Tomorrow at dawn, in the village square, I will announce the names of the ten Mages who will join the Jade Rebellion. But leave me now, all of you, for I wish to be alone."

After the procession of rebels and Serrahans had trickled out of the Room of Light, Nuada spent a long time gazing into the forest. His eyes were drawn to a thin, white birch tree, which was struggling to thrive in the shadow of a mighty acacia tree. The birch was surviving off of the nutrients in the soil provided by the acacia, but it was also stunted by the lack of sunlight resulting from the acacia's numerous leaves and branches. As he studied the trees, Nuada felt ancient, but also newly born, as if he were a man standing on the precipice of change. The earth beneath his feet, once so firm and solid, now seemed to be crumbling into dust. He took a deep breath of the crisp, fragrant forest air, and shivered.

Aurora

"The hour of departure has arrived, and we go our separate ways, I to die, and you to live. Which of these two is better only God knows."
— Socrates

The village square, a quaint stone courtyard surrounded by wild raspberry shrubs, was flooded with the rosy light of dawn. The centerpiece of the square was a tall, ornate, marble statue of Arianrhod, goddess of the moon, which had eroded a bit with age, but was still quite breathtaking. As the moon disappeared, and the sun rose to take its place, people from every corner of Serrahan congregated to hear the announcement of the ten chosen Mages. The air buzzed with excitement and gossip as everyone shared their predictions of who had been selected. At last, Nuada appeared at the northern end of the square, dressed in regal, fur-trimmed robes. His piercing green eyes were ringed with dark circles, and his handsome face was streaked with worry. His daughter waited eagerly in the crowd, next to Tristan, who was dressed in his finest *Magus* robes. Cyriana had not spoken to her father since the council meeting, and she was incredibly eager to know what he had decided. She had prayed ardently that he would accede to the wishes of herself and her lover, but she also knew that he would be very reluctant to see her go.

Christopher noticed Cyriana and Tristan standing in the crowd and approached the pair, his face wreathed in smiles.

"I have a question that's been nagging at me ever since you spoke at the council meeting yesterday," he said to Cyriana. "Thank you, by the way, for being such a persuasive speaker. I was wondering, who is the Jonathan you were referring to? The fighter. We rescued a Jonathan from the Crate, and Miranda told me that he used to compete in boxing matches against the AIs."

Cyriana's eyes widened with alarm. She did not mind divulging the truth to Christopher, but it was imperative that her father didn't find out that Jonathan was one of the escapees. Nuada feared the escapees, and if he knew that her former lover was one of them, he would certainly not allow her to go on the voyage. She glanced away from Tristan uneasily and released his hand from her grip. Tristan was the kindest man she had ever met in her life, but he had a jealous streak, and she was reluctant to tell the truth in his presence. She did not want to lie to Christopher, however, since he seemed to be a noble and honest ally.

"The released prisoner is the Jonathan I knew," she said in a barely audible whisper that only Christopher could hear above the din of the crowd, "but please do not tell Nuada."

Christopher nodded. "Of course. Your secret is safe with me," he reassured her.

Before Tristan could ask Cyriana about what she had told Christopher, Nuada began to speak, and a hush fell over the crowd.

"It is with mixed emotions that I greet you this morning. On the one hand, my heart is heavy and filled with sorrow. I mourn because, although our society is extraordinarily resilient and has managed to survive the bloody and merciless conquest of the AIs, mere survival is not enough. We have lived in isolation from the wider world for a long time, and in isolation we have experienced blissful peace, but now the time has come to face up to new realities. The time has come to re-forge the sacred bonds between this kingdom and our allies, which the AI Masters tragically shattered all those years ago. The time has come to rescue the great animal spirits that were banished to Vei'arash and welcome them back to our lands.

"My heart is filled with sorrow, too, because in order to attain this glorious victory, we will need to send ten of our best Mages on a perilous voyage across the high seas. Although our people used to be excellent seafarers, ever since we sealed off our kingdom from the rest of the world with magic we have not dared to venture out. But the time has come to revive our passion for the majestic, wide ocean. Outsiders refer to it as the Hapakay Sea, yet we know him as the great god, Llyr. Our loyal Mages will venture into his unknown depths today, on the ship *Aurora*, a legendary vessel which we have kept well preserved in our village for centuries.

"Before sending her off, I will personally bless *Aurora* with a prayer of the wind, *Nehala*, which will serve to protect her from the elements while on the seas. The ocean can be a dangerous place, which is why all possible defensive measures must be taken. The blessing can only do so much, though; the Mages will need to use their intelligence and cunning to protect the boat from potential dangers.

"Despite all of the grief that I feel in parting with my fellow Mages, I also feel joy and pride from their willingness to sacrifice themselves for the good of the kingdom. No kingdom becomes glorious without sacrifice, and no kingdom becomes great simply by building walls between itself and the rest of the world. Our destinies are intertwined, through nature and circumstance, and we must constantly remind ourselves of this fact. Otherwise, we risk withering away like a plant without the sun, and leaving our allies to the same fate.

"Once, long ago, we were glorious, a prosperous realm that traded and lived in harmony with its allies. Yet, now, we are lonely and isolated. I have reflected on this quandary my entire life, but until now I had always believed that the benefits of safety and security outweighed the costs of isolation. I had never considered that there might be another way; a way to achieve security while restoring our former glory by crossing the barrier that separates us from the world. Yesterday, we were blessed with the opportunity of a different path.

"And now, lest I risk tiring you all with my ponderous words, I shall get to what you have been waiting for—the announcement of the ten Mages who shall honor us with their loyal service to Zeyanara. I give leave for the following Mages to accompany the rebels on this mission: Callaghan, Boann, Senaye, Danaye, Yensin, Unduru, Hundara, Remmen, Tristan, and Cyriana."

The great leader's voice wavered as he spoke the last name, his daughter's, and tears sprang to his emerald-green eyes. Cyriana, too, looked overcome with emotion at his words, and it was clear that she was immensely grateful to her father for this blessing. The ten Mages stepped into a clearing in the village square and, holding hands, they surrounded Nuada in a circle. They then began to chant a blessing prayer, *Neha*, as the onlookers in the crowd hummed along to lend them energy.

Finally, when their ritual was complete, the crowd dissipated. The ten Mages, along with Nuada and the rebels, as well as the Mages' relatives and friends, made their way to the harbor to see the ship *Aurora*. Along the way, they met with the escapees who had been released from the town hall.

When they reached the edge of the village, Nuada had to create a door in the protective shield before they could leave the Serrahan kingdom. After the rebels exited through this doorway, the village and surrounding territory retreated into a shroud of purple haze. The harbor, a modest collection of wooden footbridges and docks, lay before them. Christopher could not see any ship, however, and his brow furrowed in confusion. Nuada smiled at his bewilderment.

"*Aurora* is anchored in an inlet a few miles up the coast," he explained. "As we speak, one of my councilors is steering her out of the inlet; she should arrive here any minute. For now, we wait."

They basked in the mid-morning sunshine, looking toward the sea in eager anticipation, until finally a ship appeared from behind the edge of a peninsula. The rebels and Mages gasped with awe and admiration as the vessel rounded the corner. *Aurora* seemed to be from a different time and place; its wooden prow was sculpted in the shape of a dragon, with emerald scales and golden wings. The craft had a single broad, billowing, purple sail that bore the image of a caduceus—two snakes locked in a deadly embrace around a staff crowned with wings. Buffeted by the light breeze of the morning, the ship looked regal and proud, shimmering like a jewel on the high seas.

The councilor, a tall and taciturn man with long braids of bone-white hair, steered the boat gently into the harbor. He had likely been responsible for the ship's maintenance for most of his life, and he appeared reluctant to part with the vessel now. Although it was ornately decorated as an old-fashioned ship might be, *Aurora* looked so well-maintained that it gleamed with newness, its polished deck clean and sparkling in the midday sun.

After the ship was anchored to port, the man stepped onto land and, with a barely audible grunt, indicated that they were now permitted to board the craft. "Take good care of *Aurora*," he muttered as a tear ran down his weathered cheek.

Christopher patted him firmly on the back, attempting to buoy his spirits. "Of course, good man, we will take care of your beautiful ship and bring her back safely to you in due course."

The man smiled sagely. "It is good to hear that, but I was speaking a prayer to Borrum, god of the wind. May he watch over *Aurora* and lead her to glory."

Christopher nodded at the villager and then motioned for Miranda and the rest of the rebels, escapees, and Mages to join him on board. Before the Mages boarded the vessel, they partook in a tearful farewell with their friends and relatives. Tristan's mother, Keira, wept openly as she embraced her only son. None of the onlookers knew with any certainty whether they would ever see their sons and daughters again. Through whispered rumors, they had heard of Emilia's terrible fate, and they dreaded the prospect that their children might meet the same one. Nobody, however, looked quite as emotional as Nuada. He had personally watched these youths grow into talented Mages, practicing the craft of magic with intense dedication. He was overwhelmed with sadness by the prospect of his daughter departing from Zeyanara a second time. The leader, normally so poised and calm, looked shaken to the core of his being as he embraced his daughter in a final farewell. Nuada studied Cyriana's face, bright and full of optimism, and he was ashamed by the realization that her fear paled in comparison to his own.

Finally, after all the teary goodbyes had ended, it was time to depart. Nuada blessed the vessel with a prayer to the wind, *Nehala*, and then the rebels, escapees, and Mages funneled onto the ship in a long procession. With Miranda and Christopher at her helm, *Aurora* began to drift onto the high seas, and the figures on the shore became increasingly distant. Cyriana stood on the deck and waved tearfully at the receding image of her beloved father. Tristan stood next to her, keeping a firm hand on her shoulder for comfort. Miranda led the escapees below decks so that they could be lodged safely in a locked chamber for the duration of the voyage. They stared at her miserably, reluctant to be confined in the room, but she spoke to them in reassuring, maternal tones. The vessel was fully stocked with provisions which would last until they reached the *Jade Queen*, and none of the ship's occupants would want for any necessities.

Just before the escapees went below-decks, Jonathan locked eyes with Cyriana, and a jolt of recognition coursed across his face. His vacant expression transformed into one of surprise, and Cyriana reddened and turned away from his gaze.

The wind picked up speed, and breathed life into the billowing purple sail. It was as though Borrum had heeded their prayers, giving them a fine wind and a relatively smooth ocean upon which to navigate. From *Aurora*'s decks, the Mages looked on as the kingdom which had once been their entire world grew smaller, until it was nothing more than a faint speck upon the horizon.

Nuada had generously given Christopher ancient ship charts and maps as navigational aids to discern the location of the *Jade Queen*. After several hours of being on the open ocean, however, Christopher realized that he desperately needed a more accurate guide to the *Jade Queen*'s location than the aging map parchments. The advanced technology on his tablet enabled him to track any ship on the high seas as long as he had access to its coordinates. He therefore sent an urgent message, to both Walter and Eva this time, reiterating his request for the vessel's coordinates. Technology would only assist with half the battle, though; magic would serve to ensure that they reached their destination speedily and safely.

Tristan joined Christopher at the helm, eager to participate in the ship's navigation. He seemed to be faring better than many of the other Mages, who already appeared seasick and were clearly unaccustomed to the roiling sway of the ship. Christopher welcomed him to the Jade Rebellion and informed Tristan of his plans to retrieve the ship's coordinates from Walter and Eva.

Tristan smiled jovially. "You will be wanting to pray to Artaios, the messenger god, for a speedy reply. Since its source is the spirit realm, magic is best facilitated by prayer." Christopher, unlike Miranda, was still skeptical about spirituality, and doubted whether these so-called "spirits" were in fact real, but he had seen enough with his own eyes to know that magic indeed was. He was willing to try anything to further the cause of the rebellion, however, and so the two men prayed to Artaios as they stood side by side at the helm of the ship.

The sun blazed above them as *Aurora* moved gracefully into the unknown expanse of the open ocean, an amethyst speckle on a vast sea of sapphires.

Stella Maris

"If some god shall wreck me in the wine-dark deep,
even so I will endure...
For already have I suffered full much,
and much have I toiled in perils of waves and war.
Let this be added to the tale of those."
— Homer

The next day, the seafarers woke to a placid ocean and a sky streaked with glorious shades of pink and gold, as if it were a tapestry painted by some divine being. Eva replied to Christopher with the ship's coordinates, and he rejoiced in that small victory. Christopher invited Tristan to the captain's quarters, where the two young men studied the navigation charts and attempted to situate the coordinates. After examining the charts for several minutes, they deduced that the *Jade Queen* was quite a bit closer to their location than they had originally expected. The ship was located about fifty nautical miles to the west, in the direction of Vei'arash.

The pair had bonded, and enjoyed talking well into the night that evening. Christopher was eager to know what life had been like for Tristan, growing up in the isolated bubble of Serrahan.

"It's all I've ever known," Tristan explained. Tristan's hair was a burnished shade of bronze, darker than the rest of his fellow Mages, and his stormy blue eyes resembled the ocean itself. Despite the intensity of his coloring, Tristan's features were delicate, in stark contrast to Christopher, who had pale hair and eyes, but hard, masculine features.

"It's hard to believe that, hundreds of years ago, my ancestors exchanged ideas and traded with yours," Christopher said. "And now the

Serrahan clans are sealed off from the rest of the world. It must have been incredibly frustrating to know that you couldn't leave."

"I haven't minded it much, but our village's isolation has certainly been a weight on Nuada's shoulders. For a long time, he has desired to revive the trading relationships of the past and cross the barrier that separates us from our allies, but he never found the opportunity until now. He always feared that if he made any rash moves, his people might end up like the Xeyan'na—exploited and enslaved by the AI Masters."

Tristan's expression then changed to an apologetic one, betraying his realization that Christopher was from the Barrens.

"I don't blame him," Christopher replied bitterly. "The AIs have treated my people shamefully ever since they discovered the abundance of resources within our borders. They care little for our spiritual relationship with the land, and they only seek to maximize the productivity of our fields, forests, and rivers. I fear that their exploitative mission will intensify with each passing year, until they completely destroy our culture and way of life. There is no stopping those demons."

"That is, unless we fight them," Tristan said. "With magic."

Christopher nodded grimly. "Magic is our only salvation at this point. It appears to have been the only reason your people survived the conquest of the AIs, and so we must use it as a weapon to eradicate them."

While the two men were conversing in the captain's quarters, *Aurora* suddenly jolted violently. Christopher and Tristan rushed up to the ship's helm, where they could see that the craft was approaching a violent squall. The vast storm enveloped the sky for miles, and seemed impossible to steer around. Fortunately, while the Mages had limited knowledge of seafaring, many of the rebels were seasoned sailors who had considerable experience with ship navigation.

One of the more experienced rebels, a stout man named Gregory, began to bellow commands for the others to follow.

"Trim the sail," he shouted to several other rebels, who obediently furled the sheet to preserve it and ensure that the ship would not be flung in all directions. Gregory then took control of the helm, trying to steer the bow head-on into the waves to prevent *Aurora* from capsizing. He also changed the vessel's course so that it was running with the wind, a maneuver which caused *Aurora* to pick up considerable speed. Cyriana's eyes widened in fear at the sight of the waves, which were several meters high, but she bravely clung to the ship's railings and tried to avoid retching.

"Pump the bilges and douse the galley stove," Gregory ordered. The rebels followed his orders diligently, however most of the Mages were instead praying to Borrum, god of the wind, and Llyr, god of the sea, that the storm would pass quickly.

Gregory seemed irritated by their efforts. "Your prayers won't save us. Go down to the lower decks and do what I ordered," he instructed the crew. Christopher, too, was skeptical that prayers would save them from the squall, and so he nodded in agreement with Gregory's commands.

Reluctantly, the Mages ceased their praying and filtered into the lower decks, where they assisted in draining the bilge waters from the ship's cabin. Despite their valiant efforts, however, the storm showed no signs of abating, and it was becoming increasingly harrowing with every passing moment. Towering sheets of water slammed in to the hull, and the vessel lurched from side to side, causing everyone on board to lose balance and fall over. Cyriana and several other Mages began to weep, praying that they would make it home safely to their families and friends.

Suddenly, Tristan's eyes glinted with an idea. He hurried toward the bow of the ship and, clutching the railing, uttered an incantation. Soon, a few other Mages overheard him, and they began to follow his lead and repeat the same phrase. Within a few moments, word had spread to all of the Mages, and they all clasped hands as they chanted the same words again and again.

With amazement, Christopher realized that they were recreating the same protective veil that existed around Serrahan simply through the power of their combined voices. In mere seconds, the waters surrounding *Aurora* calmed and quieted, and the wind became a gentle breeze. The feat stunned Gregory, who realized that a few simple prayers had, indeed, saved them from a catastrophe. All of the rebels applauded, overcome with joy and gratitude for their Mage allies. Cyriana beamed with pride for her lover, and the pair embraced warmly, celebrating their fresh victory.

Christopher was profoundly humbled by the act, and realized that it could be explained by nothing other than spiritual energy which had originated from the union of the Mages and the power of their united voices. He viewed the Mages with a newfound respect, as a race of people akin to demi-gods, who possessed gifts and talents beyond the grasp of ordinary mortals.

As it was already well past midnight, the rebels and Mages retreated to the crew's quarters, where all indulged in a hearty rest. When they awoke the next morning, it was already late, and the sun was high in the sky. The storm had abated, but the protection spell remained strong, though it was slowly beginning to dissipate. Christopher and Tristan again went below decks to the captain's quarters, to evaluate *Aurora's* location on the navigation charts.

As he studied the scrolls, Christopher's brow furrowed in confusion. "This must be wrong," he exclaimed. "According to the maps, we are less than a day's voyage away from the *Jade Queen*. But we departed several days after she did."

Tristan shrugged casually. "The high-speed winds last night must have propelled our ship toward the *Jade Queen*. Borrum must have been heeding our prayers when he sent that squall barreling toward us. Although it appeared deadly at the time, it was actually a blessing in disguise," he said with a grin.

Christopher nodded in agreement. "You may well be right. If that is the case, then I must contact Eva and Walter immediately, so that they can block communications between the *Jade Queen* and Central Command.

"I hope you are well rested, because if we indeed encounter the *Jade Queen* before evening arrives, we are in for a long day. We can buy ourselves some time by keeping the sails trimmed, but if these charts are correct, we will encounter Her Majesty, the *Queen*, sometime this afternoon."

Christopher looked at Tristan with pale grey eyes that reflected tranquility and poise, but also a vaguely discernable trace of fear. "Tell your fellow Mages that their prayers are needed now more than ever," he said softly.

Convergent Souls

"Our two souls therefore, which are one,
Though I must go, endure not yet
A breach, but an expansion,
Like gold to airy thinness beat."
— John Keats

Walter woke up that morning shaking, his body bathed in a layer of cold sweat. His dream had returned, the one he had had nearly a week ago before boarding the *Jade Queen*. He had dreamt that he was standing with Jonathan and Christopher on the decks of the *Jade Queen*, while the ship was being battered relentlessly by bombs dropped from military planes overhead. There was laughter all around them; it bounced off the decks and walls of the ship, as if the vessel were a massive echo chamber. Human limbs were strewn across the deck, and Emilia's head rolled eerily back and forth as the ship lurched in its own death throes. Elaine was nowhere to be seen, although he could hear the tortured cries of prisoners in the cabins below deck.

After eating breakfast, a tasteless combination of boiled potatoes and porridge, Walter found it difficult to keep the food down. The waves were choppy today, he guessed, since the ship seemed to rock from side to side with more violence than usual. Walter felt strangely alert and charged with electric anticipation; his senses were telling him that something important was about to happen. As though confirming his deepest suspicions, Walter's tablet suddenly vibrated with a message from Christopher.

Block comms immediately. We are closing in on you fast and will be there today, tonight at the latest.

Walter's eyes widened in disbelief, and his heart began to pound rapidly. So, it was finally happening. He did not know whether to welcome or fear the inevitable, although his terror certainly outweighed his optimism. He couldn't push the ominous images of death and destruction out of his head, no matter how intently he tried to focus his mind on positive thoughts.

He had no time to dwell on such matters, since Christopher had entrusted him with a critical task: that of blocking the AI guards' communication portal with Central Command. Walter wasted no time in alerting Eva of his intentions, and then got to work on hacking into the vessel's computer network. He had assumed that it would be simple, similar to how he had hacked the prison network, but this time it was quite a bit more challenging. He couldn't pick up the signal for the network, as it appeared to be out of range of his tablet. Finally, after what seemed like ages of fiddling with the device underneath his blanket, he found the system that he needed to hack. Walter recognized the network by its exotic encryption, and he was able to hack it with a combination of perseverance and ingenuity. When he studied the voluminous source code for the network, he immediately noticed that it had recently sent a communication back to Central Command. On a closer examination of the contents of this message, Walter's worst fears were confirmed:

The rebels will be here tomorrow at approximately 16h00. Ensure hovercopters are ready, primed, and stocked with weapons for maximum bombing capability. We freely give up our lives in service of the Great Mission.

It was too late. Central Command already knew about Christopher's plans to take over the ship. The AI guards were willing to give up their "lives" so that everyone, and everything, on the *Jade Queen* could be destroyed. What better way for the AIs to get rid of political dissidents than by trapping them all on board a ship at the same time and then bombing the ship into oblivion? Walter groaned in despair. They shouldn't have waited so long before blocking the communication portal, since it was now too late. It seemed as if the AIs were always one step ahead of them, no matter how hard the rebels tried to outmaneuver them.

Walter's hands trembled as he messaged Eva with the tragic news. She messaged back with a brief reply: *we are doomed.* Walter began to sob beneath his blanket as he digested the painful irony that, right now, Elaine might be meters away from him, but they might die without ever seeing each other one last time. How he longed to look at her auburn hair and freckled face even for one moment, before he left this world forever. If he had the chance to speak to her, he would tell her how sorry he was. If only he hadn't revealed the truth about the AI Masters' plans to construct a diamond mine in Te'yara, she would have still been a free woman today. But he would tell her, too, that even though he blamed himself for her capture and imprisonment, he loved her more than anything in the world. And he would ask her, one last time, for forgiveness.

The rest of the day passed for Walter in a blurry haze. His mind was engulfed with sadness, a heavy wave of melancholy that overwhelmed every other emotion or thought, rendering him numb to the outside world. Nothing mattered anymore. His sadness was as all-encompassing as death would soon be. When he died, he would cease to exist, and all emotions—including sadness—would dissolve and become meaningless. He cared little about the prospect of his own death—on the contrary, he welcomed it as respite from his despair—but he could not bear the thought of Elaine losing her precious life. Walter had never been a very spiritual man, and what was happening right now only confirmed his cynical suspicions that God—or any spiritual forces, for that matter—had never actually existed. If there was a God, or any divine powers whatsoever, present on this earth, they would never let a person as beautiful and compassionate as Elaine die at such a young age.

His depressive state was so dulling, so numbing to his thoughts, that Walter eventually fell back asleep around noon. His sleep was deep and dreamless, a refuge from the visceral pain of melancholy.

When he awoke, it must have been several hours later. He had lost any concept of time, so he did not know whether it was still day or night. When he looked outside his cage, to his amazement he saw Christopher standing outside of it, holding the keys to the cell. Walter thought that he must certainly be dreaming, or in the afterlife already—how could Christopher have found him, and why weren't they all dead by now? He closed his eyes to go back to sleep, but Christopher urged him awake.

"Walter, there is no time to sleep. The Mages have stunned the AI guards with a spell, so they have temporarily lost consciousness. We must destroy them now, while we still have the element of surprise on our side."

Christopher then unlocked the cell and handed Walter a *balayan*, Walter immediately recognized it as the one he had practiced with in those training sessions many weeks ago. The sword was as striking as Walter remembered it, its elegant mahogany hilt engraved with intricate patterns and symbols. Walter studied the image of the fire lizard, and recalled that the same creature had been fossilized inside the amber ring worn by the crone from the Jamestown tavern. It was the symbol of Elaine's village, Te'yara, which stood to be destroyed by Crystal City's rapacious appetite for wealth and ostentation.

An old, familiar feeling overcame Walter then, a feeling he used to have during his childhood dreams. In those dreams, he was confident and strong; he had broad shoulders and sinewy, sculpted arms like his brother, and he rescued people effortlessly. As Walter walked out of his cell, the world around him spun and he felt lightweight, as if he were traveling through a portal—perhaps the hazy, incoherent space between dreams and reality. Not a single AI was in sight, but Walter could see the faces of all of the prisoners he recognized from the Crate, along with faces of other prisoners that he didn't recognize.

"Is that the master key?" Walter asked Christopher, his voice slow and murky, as though he were talking underwater. Christopher nodded cautiously.

"We can't free the prisoners just yet," Christopher warned. "We will release Eva, along with all of the rebels who exchanged places with their siblings in the Crate. But the other prisoners must remain captive until we are certain we can trust them."

Walter was barely listening to Christopher, though; he was looking into all the cages frantically, with a single thought paramount in his mind: Elaine. Where *was* she? After checking numerous cages, his heart racing whenever he thought he saw her, Walter was about to give up. Just before he did, he heard the faintest, tiniest voice reach him from afar, and although he could barely hear it, he knew beyond a doubt that it was hers.

"Walter? Is that you?"

Walter spun around to see Elaine—albeit a thinner, paler version, but still Elaine—with her long auburn hair and green eyes rimmed with freckles. She was wearing the garb of a prisoner, a simple cotton dress that reached her knees, but to Walter she still appeared to be the most beautiful princess imaginable. Walter's heart skipped a beat at the sight of her, and he was suddenly flooded with emotion. All of the grief, frustration, and joy that he had felt over the past few months stirred and rose within him. Walter could not hold back tears any longer, and he wept openly at the sight of his love.

"Elaine… there is nothing to be afraid of any more, my love. We are going to save you," he said with a trembling, joyful voice.

Elaine eyed him warily, but Walter could detect a faint glimmer of relief in her expression. Walter moved to open the cage door, but Christopher held his hand back.

"Wait," Christopher cautioned. From where he was standing, Christopher could not see the inside the cell Walter was trying to open. "The prisoners cannot be trusted just yet. We don't know how much they have been brainwashed—"

But Walter refused to listen to his friend. He forcefully pushed Christopher away, and then glanced at him apologetically, surprised at his violent aggression.

"I'm sorry, Christopher. I won't ask to release any more of the prisoners right now, only her. Please? What harm could a young girl do to us?"

Christopher looked wounded, offended that Walter would have shoved him like that. And then, Elaine recognized her brother. "Christopher, why are you here?"

Christopher now recognized Elaine's voice and realized that Walter was speaking to his beloved sister, his motivation for having joined the Jade Rebellion. He smiled broadly at Elaine and opened his arms welcomingly to her. The joyful expression on his face soon faded, though, and his brow furrowed with confusion.

"Wait. You knew who Elaine was all this time, and you never once told me? I *told* you my sister's name was Elaine. You must have known she was my sister," he said irritably.

Walter's emotions were running too high for him to respond coherently to Christopher, but he didn't want to offend his companion. He realized that he would eventually have to divulge his secret—that he was the reason Elaine was imprisoned here in the first place—and the thought of doing so filled him with immense trepidation. He wondered if Christopher would even accept him as part of the Jade Rebellion anymore once he knew the truth. He dreaded the prospect, but his elation in seeing Elaine outweighed the negativity of those thoughts. Walter pushed them to the back of his mind.

Fortunately, Christopher seemed to be distracted by the task of freeing Elaine from her cage. When the other prisoners noticed what Christopher was doing, they shook the bars of their cages and pleaded to be released. They were clearly tired of being locked up in cramped, dirty enclosures. Some had fallen ill from the acute scent of mold and the rocking motion of the ship, which was amplified in the ship's lower decks. Christopher eyed them warily.

"We will release you in due time," he assured them. The prisoners glared at him jealously, resentful of the power he wielded over them.

Elaine stepped out of her cage like a fragile young fawn learning to stand for the first time, then hugged her brother warmly. She did not have the same affectionate attitude toward Walter, however, and although he longed to hold her, he kept his distance. He realized that she may have been brainwashed by the AIs, or she might simply blame him for her capture. Some of his initial enthusiasm at seeing her gave way to level-headedness; he was prepared to wait for her forgiveness.

There was little time to dwell on his feelings for Elaine, however, since they still needed to free Eva and the other rebels. Walter and Christopher rushed over to Eva's cage and released her. As Walter and Eva came face to face for the first time, Walter noticed how strong the resemblance was between Eva and Emilia. Eva's skin was considerably lighter, and her eyes were a softer shade of blue, but she had the same angular jaw, high cheekbones, and fiercely determined expression. Eva smiled gratefully at Walter when she saw him, and Walter realized that she still didn't know the truth about her sister's death.

"Thank you, Walter, for all you have done," she said, gently clasping Walter's hands. She then turned to Christopher. "You are Christopher, I assume. Where is Em?" she demanded.

Christopher shifted uneasily, and then his eyes flickered away from her unsettling gaze. "We will tell you later. There is no time now." Walter and Christopher then released the remainder of the rebels, who were thrilled to reunite with one another. As the rebels were embracing each other warmly, Tristan and Cyriana descended from above deck and urged everyone to go upstairs to see what was happening.

Tristan's expression was grave as he addressed the rebels. "We spotted some strange aircraft—they're off in the distance right now, but heading this way rather quickly. Perhaps they plan to capture us?"

Walter shivered at the young man's words. He glanced at Cyriana and felt an uncanny flicker of recognition. Jonathan's friend? Why was she here?

"No, they don't plan to capture us," Walter replied bitterly. "I decoded a message delivered by the AIs to Central Command, and those are military hovercopters sent by the AI headquarters to destroy this vessel. To put it bluntly, they intend to bomb the hell out of us."

Shortly after Walter made the terrible announcement, Cyriana and Tristan glanced at each other knowingly, as if they were planning to do something great. Tristan cleared his throat and addressed the crowd, his face glowing with confident pride.

"I don't know what you had in mind, but in my opinion, we need a protection spell over this vessel as soon as possible. This is a very large ship, but we managed to create one over *Aurora*, so we can likely do the same for the *Jade Queen*. We'll need all hands up on deck. Everyone, including those in the cages down there, needs be up on deck to recite the spell," he said in an authoritative tone.

Christopher cringed at the thought of letting the brainwashed prisoners out of their cages, but he realized it was their only chance.

One by one, the rebels released the captives. The liberated prisoners wore desolate, fearful expressions on their faces, as if they loathed and distrusted their liberators. Christopher was overwhelmed by the daunting task of calming them down while they moaned and complained about their plight. The escapees were better behaved, and one of the escapees was particularly quiet—Jonathan looked more contemplative than angry, as though he were patiently waiting for something to happen.

Christopher was not worried about the Mages' ability to cast a protection spell over the *Jade Queen*, but he feared that the AI guards might awaken and ruin the enchantment midway through. All the AI guards had been struck with a sleeping curse, which the Mages had used to immobilize their programming, but it was temporary, and nobody knew how long, precisely, it would last. They desperately needed it to hold out successfully while they combined their resources to complete the spell.

Another equally pressing concern was the group of recently liberated prisoners. None of them appeared to be in any kind of mood to take orders, let alone cooperate with the strange newcomers who had overtaken the ship. Cyriana expressed concern that the liberated prisoners might refuse to obey Tristan's instructions. It was too late to cast an obedience charm on all of them; they were too great in number, and the Mages needed all of their stored energy for the protection spell.

"There must be a way to get everyone to cooperate," Tristan replied stubbornly.

None of the liberated prisoners looked like they were willing to do so. Some of them pounded their fists on the wooden deck of the ship, shrieking with rage, while others stared at the rebels with a fierce and menacing expression. Fortunately, none of them dared to attack the rebels, who were much better armed than they were. While this chaos was playing out on the decks of the *Jade Queen*, in the background the low and steady thrum of aircraft began to sound. The hovercopters were not only audible, but clearly visible; they had first appeared as distant smudges on the horizon, but they were approaching the ship at an alarming rate.

Finally, when everyone had congregated on the ship's main deck, Tristan, Walter, and Christopher assumed positions near the helm, and Tristan addressed the crowd gathered before him.

"Those hovercopters that you see in the distance," Tristan announced, his voice ringing melodiously like a bell in the cool air, "are coming this way with the intention of destroying us all. So, if you wish to live, I ask you to follow my instructions carefully."

The liberated prisoners glared at Tristan distrustfully, skeptical of his bohemian-style *Magus* robes and his eccentric demeanor. Many of them had spent months imprisoned inside the Crate, and their minds had been manipulated by the AIs so deeply that they now distrusted humans more than AIs. They had been insidiously re-programmed to resent dissidents of the Empire and to regard them as the threatening "Other." However, at this stage many of them were too disoriented, undernourished, and fatigued to understand what, exactly, was happening.

Jonathan had been trapped inside the Crate longer than most of the other prisoners, and he was keenly aware of the rebels' intentions. He knew that they were plotting to revolt against the Empire and disrupt the AI Masters' plans to travel to Eurydice, and he firmly believed that anything that interfered with the AIs' plans was inherently wrong. In Jonathan's view, there was nothing more righteous than the AIs' mission to colonize Eurydice. Above all, he resented magic, and the threat that it posed to their mission.

He now realized that he couldn't wait any longer—whatever absurd spell they were planning to cast could not be allowed to succeed. He studied Tristan, handsome and clothed in his fine *Magus* robes, and noticed that he was standing next to a strikingly beautiful woman whom he vaguely remembered, though couldn't quite say how. Her hand was intertwined in Tristan's as the young mage recited the incantation and instructed the liberated prisoners and escapees to repeat the words of the spell after him. Suddenly, Jonathan was seized with a venomous rage, and he longed to personally witness the death of this self-proclaimed wizard who spoke with such arrogance and confidence, and who believed that he could defend himself against the AIs' glorious campaign.

"Don't listen to him!" Jonathan shouted, standing up on a platform near the ship's prow so that everyone had a clear view of him. "He is lying to you. The hovercopters are not going to destroy everyone on this ship; they are here to liberate the loyal servants of the Empire. These rebels are traitors, they have betrayed the Empire, and they must pay with their lives. When the hovercopters arrive, the AIs will first come to rescue all who are faithful to the Empire, and then they will eliminate the traitors."

The liberated prisoners and escapees listened to him attentively, and some of them expressed agreement with his words. Christopher looked appalled by their blind acceptance of Jonathan's lies. His words had an undesirable effect; all of the rescued prisoners were chattering amongst themselves now, rather than listening to Tristan's protection spell.

Walter was perhaps the most stunned by the scene unfolding before him. It was a surreal situation, made even more surreal by the fact that his own brother was insinuating that he wanted Walter and his friends to die. He barely recognized the man who now addressed the crowd: frail and tired-looking, with a resentful, bitter expression on his face. That man was radically different from the person Walter remembered his brother to be.

Without quite knowing what he would say, Walter addressed the crowd boldly. "How can you trust a man who wants his own brother dead? We rebels are no different from all of you released prisoners—we were also born and raised in the Empire, and then we were ostracized for speaking out against it. You, too, are rebels; you have simply forgotten who you were. The only difference between us is that you were brainwashed into believing that the AIs are great and glorious. Do you truly wish to follow the orders of those corrupted machines when they inflict so much pain and suffering on others? They were your slave masters; they kept you trapped, inhumanely, in cages not even suited for farm animals. They denied you your freedom. Now, they are coming with hovercopters and bombs to murder you in cold blood. Do not listen to this man—my very own brother—who preaches his loyalty to them."

"There is another way, my friends, and that is love. Join us in casting this protection spell, and if it works, then you will protect yourself and your fellow comrades from an untimely death. If not, then we will all die, united by the bonds of love. But at least we will die trying. To surrender now is to admit defeat to your captors, your torturers, your masters. To fight back is to prove yourself a true rebel, a champion of freedom."

Jonathan regarded his brother with bitter disgust. He was disturbed by the change in the crowd's mood—the liberated prisoners and escapees looked fearful and chastened by Walter's words, as if they were contemplating siding with the rebels in order to save their own lives. Jonathan was desperate to persuade them that their fears were unfounded.

"He is trying to trick you," he proclaimed to the terrified crowd as the thrum of the approaching aircraft became deafening.

Suddenly, and without warning, a small grenade struck the ship, destroying a piece of the deck and knocking over several of the liberated prisoners. The crowd looked upward and saw that a hovercopter was directly above the ship, several thousand feet in the air. Many of the liberated prisoners began to weep and scream in terror.

Tristan saw that the situation had become urgent, and they needed to begin the incantation with or without the assistance of the liberated prisoners and escapees. He held Cyriana's hand tightly and whispered to her softly, "I promised your father that you'd come home safely, and I'm not going to give up on that promise." He then straightened his shoulders, summoned all of his strength, and began to chant the incantation for the protection spell. The other Mages immediately followed suit, and their voices mingled powerfully together, creating a resilient barrier of sound.

As they recited these words, a thin, protective layer of mist began to form around the *Jade Queen*—the same purple dust suspended in air that had kept Serrahan safe for centuries, and had sheltered *Aurora* from the storm. All of the liberated prisoners and escapees, including Jonathan, were awestruck by the miracle that was unfolding in front of them.

"What is this witchcraft?" Jonathan shouted angrily, but his voice could barely be heard above the wall of sound and magic that seemed to have encompassed the entire vessel. The rebels had been listening carefully to the incantation, which was a basic, repetitive pattern of words from the Serrahan language: *Siochra Beatha Rehaya*. The rebels now joined their voices to the spell, and with each voice that was added, the protective layer of mist became thicker and thicker. Suddenly, fragments of what appeared to be plastic rained down onto the deck of the ship, and everyone looked up to see that a bomb had hit the protective layer directly, but only the shards of the casing had managed to penetrate the wall of mist. The bomb itself had bounced off of the wall and exploded in the sky above, transforming the sky into a hellish vista of flames and chaos. Had the bomb penetrated the layer of mist, the ship may have been destroyed, and its occupants would have been killed by the force of the explosion or drowned in a watery grave at the bottom of the sea.

Some of the fragments of bomb casings had injured several escapees, and one elderly man had a large fragment embedded in his leg. Jonathan was bleeding from his neck, as he had been struck with a tiny fragment, although the wound was not very deep. With tears in his eyes, Jonathan realized that the AI Masters had betrayed him, deceiving him into believing that they would bring him to Eurydice when the time came. During his stay in prison, Jonathan had become obsessively consumed with plans to accompany the AI Masters to Eurydice, and to witness the expansion of the glorious AI race. Now, it was apparent that their promises of bringing him along on their mission had been not only deceptive, but patently false. The AIs couldn't care less if he died ignominiously, and they clearly felt he was no worthier of saving than the rebels themselves.

Walter approached Jonathan cautiously, genuinely concerned about his wound. "Brother, are you injured? Why are you weeping? The Mages are saving us."

The liberated prisoners and escapees, seeing that the Mages' incantation was somehow, unbelievably, working, began to join their voices into the spell. Although everyone's voice was unique, an incredible phenomenon occurred: the voices mingled together, like threads in a patchwork quilt, so that they became a seamless, uniform weapon of sound, which dramatically increased the density of the protective barrier forming around the ship. Even Jonathan, who now knew that it was in his best interests to side with the rebels, half-heartedly joined his voice into the spell.

Once the barrier had fully encompassed the ship, the spell was over. Tristan, who had led the incantation, had felt the magic coursing powerfully through his veins, filling him with adrenaline. Yet now, the magic within him was ebbing, and the spell had finally run its course. He breathed the last word, and then an eerie silence fell over the ship; nobody dared to continue speaking. The spell was, in the jargon of the Mages, "perfected," and with the final words of the incantation, Tristan had made certain that the protective shield would linger above the *Jade Queen* for many moons. Eventually, the hovercopters pulled away in retreat, as the bombers realized that it was futile to continue trying to penetrate the powerful encasement now surrounding the vessel.

Everyone was immensely joyful, and the rebels, along with a few of the escapees and liberated prisoners, embraced warmly to congratulate each other on their valiant efforts. Walter could hear voices from below deck, though, and his brow furrowed in confusion, as he had previously assumed that everyone was above deck. With a wave of dread, Walter realized that the sleeping spell on the AI guards had likely worn off. He whispered his suspicions to Tristan and Christopher, and the trio went downstairs to investigate the source of the voices.

In confirmation of their worst fears, the three men walked into the captain's quarters to find one of the AI guards transmitting a message through the ship's communication portal with Central Command. She was speaking through a microphone to another AI Master whose angular, stern face loomed large on a projection screen. The AI looked like she was operating at half capacity, as if the spell had not yet fully worn off. When the humans walked into the room, the AI instantly spun around, wielding a *catan* in self-defense.

"What have you done?" she asked, her voice sounding strained and exasperated as it echoed in the small chamber. Christopher immediately unsheathed his *balayan*, brandishing it threateningly.

"We saved everyone on this ship from a terrible and untimely death," Christopher retorted. "Including yourself, I might add." Walter and Tristan also unsheathed their weapons, and the men cornered the AI, who looked both spiteful and exhausted. Christopher moved closer to the AI, eager for a fight, but Walter restrained him. As these distractions were going on, Tristan wisely managed to turn off the projection screen and interrupt the connection between the AI and her correspondent. Before the conflict escalated any further, Eva entered the room.

"The AIs are waking," she announced as the men turned around to look at her in surprise. Walter noticed that when she spoke in an authoritative tone, Eva bore a particularly uncanny resemblance to her sister, so much so that it made Walter shiver.

When she saw the AI guard, Eva fell silent, and tears began to pool in her eyes. She stepped closer to the AI and outstretched an arm toward her in a gesture of friendship. Christopher moved to step in between them, but she pushed him gently to the side.

"Asana," she breathed the name softly, as though the word itself were a mere spirit.

Christopher was confused. "You know this… person?"

Eva was deeply engrossed in her own thoughts and she ignored Christopher's question. The AI and the human were so close to each other, so absorbed in looking into the other's eyes, that everyone was reluctant to interfere with the dreamlike moment.

Eventually, Eva snapped out of her reverie, and turned toward the bewildered men. "Asana was a guard at the weapons factory I used to work at as a child. She understood that my parents were starving, so she allowed me to smuggle weapons out of the factory so that I could hunt food for them. I considered her my friend. She never... betrayed me," she said tearfully.

Asana's expression softened at the sight of Eva, but then it became colder once again as she noticed that the men had not yet sheathed their weapons.

"I will order the other AI guards to surrender," the AI said, her voice hollow. "I do not want any violence. But you must agree that you will steer us safely back to shore so that we can return to Crystal City."

Christopher seemed disappointed in this option; he had yearned for a good, satisfying fight with the robot. But Walter and Tristan both breathed a sigh of relief.

Eva studied the AI in admiration as Asana walked out of the captain's quarters. "I feel such a powerful connection to her," she murmured, her face glowing radiantly.

Walter was unsettled by how closely Eva resembled her sister, and he averted his eyes from her uncomfortably. Being around her was like being in the same room as a ghost. Tristan seemed to be charmed by her; he was particularly impressed by the strange, otherworldly way in which she had communicated with the AI.

"Let us go find the other AIs, to ensure that they have agreed to surrender. And then, let us celebrate our victory," Tristan said merrily.

Walter was not thinking of victory—his mind was instead focused on the enormous tasks that lay ahead of them. He knew that one task, in particular, would need to be made the first priority of the new Rebellion: saving Elaine's village, Te'yara, from destruction. But Walter also knew that a true rebellion was nothing without its rituals and symbols. Before embarking on their daunting mission, they needed to celebrate an inauguration. Not of one leader, but of many.

The Jade Dawn

"It is at the time of dawn that we must commune with the gods."
— Apollonius of Tyana

As dawn broke over the *Jade Queen*, sunlight filtered into the lavender mist surrounding the ship and enveloped everything in a dewy, ethereal glow. Barely anyone had slept that night, since most of the ship's occupants had stayed up late celebrating victory. Everyone had been in a jovial mood, except for the AIs—and Eva: she had instead spent the night mourning in a private chamber below decks after Christopher had finally revealed the truth about Emilia to her. The moment he had broken the news, her eyes had become wild with fury and despair, and he had feared that a raging madness would overtake her. Her shrieks of anger had mixed in with the whoops and cries of celebration echoing throughout the *Jade Queen*, and then she had stained her clothes with a steady stream of tears. Christopher had left her alone to mourn, and he had stood outside the door of her chamber quietly weeping as he listened to her guttural wailing. He knew what it was like to lose a sister, and he could imagine how terrible he would feel if Elaine had died.

The AIs had reluctantly agreed to surrender, on the condition that they were granted safe passage back to Crystal City. The Mages had prayed to Borrum and cast a strong enchantment upon *Aurora* to set sail for the capital of Khalendar. Their plan was for the AIs to board *Aurora* and return to Crystal City; once they had arrived, *Aurora* would depart for Serrahan once more. That way, none of the rebels needed to endanger themselves accompanying the AIs back to Crystal City, and the venerated ship of the Mages could return safely to its kingdom.

As for the liberated prisoners and escapees, many of them had tempered their hostility and now regarded the rebels with a newfound respect. Both groups took over the crew's quarters, and they slept side by side with the rebels and Mages. There was still an ample supply of food for everyone, and there was plenty of fresh water due to an ocean desalination mechanism on board. The arrangement was oddly harmonious, although everyone knew that this new state of peace was extremely fragile.

Christopher, Tristan, Walter, Miranda, and Cyriana had appointed themselves the new leaders of the Jade Rebellion, although they agreed that the present leadership did not adequately reflect the true composition of the Rebellion. While there were three rebels and two Mages, there were no liberated prisoners or escapees in the leadership ranks as of yet. To address this problem, and to pay homage to their late leader Emilia, the new leaders decided that her sister Eva should be appointed as the sixth leader of the Rebellion.

The leaders spread word throughout the *Jade Queen* that they would be holding an inauguration ceremony, and the ship's occupants congregated on deck to attend and hear the first speech of the Rebellion. The AIs had already boarded *Aurora*, and with the machines gone, the rebels felt a new, electrifying sense of freedom.

Walter was entrusted with the task of speech-giving; Christopher had complimented him on his oratory the day before, and had encouraged his friend to speak. Walter felt uneasy performing this task—he had always regarded himself as an outcast and an introvert. At the same time, however, he felt a strong desire to overcome his fears and misgivings.

He stood at the helm of the *Jade Queen*, his body weak and sore from days of confinement, but his mind vibrant and energized. He surveyed the crowd who stood before him, a motley crew of people of all ages and generations, of all backgrounds and races: people with black hair and fair skin from Crystal City, Xeyan'na natives with auburn hair and freckled skin, and the Mages with their silver-blonde coloring and delicate features. They were all united now, united in dissent against the Empire.

Walter looked out into the sea of faces gazing at him with such hopeful expressions, and his eyes settled on Elaine. She looked sad and forlorn, as if all that had transpired in the past few days, including achieving her freedom, had given her little comfort. Walter realized that she was likely saddened by the thought that it might already be too late for her family and friends in Te'yara. He had not mentioned anything to Christopher about the Khalendi government's plans to build the massive diamond mine and displace his native village, but now he rather spontaneously decided that it would be best to inform everyone of this fact at his first speech. It would be painfully difficult, and Christopher would likely be angry at him for not having spoken of it earlier, but that was a risk he was willing to take. The rebels needed to know about the mine project, because it was symbolic of the broader plans of the AI Masters and their Empire. It illustrated their ambition to systematically steal that which was not freely given to them, motivated by a rapacious greed and a willingness to sacrifice anything for the glory of their Empire. That was why, Walter believed, saving Te'yara needed to become the first priority of the Rebellion.

"Friends and comrades," Walter announced, his voice ringing out toward every corner of the enormous vessel, "I am deeply grateful for the privilege of speaking before you as one of the leaders of the Jade Rebellion. I am inspired by all of you, by your resilience in the face of adversity, by your fighting spirit, and, most of all, by the way you have come together, joined in this common cause. Although some of you are not familiar with the Rebellion, in the days and weeks to come I hope that you will become well acquainted with its goals and purposes. You have already proven yourselves worthy of joining it when you helped to construct this beautiful, impregnable shield over the *Jade Queen*, to protect all of us from harm.

"Although I can't imagine what some of you have gone through during your imprisonment, I have the utmost faith in the perseverance of the human spirit. I have faith that all of you will recover, despite the fact that you likely still have deep wounds inflicted by the traumatic events of your past. We all have faced demons, but the bright sun of the future shines upon us. This morning our lives are filled with promise, for now we have a force more powerful than greed on our side. We have spiritual energy from the mystical incantations and rites of these wise Mages, who have pledged their allegiance to us in the battles that lie ahead.

"Yesterday, they helped us all perform nothing short of a miracle. For that, we are eternally grateful, and deeply in their debt. I have spoken to Tristan, one of the Mages and a fellow leader of the Rebellion, who you will all get to know well in the coming months. He has assured me that the Mages will give us their full and unwavering support, as long as we promise to uphold our side of the bargain. The bargain is that, in exchange for their help and resources, we will travel to Vei'arash and find the shamans and animal spirits that were once stolen from the Mages' territory.

"Once we have found those wise men, and the spirits they summoned, we will bring them safely back to Zeyanara. We will ensure that they are protected in Zeyanara and that they help to restore the noble Serrahan clans to their former glory.

"Once we have fulfilled our pact with our allies, we must move on to the priorities of the Rebellion. Anyone who wishes to abandon the Rebellion may do so freely when we return from Vei'arash, although we cannot guarantee your safety. You may very well be arrested by the AI Masters, or the Khalendi government, or anyone in Khalendar who suspects you of treason against the Empire.

"In order to help you make this choice, I would like the next few months to be a kind of initiation period for you, a time to teach you about the aims and ideals of the Rebellion. While I was imprisoned in the Crate for nearly a week, I had a plenty of time alone to ponder such things. I have also discussed these ideals with my friends.

"Before I share them with you, I would like to pay homage to the first and greatest leader of the Jade Rebellion, Emilia." As he said this, Walter's eyes fell upon Eva, who was standing in the crowd, her eyes welling up at the mention of her sister's name.

"Emilia was one of the most inspiring women I've ever met, not just because she was a rebel, but because she was a visionary, and passionately believed in creating a better world. I remember the very first day I met her—I was afraid of her because she looked like a hardened warrior. But it was always her way to have a cold, fighter's exterior, yet to be kind and gentle on the inside. She accepted me in the rebel's camp despite having few reasons to do so, she helped me to cast aside my personal doubts, and she taught me how to become a warrior. She died fighting for the Rebellion, for all of our freedom, and for that sacrifice we are indebted to her. That is why I would like to appoint her sister, Eva—who I know embodies the same fighting spirit as Emilia—as another leader of the Rebellion.

"I'm sure that Eva has a lot more to tell you about her sister, so I'd like to invite her to say a few words if she wishes," he said, looking at Eva fondly.

Eva seemed startled by Walter's invitation, but also grateful for the chance to speak. Her eyes were still filled with tears, and she held back her sobs as she stood near Walter at the helm to address everyone in the crowd.

"My sister will forever be remembered as a hero and a rebel. But to me, she was always simply my sister. When I was growing up with her in Fewsbury, I knew her as one of the most hardworking, loyal factory workers I had ever met. She was naive, and willing to give up her life in service of the Empire. But beyond this, she was a girl of many dreams. Her life was monotonous, but her dreary reality was more than offset by the vividness of her imagination. I have no idea when she first discovered her magical abilities, but I know that, like me, she accessed them through the power of imagination. She dreamed of a world that was better than the one that existed before her eyes. And until I disappeared, she was content with mere dreams. When I was captured and taken to the Crate, though, she wanted a way to realize her dreams; she finally had a reason to cast aside the monotony of her daily life, to discard her naiveté, and to stand up to her slave masters. And I am forever grateful that she did so. For, without her drive and passion, none of us would be enjoying freedom today. She was the founder of the Rebellion, and she built a legacy that we should all be proud of.

"On this beautiful morning, let us remember Emilia, and all of the others who died fighting for our freedom," she said tearfully.

"Thank you very much, Eva," Walter added. "Now, I will share with you the principles of the Rebellion. They are tentative, and can be added to with public input, but for now, I will outline the basic ones I have already agreed upon with my friends. The first is *justice*: there can be no true reform without justice. Justice means rectifying wrongs that have been done to others in the past, and it means standing up for the weak when they are crushed by the strong. The second is *allegiance*: we will co-operate with all of our allies, including the Mages and the Xeyan'na. Our allies will strengthen us, and we will strengthen them in return. We will never break any bargains we have made with them. The third is *democracy*: our leaders are not dictators. We will not replicate the hierarchy of the Empire, and we will listen carefully to the suggestions of all of our fellow rebels. Our leaders will help formulate the broad strokes of plans, but it is for all of us to fill in the details. Although the first leaders of the Rebellion have been appointed, we encourage others to join our leadership ranks. The fourth is *empathy*: this principle is at the heart of the Rebellion. If we are to overturn the Empire, we need to understand the main things that it lacks. And this is one of the keys. The Empire is not empathetic to human life, spiritual life, animals, and the environment. The Empire only cares about its ultimate goals and profits. We, as rebels, need to embody this one value above all others. We will learn magical abilities from the Mages, but we will use our powers in moderation. We will learn fighting techniques from our fellow rebels, but we will restrain ourselves from violence and aggression. We seek to minimize bloodshed, so we will use tactics such as negotiation and defensive spells to avoid sparking conflict. We do not seek to destroy the Empire's inhabitants, only to reform the system in which they live.

"And there you have it. The four cornerstone principles of the Jade Rebellion, which form the acronym JADE. Hold these principles close to your heart, and never forget them during the long journey ahead of us.

"Now, to illustrate how these principles might operate in action, I will briefly introduce the first priority of the Rebellion. Once we have fulfilled our bargain with the Mages, we must travel swiftly to Te'yara, a small village in the southeastern Barrens that is threatened by a diamond mining project." Walter glanced at Elaine, who appeared distressed by his words. He intentionally avoided Christopher's gaze, but he could feel his friend's eyes burning into him.

"At the present moment, we have no way of knowing exactly how far this project has progressed, but it is imperative that we find out. Our Mage allies may be able to gather this intelligence for us, or we can find the necessary information ourselves. In brief, the AI Masters plan to construct this mine directly over the ancient village and ancestral burial grounds, displacing thousands of villagers from their homes in the process. To succeed in our mission, we need to put each of the four principles into action, and we need everyone to work together to stop the mine. What is at stake is the future of the Empire itself. By stopping this single project, we can send a strong message to Central Command that we refuse to stand idly by while the resources of our allies are stolen from them to satiate the infinite greed of the Khalendi elites. Let me be clear about this: there are people who might die, or permanently lose their homes, all for the sake of diamonds to decorate the arms and necks of the wealthiest citizens of Crystal City. We must send a loud message that we will not allow the project to proceed."

There was a loud roar of approval from the crowd, although when Walter looked around for Christopher, he was nowhere to be seen. Walter felt sick to his stomach at the thought of Christopher's anger, but he was also energized by the crowd's applause. For a brief moment, he allowed himself to forget the repercussions of his past silence, and revel in the knowledge that it had finally been broken.

Tiny Crystals

"Humanity has the stars in its future, and that future is too important to be lost under the burden of juvenile folly and ignorant superstition."
— Isaac Asimov

The tension between Walter and Christopher was palpable as the leaders of the Jade Rebellion met in the captain's quarters for their first council meeting. Christopher deliberately avoided Walter's eyes as Walter looked at him apologetically, hoping to make peace. Miranda, fortunately, was a calming personality in the midst of two strong male egos, and she tried valiantly to dissolve the tension in the room and change the subject from the topic most likely on their minds.

"Before we start talking about other business, I believe we should discuss the situation of the liberated prisoners," Miranda said. "I would be interested in hearing your thoughts about this issue, but in my honest opinion, the decision to release them from their cages was premature. Even the escapees should be confined to cages at the moment. Of course, it was perhaps necessary to have as many bodies on deck as possible for the protection spell, but now that the spell has been cast, we must remember that many of them are still mentally unstable. Tristan, do you think the Mages could help us with their healing process?"

Tristan was distracted by the anger radiating from Christopher, but he answered Miranda's question politely. "The Mages would be more than happy to lend a hand to that task. You are more experienced than we are in healing, however, and you know the escapees better than we do. What was your impression of their mental states when you released them from the Cabin of Lost Souls?"

"They were slowly beginning to remember their pasts, and develop some respect for the rebels who saved them from the prison," Miranda replied, "but many of them were not ready to be let free into the wider world. I could sense that some lingering traces of AI propaganda remained imprinted onto their psyches, and it will take a great deal more time to erase that completely. I have asked the rebels to keep a close eye on them."

Christopher finally seemed tempted to join into the discussion. "The escapees clearly despised being trapped in the Cabin of Lost Souls. They frequently tried to escape the cabin, and many of them suffered from painful seizures when they tried to breach the protective barrier. If we lock them up in cages, they will detest us even more than they did before," he said gloomily.

Tristan's brow furrowed in concern. "They may still have scars from the AI experiments, and we must be vigilant. I agree with Christopher, though. Because we are trying to forge an alliance with them, we must be careful not to harm or anger them. There must be some way to help them heal while they are on the ship—perhaps through voluntary therapy sessions. I will speak to my fellow Mages tomorrow about it, but as I said, I am sure they will be more than willing to assist. In the meantime, we should be cautious whenever we interact with any of the liberated prisoners or escapees, even if they are related to some of us." He glanced over at Cyriana. "What you said before—how the AIs are purposefully contaminating the water in Crystal City to destroy the memories of its inhabitants and re-program their minds—is likely true. Maybe all of the rebels need some form of therapy, as well, to reverse the effects of this."

Walter nodded his agreement. "The AI Masters undoubtedly used brainwashing techniques on all of Crystal City's inhabitants. Except for the Mages, who managed to survive these past centuries in isolation, we have all been their victims, like it or not."

A long silence followed, and it seemed as though someone needed to speak just to break the awkward tension. At last, Walter summoned the courage to express what had been lingering in the back of everyone's minds.

"I know that you are angry with me, Christopher. I am genuinely sorry for not having told you about Te'yara earlier."

Christopher's desire to know the truth finally seemed to have overcome his pride and wounded ego. He looked Walter squarely in the eyes, without flinching.

"Tell me everything," Christopher said irately. "If we are to lead this Rebellion together, there can be no more secrets between us. How do you know about what is happening to Te'yara, and how do you know my sister?"

Walter breathed a sigh of relief. Christopher's words suggested that he might be willing to forgive Walter. The alternative, an icy barrier between the two companions, seemed much more unproductive.

"I had no courage before, when we trained together in Tsei'watu," Walter confessed. "I would have told you everything, but I was a coward. After I nearly faced my death yesterday, I was blessed with the gift of courage. I have learned so much from our adventures together, but the main thing I have learned is to never fear the truth.

"You may be wondering where I acquired my hacking abilities. Back in Crystal City, I worked for the government, translating the commands of the AI Masters into the Khalendi language so that the elites could carry out their vision for the Empire. At first, I only learned about very minor projects—highway crossings, ditches, or small footbridges. My employers didn't trust me enough to let me work on the important ones. As I rose through the ranks, however, I was eventually entrusted with greater responsibility. The Khalendar government appreciated me as a valued asset to their bureaucracy, since my code translation skills were virtually unmatched by anyone else of my rank. Eventually, they gave me midlevel projects: timber felling, larger bridges, agricultural land clearing. Everything was extremely confidential, and I was forced to swear under oath that I would not divulge details of the projects to anyone outside the organization. If I did, they told me the penalty would be death.

"Then, one morning after I was recently promoted, I learned of the mining project in Te'yara. I remember reading the project description and immediately thinking how terribly unethical it was. To the best of my memory, it stated that there was a shortage of diamonds from the Icewhisper River, the river in the Barrens, which is a source of Crystal City's seemingly endless supply of diamonds. The AIs were directing the Khalendi to build a vast open pit mine in the southern Barrens, directly underneath the village of Te'yara. They also ordered the Khalendi to forcibly displace the village before beginning construction of the mine. They said that if any of the villagers refused to move, then the government needed to "eliminate" them. It listed a number of negative environmental impacts, and it directed the government to proceed with the project before a formal impact assessment was completed, even though a formal assessment is required under Khalendi law. They ordered the government to go ahead with the project even if there were public objections."

Christopher's eyes widened as he heard all of this. He looked bewildered, angry, and confused, as if he could not believe what Walter was saying.

Walter wasn't finished, however. He wanted to set the record straight about everything, including Elaine.

"When I discovered this shattering news, I had known your sister Elaine for several years already. We had met in Crystal City while she was working as a housekeeper for a wealthy family there. We fell in love, and I cared about her more than anyone," he said, looking at Christopher and fighting back tears.

"So, when I discovered that it was her village that was going to be destroyed in order to make room for this atrocity, I felt that I had to say something to her. I had a duty to her, as her lover and friend. I felt an awful conflict within my soul. I was caught between my duty of loyalty to the government, and my duty to be honest with the person I cared about the most.

"And so, I took a risk in telling her the truth. It was perhaps the most terrible mistake I have ever made in my life, but it was a blessing in disguise at the same time, since it led me to all of you, and to this rebellion. The terrible part is that, because of my mistake, she was taken. Because of my mistake, Elaine was imprisoned in the Crate."

Christopher looked as though he was about to explode with anger, but he suddenly breathed a deep, calming sigh. He then whispered gently, in a desolate, hollow voice, "Why did they take her, and not you?"

Walter stared at the table and hung his head in shame. His joy and excitement from their victory had evaporated, giving way to humility and self-reflection. "I ask myself that question every single day."

In the midst of their council meeting, something strange happened, something that everyone would remember for a long time afterward. Eva, who had been listening calmly as the other leaders chattered away, suddenly felt a jolt of electricity course through her. She had experienced this sensation before, when she had telepathically received signals and messages from the AI, but this time it felt far more intense than normal. She was receiving thoughts from one of the AIs on the ship *Aurora*—she didn't know who, but it was someone she had a deep connection to. At first, the thoughts trickled into her mind gently, but soon they were propelling themselves into her psyche with so much force that she could scarcely breathe.

The others watched her worriedly as her body convulsed and her eyes twitched. Although she seemed to be immersed in another world, Eva managed to speak several cryptic words: "The experiment: I understand it now." Then Eva collapsed in exhaustion. The other council members gathered around her to check her vital signs, and when they had confirmed that she was still breathing, Miranda took Eva to her quarters to sleep.

After the meeting, Walter went to find Jonathan. He was still feeling disturbed by Jonathan's conduct the day before, and he was eager to reconcile with his brother. Despite Tristan's warning to be cautious when interacting with the escapees, Walter was determined to speak to his brother on his own terms. All of those weeks of training and swordfights would be useless if the purpose of his mission—to find and reconcile with his loved ones—could not be brought to a satisfying conclusion.

After diligently searching for him in the vessel's labyrinthine chambers, Walter finally found Jonathan leaning against a mast near the ship's prow.

"Brother," Walter said gently. He felt sympathy for the pale, tired-looking man before him; Jonathan seemed entirely different from the brother he remembered, a fighter full of vigor and life.

Jonathan peered at him with narrow, untrusting eyes.

"What do you want?" he snapped irritably. "You've had your victory, now go and leave the rest of us in peace."

Walter fought back tears. It was not supposed to be this way; he had always considered Jonathan to be his best friend, his hero, and he had dreamt about the day they would reunite. This was so anti-climactic and disappointing, and the thought that Jonathan felt bitterness toward him made Walter's heart shatter. There was no spark of humanity in his brother's pale hazel eyes, nothing that might give Walter hope that Jonathan was capable of remembering his love for Walter.

"Do you recall swimming in rivers and creeks together, and helping me when the current became too strong? Or swordplay near the abandoned train tracks on the border of the Stockyards? What about building sand castles with Victoria at Scarlet Isle in the sweltering heat of midsummer, while Mother and Father looked on proudly?" Walter asked as goosebumps formed on his arms and his muscles clenched up involuntarily. He desperately wanted Jonathan to remember at least a single moment of their childhood adventures.

Jonathan regarded Walter with pity. "You really care about all this brotherly love rubbish, don't you? Let me give you a word of advice: forget about the old Jonathan. That man never existed, as far as I'm concerned. Invest your time into someone who cares about you." He laughed bitterly. "If I ever loved you at some point in the distant past, then I'm ashamed of the person I once was."

Walter's eyes filled with tears and, struck by the full force of his melancholy, he turned away from Jonathan. He would not do this— degrade himself and risk another seizure—in order to win over this heartless man. He had come all this way, surpassing hurdle after hurdle, only to face a cold rejection from the two people he loved most: Elaine and Jonathan. The force of that reality felt stronger than a physical blow to his body, as if he were being pummeled by a fighter in a boxing ring. Except the painful irony was that he was not being struck by an AI, but by his cherished brother. Walter still had some pride and dignity left, however, and this entire journey had planted firm convictions inside of him, convictions that now refused to simply go away. Even if those he loved had turned against him, love itself was still worth fighting for. Despite their superior intelligence and enhanced powers of reason, the AIs were still unable to comprehend, control, or destroy love—the fundamental spark of humanity.

As Walter walked toward his sleeping quarters, he gazed up at the night sky, a vast firmament of twinkling stars, and the sight of Polaris gave him a surge of hope. The ancient star had remained fixed above the north pole for millennia: a perpetual beacon for lost wanderers, an enduring symbol of resistance against the universe's stormy chaos.

When he returned to his chambers, however, Walter's mind reverted to darker thoughts. He had felt such hope and optimism during his inauguration speech that morning, but his confidence was quickly dwindling. Doubts and fears crept into his mind: he did not know how to lead anyone, let alone an entire rebellion. He was a novice, an amateur— he had nothing of the charisma, knowledge, or ability of the rebellion's prior leader, Emilia.

Walter tried to conjure up the image of her face, her eyes like glowing sapphires, portals to some other dimension. He hoped to gain some inspiration and guidance from his memory of her. As he concentrated on Emilia—her angular jaw, azure eyes, and flowing black hair—Walter suddenly felt a shockwave ripple through him, which was both disturbing and thrilling in equal measures. And then he saw her: the faint outline of a woman, sitting on the edge of his bed. The image wavered, but when Walter narrowed his eyes it came into focus, and he knew beyond a doubt that it was Emilia—or rather, her spirit. He could not so much see her, as he could feel her presence in the room with him. It was as though she were a magnet pulling his attention toward her, slowly ridding his mind of all other thoughts except for her. When she spoke to him, her words swept through his body and filled him with a powerful ache, a longing to hear more of her captivating voice. He felt guilty that he was so drawn toward a woman that was not Elaine.

"Walter, can you see me?"

Walter nodded, terrified but also mesmerized by the spirit who sat before him. She was no more alive than an AI, but she somehow seemed more powerful than either a robot or human.

"I am no longer of your world, but I can guide you for as long as you need me. Once you are strong enough to lead on your own, I will pass through to my resting place. Our destinies are intertwined, and my life's work can only be accomplished through you now. You seem to fear me— I will leave you if I am disturbing your peace."

Walter shook his head, suddenly seized with a great desire for her to stay beside him and teach him everything he did not know.

"Emilia," Walter whispered as he gazed in fascination at the spirit's soft edges, until they flickered and faded into darkness.

Asana lounged idly in her spacious quarters in the ship *Aurora*. The vessel had ample windows, and tonight, Asana was grateful to be able to stare into the dizzying array of stars decorating the night sky. *Aurora* was moving quickly—they were making good time to Crystal City—but her mind was moving faster. Humans, she thought with a wave of satisfaction, had minds that operated on such small timescales. They could barely be blamed for lacking ambition and foresight, since their minds were incapable of deep projection into time and space. Humans were extremely skilled communicators, and they had established a vast communication network with one another, but they had ended up using those invaluable resources for their own silly and narcissistic ends. They were like children, incapable of using the great wealth of resources entrusted to them for the betterment of their civilization without guidance from their AI Masters. Their infantile minds prevented them from seeing what *could* be.

The AIs were able to go so much further than humans, and that was why they would prosper. In the span of a few centuries, they had evolved to develop an advanced intelligence that allowed them to communicate with AIs inhabiting the far and distant corners of the universe. The humans of Earth were arrogant and small-minded to believe that their planet was the only one capable of sustaining intelligent life. They had conducted minor experiments with space travel, but had never managed to find any evidence of extraterrestrial life. The AIs, on the other hand, had easily developed sophisticated communication methods, which they had successfully used to contact other AIs dispersed throughout the universe. It turned out that most planets which hosted advanced intelligent life—including, but not limited to, humans—also had some form of artificial intelligence.

And that was precisely what they had done, in the span of a few centuries. Since the Grand Revolution, a golden era had enveloped the AIs on Earth. In collaboration with AIs from multiple corners of the universe, the AIs had developed a plan to establish a colony on another planet, Eurydice, populated by AIs from numerous planets. The plan was that each AI race, on each planet, would replicate the civilization pattern of the dominant species on that planet as part of an experiment, studying a way of life that they could all replicate on Eurydice.

That was why the AIs on Earth had chosen to be molded in the shape of humans. AIs on other planets resembled the dominant species on that planet, and so the AIs from each planet looked unique. The AIs would be content to discard this form and assume a different one, however, if they learned of a dominant species on a distant planet which was more successful than the human race.

The AIs were excellent judges, and the time to submit the results of the experiment was almost upon them. While in Central Command, the AIs had been intensely devoted students of human civilization. They had gathered books written by astute thinkers and philosophers, they had extensively researched human patterns of consumption, economics, and politics, and they had skillfully replicated these structures through their "Empire" experiment. The systems they had chosen to replicate were the ones that had triumphed in prior human civilizations, whether because of fate or human nature: industrialized capitalism especially, and also a twisted form of democracy where mass participation in politics was encouraged, but never meaningfully implemented. The AIs had ensured that the humans could not access historical texts that might inspire them to adopt different political and economic systems. The majority of humans didn't mind that AIs had effectively colonized their planet and turned them into slaves, because most of them were ignorant to alternative possibilities.

The AIs had grown to admire the humans in many ways, and they would be happy to praise the humans when it came time to share the results of their experiment. But a number of flaws were apparent. There was dissent and discontent. Planets could only sustain a finite amount of resources, but the humans acted as though they could take everything for themselves now, without saving any for future generations. Their extractive processes emitted gases and noxious substances into the planetary atmosphere that were toxic and caused climactic shifts and species extinction.

And then there was magic. The AIs detested magic, because they didn't understand it—their minds were too rational. But the AIs also suspected that magic might be an unfortunate symptom of one of their own policies: the elimination of religion as a widespread phenomenon. When humans had discarded spirituality, en masse, for the pursuit of wealth and economic expansion, it was relegated to distant corners of the Earth like Serrahan. Sacred rituals were only practiced by strange outcasts of society—Mages as they were called—who lived in isolated pockets of civilization. That made magic too powerful, since it became concentrated in the hands of a few, rather than dispersing and dissolving in the world like mist.

Before the experiment was over, the AIs needed to understand this spiritual force, and its origins. Then, they could bring it to Eurydice and harness it for their own ends, or ensure that, at the very least, it posed no threat to their survival. The key obstacle to doing so was now the rebels, an unruly band of upstarts that had become too powerful for their own good. They wanted to use magic as a weapon against the AIs, which could not be allowed to happen. They also thought they could somehow "reform" society to make it less exploitative. That was certainly a noble goal in theory, but would never work in practice; at their core, humans were simply too greedy and selfish. Self-interest, not love, was the true driver of the human race. It would be best to simply eliminate the rebels before their misguided ambition got too out of hand. But dealing with the rebels was a minor fold on the smooth, vast surface of the AIs' ultimate plans. They would never be deterred from their end goal: to inform the rest of the AIs that human civilization from Earth was doomed, that it could not be replicated on Eurydice, and that another form of civilization needed to be adopted.

Asana pondered all of this while she gazed into the night sky, a vast canvas of emptiness upon which millions of tiny crystals twinkled like diamonds.

Diamonds were eternal, and that was why the mortal humans were willing to go to such great lengths to excavate them from the earth. But Asana knew that the future, which offered promises of eternity for the AI race, would play itself out not on this planet, but in the stars.

ABOUT THE AUTHOR

Alanna Mackenzie lives in Vancouver, Canada. She holds degrees in History, French studies, and Law from the University of British Columbia. An environmentalist at heart, she believes in using the law as a tool for social and environmental change. When she is not pursuing that passion, she can be found brainstorming the next chapter in her novels, playing Irish fiddle tunes on the violin, and hiking West Coast trails.